THE SEEKERS OF DUAT

The Art of Darkness, Book 2

A Supernatural Adventure

The underworld is closer than you think

BY KEITH CADOR

KEITH CADOR

Copyright (©) 2023 Keith Robinson
ISBN: 9798870823713

This book is copyright under the Berne Convention
No reproduction without permission
All rights reserved

The right of Keith Robinson to be identified as the author of this work has been asserted by him in accordance with sections 77 and 78 of the Copyright, Designs and Patents Act 1988.

This book is a work of fiction. Names, characters and incidents are either a product of the author's imagination or are used fictitiously. Any resemblance to actual people, living or dead or events is entirely coincidental.

Prepared for publication by Wise Grey Owl
www.wisegreyowl.co.uk

THE SEEKERS OF DUAT

Revenge is like a ghost. It takes over every man it touches.

Its thirst cannot be quenched until the last man standing has fallen.

Vladmir Makrov

KEITH CADOR

Thank you to my family and friends for supporting me in writing this second novel in the Art of Darkness Series.

Book 1 is The Search for Orion.

Book 2 is The Seekers of Duat.

Book 3 is coming soon – the story continues.

CHAPTER 1

The night in Brunswick was as dark as the secrets hidden beneath its streets. Two local heroes lie asleep unaware of the extraordinary journey that would await them. For soon, their nightmares would become reality and their home a battleground between forces unseen.

Startled, Olly awoke from his slumber as the phone's incessant ringing continued; he was the only person who could answer it. His parents were working a night shift at the hospital and his friend, Leo, who was crashing in the room next-door, was dead to the world. The phone was insistent as Olly's mind focused. He dashed downstairs and snatched the beige telephone receiver positioned centrally on the hall side table.

"Hello, Olly speaking," he said while his dog, Maddie, sniffed his pyjamas.

"Hey Oll. It's Jimmy."

"Jimmy?" Olly muttered, trying to put the name to a face.

"From the exhibition yesterday," Jimmy confirmed in a whispered voice.

Olly's mind bounced into gear. He remembered – Jimmy was the security guard who'd helped out at the exhibition over the weekend, one that celebrated the first-year anniversary of the Brunswick Tunnel adventure. Jimmy was over six-foot tall, rotund with a tattoo of a skull decorating the rear of his shaved head. He seemed menacing but it was a show. His gentle voice betrayed his kind nature immediately.

"Oh, hi Jimmy … how can I help you at … four in the morning?"

"Yeah, soz about that, I found your phone number in the emergency contacts. I hope you don't mind," Jimmy replied nervously, "Something's happened down here and I thought I'd better let you know first before I call the police."

"I'm all ears. What's happened?"

"A break-in. I'm in my office overlooking the main hall right now."

Olly had chatted to Jimmy twice over the weekend; he had a penchant for exaggeration. His office was merely a chair next to a wall-phone on a balcony.

"I was having a kip when I heard a loud bang. It made me fall off the chair, especially when I detected the sound of glass smashing. I pulled myself up to glance over the balcony."

Olly tried not to laugh at the thought of Jimmy falling. "Well ... and what did you see?"

"That box thing you told me about. It was open." A pause interrupted the conversation. "Are you there, Olly?"

"Yeah ... yeah, I'm here," Olly said, a veil obscuring his thoughts. "You mean the cube... the cube's been opened?"

"That's it. It's still on the pedestal, but the lid's on the floor."

Olly was puzzled by what he was being told. The cube held Victor Golding's ghost, captured by Leo deep in the tunnel the previous year. "Have you seen anything else ... anything ghostly, say?"

"No, why – should I?" Jimmy replied, his breathing quickening.

Olly gulped. "I need to get down there. What time will people start arriving to take stuff back to the museum?"

"Not for a few days. There's no event on for a while, they're taking their time. Should I call the police now?"

"No!" Olly barked down the phone. He knew the police wouldn't believe the truth. A year ago, Olly had been seated in an interview room at the police station and recalled that any words uttered about supernatural or ghostly happenings were dismissed without consideration by the sergeant. Luckily the police found enough evidence at Marshall's home to detain him and his Uncle Lance at Her Majesty's request. "Just wait there. Me and Leo will be right over."

A relieved Jimmy answered, "Well if that's what you want, that's fine by me. Hurry up though, I don't feel too comfortable hanging around here on my own. When you arrive go to the fire escape, it'll be ajar. I nipped out for a ciggy before I rang you … my nerves are shot. Oh, on your way, you wouldn't grab me some food would ya, maybe a sandwich and a aaaarrgghh!"

"Jimmy! …Jimmy!" Olly shouted down the phone but he was met with the sound of footsteps followed by silence as the phone went dead.

Olly replaced the receiver and bounded upstairs two steps at a time. Running down the landing he came to the spare room, Leo's room for the night. Even with the commotion, Leo was snoring in a deep sleep. Olly opened the creaking door, causing Leo to twitch and mutter the words. "Set free … Set free."

Olly placed his hands on Leo, shook him and shouted, "Leo mate, wake up. Something's happened."

"Uh, who's that."

"Who do you think it is? It's me, Olly. You need to get up, we need to talk."

"Five more minutes."

"No, now!" Olly said, pulling the duvet away. "The cube's been opened."

Leo's moaning stopped as he spun around on the bed and stared at Olly, eyes like a startled owl.

"That got your attention."

"Are you serious?"

"One hundred percent mate. I've had a call from that guard we were talking to at the exhibition, the one with the tattoo."

Leo moved his legs round, dangling them off the bed, leant forward and shook his head. "So, what do we do?"

"We get down there sharpish," Olly replied, throwing Leo his t-shirt discarded onto the floor. "I heard Jimmy scream before he was cut-off. Something's going on down there. Ring your parents, have them pick us up will you?"

Leo leapt from the bed and dashed downstairs to the phone.

CHAPTER 2

"Stop … stop! Get off me!"

"Orion, wake up! Please wake up, you're having a nightmare," Melanie said, watching Orion lying in bed, struggling with an imaginary attacker. Beads of sweat flew everywhere as he wrestled in fright. His hands gripped his pyjama top, pulling it open, buttons flying across the room peppering the windowpane. Restraining his arms, Melanie shook him from his nightmare until he relaxed.

This was a regular ritual for Orion's devoted wife. The year had been arduous since Orion's rescue. The media interest had been relentless following his discovery, causing a breakdown for Orion.

Melanie decided to move her family to the town of St. Prion, five miles north of Brunswick, finding a modest terraced house looking out onto a meandering river abundant with wildlife. It was a perfect place to recuperate, escaping from the craziness that had become their lives and improve Orion's well-being – he'd recovered significantly over the few months since they'd uprooted.

With the sound of the phone ringing, an exhausted Melanie made her way downstairs. "Hello, the Hart residence."

"What accent was that?" Leo said.

"Oh, hi Leo. You know I always put my posh voice on when I'm answering the phone. Anyway, what on earth are you ringing at this time for? Is everything Okay? Did the book signing go well?"

"Yeah, yeah, the signing was great Mum. Erm …"

"What is it? What's happened?" Mothers know when something isn't right. "Come on tell me. You don't just ring your parents in the middle of the night to say hi."

"We need you to pick us up."

"Well, that's fine. I said I'd be over about ten o'clock," she said glancing at the grandfather clock to make sure it really was the middle of the night.

"No, now. We need you to pick us up and take us to the exhibition halls. Olly thinks there's been a break in."

"Shouldn't burglaries be reported to the police?"

"The police don't look for ghosts."

"What do you mean?

"It's the cube. It's been opened."

Melanie closed her eyes to compose herself. "Okay, well your dad will have to stay here. He's had another nightmare and is in no fit state to travel, especially given the circumstances. I'll tell him a white lie and I'll be over as quick as I can."

"Thanks Mum."

Twenty minutes later the boy's heard a familiar sound approaching. Olly peeked through the living room curtains and witnessed a green Volkswagen Beetle speeding up the road, a cloud of black smoke belching from its exhaust, visible in the light from the cast-iron lamp-posts. Noticeable too was the twitching of a neighbour's curtains — to Olly's amusement. In the past year, Olly's street had been inundated with TV crews and reporters vying for a story. *What better way to tell the world than producing a book ghost written for them by a family friend?* Olly thought.

Melanie pulled onto the driveway, exited the car and hurried to the door. Before she had time to knock, the door flew open. Although they'd been apart for less than two days, Leo ran to his mum and embraced her like a limpet to a rock. He could always count on his mum to help out; she was the rock of the family, the one who kept them safe.

"Thanks for coming Mum."

"Yeah, thanks Melanie," Olly said standing in the hallway, a rucksack slung over his shoulder.

"It's no problem boys," Melanie said, taking a deep breath while tidying her hair. "Now, are you sure you don't want me to call the police? It is burglary that's happened, you know that, yeah."

"We're sure," Olly said. "They're not the Ghostbusters, are they? We put Victor's ghost away before ... and we'll do it again."

Melanie believed what Orion and the boys had told her from their time in the tunnel; the police had laughed at the ghost stories so she understood Olly's reluctance. "Okay, we'll go and take a look but if there's any sign of someone lurking then we're out of there. Do I make myself clear?"

Olly and Leo nodded as they prepared to leave, Olly leaving his dog some food before writing a note for his parents to find. He locked the front door and accompanied Melanie and Leo to the car.

"Are you sure you've got everything?" Melanie asked, starting the engine.

"Think so." Olly tapped his bag. "Torch, binoculars, penknife and food."

As the Beetle left, a plume of smoke in tow, the boys sat quietly. Staring from the windows, they tried to recall anything from the previous day's book signing at the exhibition halls – had something odd occurred?

CHAPTER 3

"Next!" shouted the volunteer overseeing the book signing for *My Dad's a Dragon Slayer* by Oliver Webber and Leo Hart. A queue of customers zigzagged through the hall, past the giant glass doors and into the gardens. This was no ordinary meet and greet, it was to celebrate the one-year anniversary of the Brunswick Tunnel adventure. The authors were well-known children of Brunswick after they found Orion Hart and countless jewels deep in the tunnel.

It was only a year but that's a long time for young boys. Leo had since turned thirteen, transforming into a typical teenager. He loved music – thanks to Olly – had mood swings and played on his Super Nintendo most of the time. Olly was well ... still as carefree, but considerably taller than his friend.

"This is taking ages," Leo whispered, fiddling with his pen.

"I know, mate," Olly said. "But just think of all the books we're going to sell. We released this four months ago and up until now, sold only to our friends. This is great promotion. Another few hours, we'll be done."

"Hi there," said two voices in unison.

The boys looked up to see two girls, a brunette and a blonde, both dressed in black jeans, sporting similar dark jumpers and matching pale make-up.

Olly smiled. "Hiya Katie, what are you doing here? You never told me you were coming."

Olly had met Katie at a previous book signing in the Brunswick library three months prior. She'd asked him for his telephone number plus an autograph — he'd obliged. They attended different schools, Katie at the Grammar, but managed to meet up, including dates to the cinema and the bowling alley. Katie's family had decided to move to St. Prion, five miles away; to two teenagers besotted with each other, it seemed like they were on another continent.

"I thought we'd surprise you," Katie said leaning over to kiss Olly on his cheek. "This is my cousin Claire; she's come to stay for a week over Easter."

Claire blushed, smiled and started playing with her long blonde hair. "Hi."

"Err ... hi." Leo said, his face reddening.

"I'm sorry about him," Olly said. "He's shy around girls. I'm Olly by the way and this is Leo."

"I'm not shy."

The girls giggled. "Claire knows who you both are. She couldn't wait to meet you; I sent her a copy of your book so she knows about your adventure."

"You're the one who's bought it then," Leo said sarcastically.

"You're funny," Claire said, turning redder.

"Next!" came the voice again.

"Well, thanks for coming," Olly said. "I'll ring you soon."

"Look forward to it." The girls waved and scurried out of the hall into the gardens.

Leo sat back, running a hand through his highlighted ear-length hair. "Claire seemed nice."

"Do you fancy her? Tell you what, we'll go on a double date over the Easter holidays. It'll be a right laugh."

Before Leo had chance to reply the next customer strode forward, casting a shadow. "Hello, young men," he said in a refined accent. The gentleman was in his fifties, six feet plus tall, and wore a loosely fitting light grey suit with a matching trilby. He placed his copy of the book on the table.

"Hi," Leo said straining his neck upwards. "Would you like a dedication?"

"To Horace Griffin please. I have to say what an absolute pleasure it is to finally meet the both of you."

"It's okay," Olly said trying not to snigger at his posh name and accent. "How exactly do you spell your name?"

"G. R. I. F. F. I. N."

"And your first name? That's quite unusual too," Olly replied.

The gentlemen leant forward, "It's an old-fashioned name. My father took it from Horus, the Egyptian god."

With an innocent voice, Leo spoke, "Well, you'll like this book. An Egyptian artefact is featured."

"Yes, the cube," Horace said. "Egyptian artefacts are the exact reason I'm here. Something happened in my …"

"Next please!" came the call before Horace could finish his sentence.

"O … K …" Leo muttered, nudging Olly's foot under the table.

"Well Horace, thanks for coming. It's been a pleasure meeting you," Olly said, scrawling his signature into the book and passing it back.

Taking the book, Horace dropped a business card in front of them, "Give me a call," he said before turning his gangly body towards the exit of the building, the boys staring after him. He waved farewell through a window. Leo reciprocated, muttering, "Yeah, see you later, Freakenstein."

Olly laughed as he shoved the card into his back pocket. "What on earth was that about? Almost scarier than being in the tunnel!"

"Yeah, give us a dragon to slay any day over that."

As the hands of the clock in the hall approached six o'clock, the last visitors left, leaving the two boys exhausted. For hours they'd shaken hands, posed for photos and sold books – until every last one was gone. The signing was the last event of the weekend exhibition, on the previous day, historians had given talks on the tunnel's past while the police officer who arrested Marshall presented his account of the day's events.

Large display cabinets – moved from their usual residence at the Brunswick Museum – were placed around the hall exhibiting the artefacts found in the tunnel, including: precious stones, which had adorned the treasure room, swords, which the slayers had used, a bow and arrow used by Orion and the original plans drawn up by George Bumble and Drake Golding to create the labyrinth rooms.

The main facet of the exhibition was in the centre of the room; on a pedestal under a glass dome, surrounded by red security rope was the cube in all of its glory. Stories of this object had spread afar, especially the secrets it might hold. Eyewitnesses had seen it move, a boy swearing that he'd seen it jump onto the floor – although that child was an unreliable witness. Could it hold the ghost of Victor, or was that a myth?

Grabbing their coats, the two boys left the hall and began the long walk back to Olly's house where Leo was staying that night. Olly's sister, Jessica, had moved into a house with her boyfriend Sam, so her old room was often used by Leo.

"Fancy going for a burger at that new McDonalds? I could eat a horse," Olly said, pointing to the distant yellow **M** lighting up like a beacon.

Leo glanced at his watch, "Do we have to? I'm knackered."

"We do have to eat; my parents are working tonight so there'll be nowt when we get back." Olly spotted some familiar faces and grinned. "I think I might be able to persuade you."

Lifting his head, Leo strained his eyes, "Is that …?"

"It is mate." Standing outside of the eatery were Katie and Claire.

"Well, in that case I'll have a double cheeseburger and fries."

"You've found your appetite." Olly laughed. "You do fancy Claire, don't you?"

"Stop it, we've only just met."

"Well, you've heard of love at first sight, haven't you?"

"We're only going to buy some food and say hi, Okay?"

Striding over, they drifted over to the girls.

"Hello again," Olly said.

Katie jumped with shock, nearly dropping her fries to the floor. "Oh my god! I wish you wouldn't do that."

19

"Just getting you back for surprising me earlier."

Claire glanced towards Leo as she nudged her cousin. "You're not following us, are you?"

"No … nowt like that. We came for food," Leo said, glancing down as he spoke.

"She's having us on, mate."

"Oh yeah … I knew that. Anyway, I'll go and order."

"Apologies again for Leo. I think you've got an admirer!" Olly said, looking at Claire hiding her red cheeks behind her hands.

"That's great, we can all hang out," Katie said. "What about going to the cinema? That King Ralph film is out this weekend, or maybe we can go ice skating or …"

"How about breathing?"

"But it's so exciting. A dragon slayer fancies my cousin."

"Let's see how we get on before you start handing out wedding invites." Olly said. "What are your plans now? We can hang around for a while … if you want?"

"Thanks, but we've got to go soon. Mum's picking us up. Do you want a lift back? She'd love to see you both again. I think she's your biggest fan."

"Err … Okay, thanks, we are pretty tired to be fair."

Leo appeared from the revolving doors which released a wave of food smells as he made his way to the wall to join his friends.

"I can't believe you fought off a dragon and those monsters to rescue your dad," Claire said, intrigued at being seated next to a dragon slayer, albeit a dragon slayer with ketchup dribbling down his chin.

"Me neither," Leo said. "It was ages ago but I do miss my powers. I felt invincible."

"You've lost them all?"

"Yeah."

"Only until you meet a dragon again," Olly said, before pausing to slurp his banana milkshake. "Then they'll be back."

"And we all know that'll never happen again," Leo scoffed.

"She's here," Katie said, spotting her mum driving up the street.

To Olly and Leo's horror – they'd never seen Katie's mum's car – a rusty faded yellow Lada Riva spluttered towards them. Getting into one was bad enough but being picked up outside the popular McDonald's restaurant was excruciatingly embarrassing. Olly prodded Leo and raised his eyebrows in shock.

"You never told me you had a Lada?" Olly said.

"Is that what it is?" she replied. "I don't know anything about cars. Is it a good one?"

"The best," Leo sniggered behind Olly.

"Hi Mum, is it okay if we drop Olly and Leo home? It's quite a walk for them otherwise."

Jean smiled at seeing the two boys, "Of course it is, the pleasure would be all mine."

Katie sat in the front while Claire was sandwiched in the back between Olly and Leo, who were trying to hide their faces from onlookers.

"How did your book signing go boys?" Jean said.

"Terrific, thanks for asking," Olly replied. "It was nice that Katie and Claire turned up."

"She thought you'd like that. She's been telling me for days that she'd surprise you."

"Mum! You're embarrassing me."

Jean patted her daughter on the leg. "That's what mums do, dear. So, what are you kids going to do over the Easter holidays?"

"I thought the cinema," Katie said.

"Maybe we could camp in my garden for a few nights. That'd be fun," Olly said.

"Yeah, then we can scare you both with our stories, mwahahaha," Leo added, doing a terrible ghost impression.

"I've never seen a ghost," Claire said, "Apart from that 'something' we saw in that barn. Do you remember, Katie?"

"I do remember. I also remember we'd had a glass of champagne to celebrate my grandparents' golden wedding, so everything was hazy."

"Oh girls, really," Jean said. "You're not even fifteen yet and you're drinking."

"Excuse us mum, but it was you who gave us the drinks and anyway, a couple of drinks doesn't turn us into raging alcoholics."

The boys chuckled in the back – not because of the girl's story, more the car's suspension was making them bounce up and down.

They were relieved when the Lada pulled up outside Olly's house. "Thanks again for the lift, it's much appreciated."

"Yeah cheers, see you again," Leo said, hoping for some acknowledgment from Claire but she said nothing. The doors slammed shut as Jean smiled and waved as she set off with the girls back to St. Prion.

CHAPTER 4

The exhibition halls in the centre of Brunswick were gigantic structures, adorned with large glass panels and tall stone columns dominating the entrance, positioned at the bottom of a steep hill jam-packed with bars, restaurants and high-end boutiques.

As Melanie drove the boys through the streets in her beloved Beetle, the surroundings offered a sinister atmosphere at five o'clock in the morning. Drunks had vacated the bars and roamed the streets seeking a taxi home or food from a kebab shop. Their staggering behaviour, tripping into raised flower beds, reminded the boys of the Drowners, zombified water creatures who'd tormented them deep in the tunnel.

"Now boys," Melanie said, "If witnessing this spectacle doesn't put you off drinking, nothing will."

Olly and Leo laughed as he watched a man talking to a tree. "Looks like fun to me."

"Yeah, a few more years and you could pick us both up," Olly said.

"Not on your life. I've enough to deal with when you're both sober thank you very much."

The Beetle entered an alleyway, leading to the rear of one of the halls. Turning off the engine left them in darkness, apart from an exit sign flickering above a door.

"Remember what I said." Melanie turned around to lock eyes with the boys. "If we see anything untoward, we get back in this car. Okay."

The boys nodded their heads as Melanie exited first, lifting her seat forward to release the boys.

"Heellloo."

"Aarrgghh!" Leo screamed.

Melanie gripped Leo's shoulders. "It's alright, he's drunk," she said as the stranger zig-zagged his way to pass them and head down the alleyway towards the noise and lights of the town. "Just be careful where you walk."

"Can't believe I jumped."

"You're becoming used to being normal again my beautiful boy."

"Yeah, welcome to the real world, Leo. You would've whooped him a year ago, but you know that."

Leo smiled at his friend and breathed deeply to calm himself down. Olly was right as usual. He always defended Leo to make him feel better. Since the boys had become famous Leo had felt the pressure, people expecting him to be the slayer described in their book. For Leo, darting up vertical walls, super strength, swordsmanship and telepathy were a distant memory.

Olly switched on his torch and walked towards the door. "Jimmy was right, it's open."

"What are you intending to do?" Melanie asked, her hand gripping Leo's – more for her comfort than his.

"I don't know," Olly said as he crept through the fire exit. "I wanted to know if Jimmy was telling the truth and if he's okay."

Leo felt helpless. "Remember, I don't have any powers ... and *we* don't have any weapons."

"I know. Look, if the cube has been opened Victor will be long gone. If it hasn't been opened, we can go back to bed."

After walking down a corridor, they turned a corner and stepped through some swing doors.

"We're here," Olly whispered as the torch light expanded into a vast hall, lighting up the display cabinets containing artefacts. Steadying his arm, he directed the beam to the centre of the room. Jimmy had been right again: on a pedestal demarcated by red security rope was the cube – without its lid. Melanie and Leo remained in the shadows as Olly slid forward. When he was closer to the plinth, he spotted flickers of light reflecting from the floor. Remnants of the glass dome that had once surrounded the cube were shattered on the ground. Within the circle of shards

THE SEEKERS OF DUAT

was the cube's lid. Olly was nervous, breathing in shallow bursts as he bent down, ducking under the security rope, his eyes fixed on the cube.

"Be careful," Melanie said, making Olly's heart skip a beat.

Olly straightened and moved his head to position it over the open box.

"What do you see?" Leo said.

"Nothing … It's empty," Olly said with a shrug of his shoulders. He leaned over, picked the lid up and shone the torch towards Leo and Melanie. "Shall I bring the cube back to my house?"

Leo and his mum stared back, transfixed like rabbits in headlights.

"I said, shall we bring this back with us!?" Olly repeated but they stayed silent. Open-mouthed, Leo raised his left arm and pointed to something above Olly's head.

Olly's senses were alerted – he realised something was wrong. In the torchlight he saw his own shadow in front. Moving his head around, a light caught the corner of his eye and he ordered his feet to move him away . They refused to cooperate, causing him to stumble backwards, fall and land in an undignified mess on his bum. Glancing up he was confronted by Victor's ghost.

"Mwahahaha!" maniacal laughter echoed throughout the room. "First, Orion took my life and my family from me, then YOU." He pointed at Leo.

"You locked me in this box like a prisoner. You will all die."

Melanie stepped in front of her son, acting as a shield. Inside she was terrified but like any parent she would protect her child to the death.

"You gave us no choice. You were going to kill us," Olly said from his position on the cold floor. "Please don't hurt us."

"We … We …We can fix you," Leo said, peering out from behind his mum.

The ghost floated over Olly and across the hall. "How can **YOU** help **ME**."

Leo moved forward to confront the spectre, feeling less brave than he seemed. "We might know how to give you your life back."

"**AND!**"

"We know of a way to find the god of the underworld. Our friend Stumpy told us of a gateway."

"How can that help me, fool."

"He's also the god of resurrection."

The ghost thought for a moment, swaying back and forth in the air. "Where is it? Where is this gateway?"

Olly stood up and shouted, "Don't tell him, Leo. He'll kill us anyway, like he's probably killed Jimmy."

The glowing apparition flew towards the display cabinets and reached its hand through the glass. It plucked one of the slayer swords out of the collection, smashing the cabinet's casing as it moved away.

"I didn't know ghosts could hold things?" Melanie said to Leo, hugging him tight.

"Poltergeists can move things, can't they?"

Gripping the sword, Victor headed for Leo. "Tell me where the gateway is?"

Mind working overtime, Olly had a brain wave. "Leo, can you remember the phrase used to trap ghosts in the cube?"

Leo, thought for a second and nodded as Olly grabbed the cube and lid.

"Say it!"

"This will hold the spirit sa ..."

Victor wasn't going to fall for that trick again. On hearing the incantation commence, he rocketed towards a large pane of glass high up on the wall and disappeared through it. The glass smashed as the sword followed the ghost into the open air.

"Right boys," Melanie yelled. "Let's get out of here."

They sprinted out, Olly holding the cube and lid tightly to his chest. After jumping into the Beetle they were soon skidding down the road.

"Where shall we go?" Leo asked his mum.

"We're going home," she said. "Olly, you can stay at ours for the time being. It's too dangerous for you to be at your place on your own. Victor doesn't know where we live; it'll give us time to think of a plan."

The green Beetle turned out of the alleyway and sped towards St. Prion.

CHAPTER 5

The morning chorus of birds twittered away outside the window as the hallway grandfather clock chimed nine o'clock. Olly arose from his sleep, stretching his arms out as much as he could on the couch. He opened his eyes, breaking the seal left by the sandman during the night. His glazed vision came into focus as he stared in horror at the TV. "Leo! Leo! get down here and see this."

In his pyjamas, Leo stumbled down the stairs in a sleepy trance. "Now what's happened?"

The local news was on. '*Lance Golding is on the run. He has seemingly been able to walk out of his cell and the prison with each door mysteriously unlocking themselves. Unexplained forces stopped guards from apprehending him and he's vanished into the nearby woods. James Marshall Golding, son of the late Victor Golding and nephew of Lance Golding has also escaped from custody. He was being transferred to another secure unit when the vehicle was hit, causing the van to turn on its side. The officer and driver were lucky to get out with only minor injuries. James Marshall Golding was nowhere to be seen after the crash.'*

"Victor's freed them," Olly said.

Leo's first thought was to alert his parents. "Mum! Dad! Come down and see this."

Melanie rushed downstairs first, fearful of what might have happened. "You okay boys? Is everything alright?"

"Not really Mum ... let's wait for Dad."

The lounge ceiling creaked, plaster dust drifting to the floor. They heard Orion's footsteps treading across the landing and down the stairs, causing the grandfather clock to chime unintentionally. Staying at home due to his anxiety, Leo's father had deteriorated physically, more than doubling his weight.

Leo embraced his father. "Hi Dad, how are you?"

"I'm getting there, son. Not sure where *there* is, but I'm getting there," Orion said walking into the lounge and plonking himself into his favourite armchair. "Hi Olly, how are you keeping?"

"I'm good, thank you Orion, nice to see you on your feet. You're looking a lot better."

"Thanks, it's been a struggle. This ageing process is hard work. I've gained more wrinkles in the last year that I've had bowls of bat soup. But things are on the up. So, what else has happened, Melanie told me last night about the cube being opened."

Olly stood, trying to camouflage his nervousness. He knew about Orion's mental health problems over the last year and how he was gradually recovering, but the latest news could cause a relapse. "Err … I woke up and saw the local news. Lance and Marshall. They … they've."

"They've what?" Orion said.

"They've escaped … both of them, last night."

"It must be Victor who's helped," Melanie said, leaving the lounge to make coffees for everyone,

"That's what we thought," Leo said. "Are you okay about it, Dad?"

Orion huffed and released an inaudible sigh. "I knew this would happen one day and they'd eventually serve their sentences anyway and be released. Hopefully the police will track them down sharpish. Everyone will know their faces after being splashed all over the news."

"But what about Victor? The police can't catch him."

"True son, I think we're going to have to sort that out ourselves."

Melanie came back in with the drinks. "We need to use the cube, that's the only way to trap Victor."

Olly took a slurp of hot coffee and replied, "Don't think it'll be that easy. You saw how quickly he vanished when Leo started the chant. The other problem is that Victor now knows that *we* know about a portal to the underworld."

"We don't know where it is Olly," Leo said, defending his earlier actions, "We can't reveal something we don't know. All Stumpy told us was that there's a pyramid portal if we need to find him again. He didn't tell us where it was or how to use it, even if we could discover its location."

"Surely it's to do with the pyramids in Egypt … isn't it?" Melanie said.

"Egypt," Olly said, thinking aloud.

"You okay, mate?" Leo said.

"Remember at the book signing? That strange man, spouting about Egyptian gods and stuff." Olly reached round to his back pocket and produced the business card the man had given him. "I'd forgotten about this … Horace Griffin, dealer in historical artefacts."

Startled, Orion nearly spilt his drink. "Griffin, that name was mentioned at the trial. Someone named Griffin had given Drake Golding the cube. I remember now, Lance mentioned it."

"Do you want me to ring the number?" Melanie said. "He might be able to help us."

It was agreed that Melanie call Horace Griffin, so Olly and Leo dressed and followed Orion into the garden for some much needed fresh air as Melanie made for the phone.

Orion was proud of his garden which had helped his recovery. Roses adorned the perimeter, with rockeries interspersed, now teeming with colour. They strolled along a meandering gravel path, under a trellised archway of scented honeysuckle, through a dense coppice of trees until they arrived at a meandering stream where Orion had built a wooden jetty to use for fishing.

"We'll catch Victor again," Olly said.

"I hope so," Orion replied. "I only wish I could help. I'm as much use as that stick floating down the stream."

In the house, Melanie was seated on the stairs as she rang Horace Griffin.

"Good morning, Horace speaking. Who is this please?" he said, in his refined accent.

"Oh … hello, my name's Melanie … Melanie Hart, the mother of Leo Hart, one of the boys you met at the book signing yesterday."

"Leo, of course. How could I possibly forget. One of the heroes of Brunswick."

"You left your business card with Olly, so I thought I'd give you a ring. You see a few things have happened since the boys saw you," Melanie said, searching for the right words. "And your name cropped up in a conversation … we were wondering, are you in any way related to the man who was involved with the Goldings. You see, his name was Griffin too."

"I am. Archibald Griffin was my father. That was one of the reasons I was at the signing. When I discovered that the Goldings were involved in their story, I knew I had to meet the boys. My father was friends with Drake Golding."

Melanie pondered for a few moments, speechless, her mind doing cartwheels at the thought of a link to Drake. "Okay ... well, could we meet up sometime? I'd prefer to discuss this with the boys there also."

"Of course, noon today? Would that be good for you all?"

"Yes, I think so. It's a little crazy for us at the moment."

"Indeed ... I saw the news last night. Terrible about them Goldings escaping. Could you come to Brunswick? There's somewhere I'd like to show you."

"That's fine, I can drive. Where were you thinking?"

"The top of Tower Lane, the location of the old snooker hall. Give me another call if you encounter any problems."

"I will ... and what was the other reason you went to the signing?"

Horace had already hung up. Excited, Melanie replaced the handset; she couldn't wait to tell everyone so rushed from the back door, down the path to the stream. "I think we have a lead," she announced.

"Well, tell us more," Orion said.

"Horace is Archibald Griffin's son ... isn't that amazing?"

"Wow," Olly said.

"Cool," Leo said, taking his fishing rod out of the water. "What did he say?"

"Not too much, but he wants to meet us in Brunswick ... today, at noon."

Exhilaration coursed through the boys' veins; they hoped to learn more from their previous adventure. Orion cast a lonely figure; He wasn't in the right place — mentally or physically — to accompany them.

Olly and Leo ran inside leaving Melanie to console her husband. "One day, Orion, you'll realise that Leo loves you whatever you can or can't do. Don't put so much pressure on yourself to be the perfect dad. Leo is a happy and healthy boy, that's all we can ask."

"You're right but I want him to be proud of me."

"I know ... and already he is."

Once inside the house, Olly decided to ring Katie, tell her about Horace and the latest news on Lance and Marshall's escape.

"Hello, Jean speaking."

"Hi, it's Olly. Is Katie around please?"

"Hello Olly, no. Katie has taken Claire into Brunswick on the bus. Is it important?"

"Kind of. Where's she gone?"

"To the shops, then they're off to the fair. You could meet them there? It'll be a surprise for them, a nice one I mean."

"Yeah okay, I'll see what we're up to. Thanks anyway. Bye."

Leo was impatient to ask Olly about the girls, though he tried to act cool. "Everything okay?"

"Yeah, thanks." Olly liked playing mind games, Leo his usual target.

"Is that it? Yeah thanks!"

Olly laughed. "Oh, what you really wanted to know was whether you'd be seeing Claire again later. Am I right?"

"Possibly," Leo said through gritted teeth.

"They're off to the fair, so it depends on what time we finish seeing this Horace bloke."

Leo hurried to the back garden and shouted to his parents, "Mum! ... Dad! What time are we seeing Horace?"

"We'll set off in an hour," Melanie said, leaving Orion to his thoughts. "And put something a bit smarter on, you're always wearing ripped jeans."

Leo rushed upstairs to change his clothes and to spray his dad's aftershave on his adolescent cheeks. His thoughts weren't on Horace – they focussed on what he'd say to Claire.

CHAPTER 6

The next hour dragged like treacle over a freshly tarmacked road, with Melanie trying her best to keep the boys occupied by feeding them a hearty breakfast followed by several cups of tea. Eventually they set off to Brunswick, Olly and Leo keeping their thoughts to themselves.

"This will be interesting," Melanie said, attempting to make conversation. "He sounded nice on the phone, I think he'll be able to help."

Leo's mum was always optimistic, the one who kept her family upbeat when it would have been easy to be overwhelmed. She treated Olly as another son, notably after what they'd been through together.

"That's good to hear. Any help is a benefit," Olly replied.

Exiting off the main Brunswick Road, they turned onto Tower Lane. On the right-hand side was an office block with a pub opposite. A row of shops followed, selling clothes and furniture, plus an old-fashioned sweet shop tucked in on the end.

"I'll stop here," Melanie said pulling up in front of Sidney's Sweets. "There's no parking ahead."

Melanie and the boys exited the Beetle and walked up the lane where they saw a sign ahead, ancient and creaking, trying to swing in the light breeze. It read: *Tower Lane Snooker Club*. Upon reaching the building they noticed that the windows were blacked out and a notice decorated the front door: *CLOSED UNTIL FURTHER NOTICE*.

"Don't believe this!" Leo said. "We can't even get in."

"Calm down, we've just arrived," Melanie said.

Olly knocked on the filthy white door, hitting harder each time. Such was his angst that he left a dent in the surface, hurting his hand in the process.

"Hello to you all," came a familiar upper-class accent.

Behind them on the far side of the road was Horace Griffin, still wearing his grey suit.

"Hello Horace," Melanie said. "It's nice to put a face to a voice. This place seems to be shut ... it's boarded up."

Within a couple of strides his long legs had transported him over the road. He held one of his bucket-size hands out and clasped each of theirs in greeting – amplifying the pain in Olly's hand from his thumping on the door.

"A Pleasure to meet you too, Melanie. I'm so glad you all made it. I've been away from Brunswick for a long time, travelling the world don't you know. I've been following your story closely but never had the chance to meet you both until yesterday. We have something in common."

Reaching into one of his pockets he produced a keyring and on the fob was a symbol: a triangle embossed with an emblem and the letters **A**, **O** and **D**. Attached to the fob were a bunch of keys, not a normal machine cut set, but chunky heavy keys like those used to unlock dungeons three centuries prior. Horace picked one and unlocked the front door which opened into a dank hallway, a wide staircase visible in front of them. Both boys glanced at Melanie for reassurance. After falling for Marshall's lies the previous year, they no longer trusted people. She nodded and smiled. "It's okay boys, I'm here with you," she said placing her hands on each of their shoulders. Flicking a switch, Leo turned on a weary light bulb that barely illuminated the top landing. Walking up the stairs they glanced at pictures of gentlemen snooker players, their names difficult to read in the dimness.

"This place is ancient," Leo said. "Everyone's wearing suits … and the photos are in black and white. How long has it been shut?"

"Probably six years," Horace said. "Some of these pictures have been here a long time. That's my father, Archibald."

The Seekers of Duat

"Archibald Griffin, Club Champion 1930," said Olly reading the inscription. "How old was he there?"

"About thirty-five."

"He looks sixty," Leo chuckled.

Around the corner, through an unlocked door, they entered the drinks bar. A panel of switches on the near wall were used to illuminate a large hall with four snooker tables.

"This is impressive," Olly said. "But I suppose we have just entered a snooker club. Is that what you think we have in common … snooker?"

"No, of course not. It's a long time since I've been in this building. My father would entertain me in here and we'd play a game of billiards when I was young. I wanted to see it again. In here is one of three things my dad told me he loved in his life: his shop, his cars and this snooker club. There's another door outside which leads to where I'm taking you, but this way is far more exciting. The real reason I bought you all up here lies beyond there." Pointing, Horace gestured to one of the oak lined segments on the far wall. The three guests strained their eyes to see anything.

Leo walked over and gave it a gentle tap with his fist. "Beyond what? There's nothing there, it's a wall."

Horace strode over between two of the tables, caressing his hand on the dusty green baize as he did so. "Don't believe what your eyes first show you, young man. Sometimes the dullest painting holds the greatest delight … if you examine it closely." He

41

reached for the scoreboard attached to the panel and slid a brass pointer back and forth over the numbers, as if he were opening a safe, until the scoreboard moved down the wall to reveal a keyhole. Using another of his keys, he plunged it into the hole and turned until it clicked. Pushing the wall open, Horace announced, "Welcome to the Art of Darkness."

CHAPTER 7

The light from the snooker hall reached into the secret entrance, revealing a cascading spiral staircase with a golden handrail.

"It's how I remember it," Horace said. "It's the first time I've entered the club this way since I've been back. The look on your face Leo takes me to my childhood. I was the same when my father first showed me this."

Leo was gobsmacked at what was behind the wall in this dingy old snooker hall and couldn't wait to descend the stairs but Olly seemed puzzled.

"Are you alright, Olly?" Horace asked.

"The Art of Darkness," Olly said. "It was mentioned at the Golding's trial."

"I'm sure it was. Down these steps is where it began, George Bumble and Drake Golding discussing the creation of the Brunswick tunnel adventure … in my father's club. My father left this to me in his will: the snooker hall, the club and he had an antique shop until he retired. He stashed the artefacts from there in a room down here."

"So, where have you been?" Melanie asked. "You told us you were travelling the world – for your job?"

"I picked up my father's interest in antiquities as a young boy. He took me on archaeological digs and that had me hooked. The world is such a huge place. People tell me it's becoming smaller with the luxury of flying, but there are so many mysteries still to be unearthed. I've spent the last seven years in the Amazon rainforest looking for a lost temple. It started off as a three-month trip but I fell in love with the place. Its magnitude and beauty is astounding."

"Did you find the temple?" Leo asked.

"Unfortunately not," Horace replied following them down the staircase. He paused for a moment before continuing. "I do remember when I first found out about your adventure. I was at an airport waiting for a transfer when I read an article in a newspaper about your incident in the tunnel – a headline maker: *Boys find forgotten man in tunnel after eleven years*. It mentioned the Golding's, which awakened memories of my dad and his meetings with Drake who called upon my father to help him retrieve treasures from the tunnel. I knew that, once I'd finished exploring the Amazon, I'd come home, sort out my father's

THE SEEKERS OF DUAT

inheritance and try to find you both. I hope you don't mind?"

"Not at all," Olly said. "You've probably arrived at the right time."

The boys reached the bottom of the stairs, Leo glancing around for another light switch.

"It's different down here, old-fashioned," Horace said turning on a torch. "They used gas lights here and it's never been updated. I'll get it fixed when I'm able."

"Fixed? Does that mean you'll re-open the Art of Darkness?" said Olly.

"I'm thinking about it ... we'll see."

The torch light piercing through the kicked-up dust revealed a spectacle that astounded the boys, leaving Melanie petrified. Spiders' webs spanned a long corridor which opened onto three rooms, two on one side, one on the other.

"I'm meant to be looking after you two and it's me who's scared," Melanie said pushing her brave warriors in front to fight their way through the silken threads. Entering the first room revealed thousands of books, crammed into giant oak bookshelves.

"Amazing," Olly said, blowing a spider off a binder to examine the title. "This one's about werewolves."

"This is about witches and warlocks," Leo said, now interested. "Wonder if there are any spells in them?"

"There will be," Horace said, leaving the room. "A remedy, spell and potion for everything magical and mystical resides down in these rooms. You just need to know where to look."

Horace strolled on, illuminating the corridor, Melanie in tow, Olly and Leo following, glancing in at the other rooms as the light flashed by. Some contained more books, while in others shelving housed skulls, jars of teeth and organs, skeletons, and deformed stuffed animals.

"This is well freaky," Leo said, standing close to Olly.

After tearing through another spider's web, they were greeted by a closed door ahead. Pulling out his bunch of keys, Horace picked the largest and thrust it into the keyhole. As it turned, they heard decades of grime grinding in the mechanism until it clunked into position. Horace permitted Leo to turn the handle and, with a gentle shoulder barge, the door groaned open. The torch light exposed a sizeable room, numerous nooks evident, fitted with green leather seats and circular oak tables. In the middle of the room stood a mahogany Victorian wind-out table of three leaves, surrounded by a dozen chairs. To the left-hand was the remnants of a bar, a couple of crystal cut tumblers gathering dust.

"This was the meeting room," Horace said. "My father used to sit in that alcove to the left of the bar."

"What did they do here?" Melanie said.

"It was an exclusive club, somewhere the well-to-do met to discuss strange occurrences around the country, arranging club outings to investigate them for themselves. My father was the founder, started the club when he witnessed odd happenings on his travels. He invited close friends at first, and so it began."

"Did you know about the cube?" Olly said.

"Ah, the cube, the saviour in your last adventure," Horace said, pulling out a chair, brushing away the accumulated dust and seating himself at the large table. "I've heard many stories and seen strange things during my life, so many that it's hard to distinguish real from imaginative sometimes. A story that my father told me has stuck with me for a long time. Would you like to hear it?"

Melanie and the boys extracted chairs and joined him. "No! Not that one. Never sit on that one." Horace exclaimed.

Leo glanced at Olly who shrugged in bewilderment before sliding the oak chair away towards the wall. "Is this one okay?"

Horace nodded and continued, "My father told me of a trip to Egypt, before I was born of course. He and fellow archaeologists discovered the tomb of Osiris, next to the great pyramid of Giza. For six sweltering weeks they dug in the Egyptian desert until the breakthrough. Behind a two-tonne slab of stone they discovered a vertical shaft forty feet deep."

"What was in there?" Leo asked.

"A room with six chambers leading off, each adorned with treasures. But there was more. Down another two shafts they reached a flooded room where a sarcophagus was lying on an elevated section, like an island. It was the tomb symbolising the god Osiris. For days, my father and his fellow archaeologists entered the dangerous shafts of the tomb, extracting items for the local historians to itemise.

"Unbeknown to the rest of his group, my dad entered an unlicensed poker game one night with locals, including Gamal – a historian he'd been liaising with. My dad had a full life, travelling several times around the world on his adventures, learning much on his journeys – one of which, was poker. Expeditions were often cancelled or extended depending on the money he'd won or lost.

"On this occasion, everyone had folded except Gamal and my father. In the middle of the table were the five cards: Ace of hearts, Ace of clubs, King of hearts, Four of spades and a Ten of hearts. Each player tested one another's nerves by piling in more chips, then real cash, watches, and jewellery. They decided that the loser would help the winner steal artefacts from the tomb to cover the bet. They shook hands across the table and Gamal made a prayer. He revealed his cards first: a pair of aces – he had four of a kind. The dimly lit room erupted with cheers. *Come on English man, show me the cards,* Gamal had said. My father stared across the cash laden table into Gamal's eyes and without hesitation flipped over his cards. all that could be heard was an intake of breath followed by a cry of misery."

"What did Archie have?" Olly said.

"The jack and queen of hearts; he had a royal flush, the best hand you can get. Gamal was overwrought but true to his word, he and my father devised a plan to raid the tomb the following night for artefacts to steal."

Silently, the boys listened as Horace continued, "The following night Gamal and father made their way to the tombs entrance. Gamal was told to wait and keep lookout while father began the decent. At the first level he ventured into a chamber room decorated more than the others; hieroglyphics were painted around the walls, a mosaic depicting heaven adorned the ceiling and hell on the floor. This was no ordinary chamber. The markings recorded details of the throne of the god Osiris presiding over the souls of the dead, transporting them to heaven or to the underworld, depending on their purity."

"What?" Olly said. "Why was this in Osiris' tomb?"

"My friends, didn't you know. Osiris was the god of the underworld and the resurrection."

"That's what Stumpy told us," Olly said. "Something to do with the portal he mentioned."

"Whatever it is," Melanie interrupted, "We can't let Victor know. That ghost will do anything to find a way to meet that god."

"I'm pretty sure they don't exist," Leo said. "And even if they did, it was thousands of years ago."

"Victor?" Horace said. "You mean one of Drakes grandchildren?"

"Yes," Olly said. "We trapped Victor's spirit in the cube but now he's escaped and seeks revenge. Thanks to Leo, it knows about a gateway to the underworld."

"I had to do something to delay Victor from killing us all."

"I know mate, sorry, I didn't mean it like that."

Horace shook his head. "This is terrible, here I am telling you stories when you need to be finding Victor."

"No, not at all," Melanie said. "I rang you hoping you could help us. Please carry on with your story."

"Yes, we need to know everything you can remember," Olly said. "Where was this? Where was the throne?"

Horace cleared his throat and continued, "Studying the hieroglyphics, my father concluded that there had to be a secret hidden in the chamber. He brushed and wiped away the sand to uncover clues until he saw it … an anomaly, different to the rest of the carved stone, one with squarer edges and defined spaces surrounding it. My father told me that he gave it a few shoves with the palm of his hand."

"Did it work?" Leo said.

"The stone shook for a few seconds, depositing sand onto the floor before sinking into the wall. My father stood in silence expecting the wall to collapse to reveal another long-lost tomb. There was nothing of interest, except the faint noise of running water. He rushed down the other shaft to Osiris' sarcophagus which – if you remember – was surrounded by water. This time the water levels were falling. A stone had moved across the wall, revealing a pipe that diverted the water from the room. Father watched in awe at what was now revealed under the casket. A four pillared structure had appeared, the sarcophagus sitting proudly on top. Between the pillars an iron throne materialised, several objects around it, sunken into the floor.

"It was then that my father heard voices from above. The expedition leader had discovered he was there. Without thinking, father grabbed loose artefacts and stuffed them into his bag. When he was found, he showed the leader the iron throne, aiming to distract them from his theft. On exiting the tomb, father was confronted by jets of water shooting upwards from the desert – it was no wonder that he and Gamal were spotted. Father was never caught for stealing, but the archaeological society had their suspicions, the lack of artefacts around the throne being a marker. My father was banished from the society and came home with a few of his treasures."

"The cube?" Olly said.

"Yes, amongst other items."

"The throne ... where is it?" Leo said.

"The iron throne was moved to an accessible site, where tourists could visit, back to Osiris's temple at

Abydos, over three hundred miles south along the Nile. This magnificent temple is now home to the throne."

"Wow, do you believe all of this?" Olly said.

"I believe that story happened," Horace replied. "Unlike young Leo, I also believe in the gods, especially after the other day – and that is the other reason I wanted to meet you."

"I was meaning to ask you about that?" Melanie said.

CHAPTER 8

Horace led Melanie, Olly and Leo over to a corridor. In the distance, light oozed around the edge of a door.

"That must be the outside," Leo said.

"Well done Sherlock Holmes," said Olly. "What would we do without you."

"You are correct, but it's this door that I want you to see," Horace said, grabbing a handle to his left and opening a door. "In this room my father stored his belongings from his shop, the one where Drake Golding was given the cube."

They walked into a room containing several rows of shelving, crammed full of boxes. "Where is the shop? Is it still standing?" Melanie said.

"It was called 'Curiosities of the World' and is long since closed but the building remains, a record shop I believe. I used to love the sound of the bell as someone opened the door. It was very distinctive."

"Which record shop?" Olly said.

"Oh, I don't know the name, I'm too old for the music you'll like. It's in Winchester Crescent."

Buzz Music, we go all the time," Leo said smiling.

"Well, there you go young man, we do have something in common," Horace said making a beeline to the back of the room. "I wanted to show you this as something happened the other day that I can't explain. I was hoping your young minds could help me."

Horace knelt down, pulling out a six-foot long metal box from under some shelves. "A few days ago, I was rummaging around and found this."

The box scraped along the floor, causing a spine-tingling screech.

"Stop!" Melanie shouted with her fingers in her ears. "That's far enough, we can see it."

Horace shone the torch onto the box. The lid was engraved with a representation of an Egyptian god. Buckled tightly around the casket, were two worn leather straps that crossed each other in the middle. More importantly, a message in white paint had been daubed across the container: **DO NOT OPEN**.

"What's inside?" Olly asked.

"All in good time," Horace answered. "I was inquisitive like you, Olly, so I re-fastened it tightly after examining it. You see, I didn't want anything else escaping."

"Anything *else*?" Melanie gulped.

"I unbuckled the straps to lift the lid, but it was corroded and wouldn't open. Where my father obtained it from, I have no idea but it *was* some time ago. So, I used a hammer and chisel and struck it harder with every blow, until ..." Horace took a breath.

"Until what?" Leo said.

"The lid of the casket blew off and out flew a red mist that bled over the edge to the floor, across to the manhole cover – the one over there – before vanishing underground." Horace pointed to the place where the mysterious substance had disappeared.

The boys stared, stepping back as if a deadly spider was crawling around in their midst.

"But that wasn't all, I heard a laugh too. Oh, not a human laugh. This sounded like it was from the depths of hell, its deep tone rumbling through the club until the essence had dissipated. I feared that I'd released ... something, though I have no idea what it was."

"Oh my, you must've been terrified?" Melanie said, regretting coming to the club. She was nervous for her and the boys' safety. "What did you do?"

"I panicked and replaced the lid, fastening the straps tightly. I've not been back since."

Unlike Melanie, the boys were enthralled by Horace's tale. "Is that why you wanted to contact us?"

"Yes Olly. I'd heard about your book signing; the perfect opportunity to introduce myself. You two boys are probably the only people who would believe me after your adventure last year."

Melanie peered at Leo in the torch-lit room and shrugged her shoulders. She had no idea about what had been released and nor did Leo but they were relieved that *it* – whatever *it* was – was no longer in the room. Glancing at Olly, Melanie noticed that he was concentrating, eyes shut, leaning against a wall, knee bent and trainer pressed against the brickwork. After seemingly an age, Olly's focus returned to the room as he pointed to an engraving on the box lid. "Who is that meant to be?"

"It wasn't hard to find a book on Egyptian history in here, so I searched for it in these tomes" Horace said. "From what I can tell, it's *Set*, an Egyptian god."

"Set … Set …" Olly thought aloud. "That name rings a bell."

"Well, I've never heard of him," Melanie said.

"Same here," Leo said.

"You have!" Olly clicked his fingers. "The other morning when I came in to wake you up. I thought you were saying 'set free'." Mute, Leo turned towards his friend. "But what you were saying was 'Set is free'. You must've received a message from someone with the telepathy stuff you can do."

Leo's temperament altered like only a sultry teenagers could. "Impossible. I'm not a slayer any more. Do I have to keep telling you? I have to be near a dragon if I'm to regain my powers ... unless any are lurking in your garden."

Olly tried to calm Leo down. "I know mate, it must be crap without your powers, but what I'm saying is someone might've communicated with you in another way. Try and think back? Do you remember a voice talking to you? It could have been in your dream or it might have been reality."

With a noisy exhale of breath, shoulders slouched, Leo dragged his feet to a secluded corner of the room, slid down the wall and attempted to recall his dream.

Horace stood, sweat bubbling up onto his brow. He took his pocket square from his suit and dabbed his forehead. "You think whatever escaped from the box here was Set?"

"Not the person but maybe his soul." Olly said. "Was anything else in that box?"

"You aren't suggesting we take a look are you?" Melanie exclaimed. "Horace has told us that he thinks he's freed a spirit. That means we should keep the box shut?"

"There might be some more clues. The more we know about this the better."

"The boy is correct," Horace said. "Nothing would be discovered if we all shut our eyes."

Melanie strolled over to Leo as Horace and Olly undid the straps. "Let's be careful about this," Horace said. "If you are correct about the escapee being Set, we are dealing with something potentially terrifying."

"Why is that?" Leo said, raising his head.

"Set is the god of war, chaos, storms, envy …"

"Okay, we get it … he's evil. Being the god of love and peace would have been just too easy, yeah? So why do you think I've been saying his name in my sleep?"

"Someone might be trying to warn you," Horace said, freeing the leather straps.

Without trepidation, Olly sprung the lid away from the box. This time nothing seeped, so Leo dashed to his feet, eager to discover what was inside. "Hey, let me see."

The box contained two packages wrapped in carpets – beautifully hand-crafted Persian rugs, ornately decorated in red and gold.

Leo couldn't resist. He bent over the casket, reached in, and took out a rug. "Look Mum, what do you think of this."

"It's beautiful," Melanie said unsure what was hidden inside. "Be careful, it looks ancient."

Leo placed it on the stone floor and unravelled it causing Horace and Melanie to gasp.

"That's amazing," Olly said.

"What is it?"

"An ankh, Leo."

"It's in the shape on your key fob, Horace."

"Ah, yes Olly. The ankh is a symbol of the afterlife. There are some more here if my memory serves me right. Father created the logo for the Art of Darkness using the ankh which he thought was a good representation of the club. He bought a few of them back each time he visited Egypt, which were many."

Without a second thought Leo picked up the ankh and regretted it immediately, dropping it to the floor with an *aarrgghh* sound.

"Are you alright? Leo? Are you Okay?" Melanie said rushing over to him. He failed to reply, instead falling to his knees, scrunching his eyes closed and holding his hands to his ears, trying to stop a noise reverberating through his head."

"What's happening to him?" Olly shouted.

"I … I can see a vision," Leo said.

"What can you see?"

"I'm in a desert, a stormy red desert, sand is flying everywhere. Oh my god!" Melanie crouched beside her son, cradling him, watching as tears streamed down his face. "I'm looking down… can see a wooden leg."

"You're seeing through Stumpy's eyes," Olly gasped. "Who else is there?"

"Fire … fire breathing monsters … coming towards me … I can't fight them off." Leo fell to the floor, staring upwards to the ceiling.

"Leo … Leo, speak to me, it's your mum,"

Leo blinked. inhaled deeply and sat upright. "That was so real, like I was there."

"I think you might have your slayer powers back," Olly was excited. "Do you feel stronger? How about doing one of those somersaults in the air?"

"Don't be daft, I feel exactly the same."

"There must be some reason you've connected with Stumpy? Maybe it's the ankh that has powers? Did it help you recall the dream of the other morning?"

Leo pulled his sweaty t-shirt away from his chest. "I remember."

"What?"

"My dream the other day Olly, Stumpy was in it with a figure in white. They were both terrified and told me they needed our help. You were right, they told me that Set is free. Mum, Stumpy's in trouble and we've got to help him."

Melanie tried to interpret her son's words but no longer knew what to believe. In the past year she'd listened to Orion's stories about his eleven years in the underworld and Leo's tales of heroics during his dad's rescue. She'd accepted what she'd been told, believing them both – though the stories were more like episodes from the X-Files. They were *her* family so why should she doubt them? This time was different. She was now involved and – yet – the story seemed make-believe. "You had a bad dream Leo. Even if it *was* real, how can you help someone who is in another world? Listen to what you're all saying? Here's a box, locked away in an old snooker club holding the soul of an Egyptian god – now escaped to terrorise the underworld. Horace, please tell these two lads to come to their senses?"

Horace plonked himself on a wooden box. "I'm not sure I can do that – even if I wanted to. Perhaps if I tell you what I've found out about Set, you'll understand. Legend suggests that he killed his own brother Osiris, cutting him into several pieces."

"The same Osiris that's god of the underworld?" Olly said.

"Yes, but remember that these are myths in our culture. To the Egyptians they represented deities to be worshipped and are believed to resurrect themselves."

"After the last year, there's not a lot I don't believe in. Stumpy himself told me that he was saved by Osiris, so he's got to be real."

"How is Osiris alive? If Set killed him?" Melanie asked Horace, her misgivings easing.

"Hieroglyphics have shown that Osiris' wife Isis reassembled the pieces of her husband, to allow her to conceive their son Horus. It was he who fought Set for over eighty years in bloody battles."

"So, *is* Set dead?"

"Everybody thought so, Leo – overpowered, conquered and then disappeared."

"Yeah, perhaps he vanished into a sealed metal box, until you opened it," said Olly.

Horace reached down to the ankh. "What are you doing?" Leo said. "Leave it, it might be cursed."

"I need to find out what it's made of... Oww!"

"Did you see anything?" Leo said, as Horace dropped the ankh.

"No, but it's hot ... and heavy. It seems to be made of iron?" Horace stood, headed to one of the bookshelves, pulled out a book and flicked through the pages, creating a cloud of dust that dispersed into the room like threads of smoke. With a waft of his hand, Horace cleared the smog as he smiled. "I thought as much."

"What? What is it?"

"Leo, I think we're onto something." Horace turned the book around to show them the page displaying a depiction of the god Set, holding an ankh identical to the one in the room.

"That's the same figure carved on the lid," Leo said.

"Whoa!" Olly said. "Set and his ankh – definitely. You told us it felt like iron but shouldn't a god's ankh be made of gold?"

"Gold was available in Egypt but Iron was believed to have fallen from another world as a meteorite – in other words, rare."

"We need to find the portal, the one Stumpy told us about." Olly said. "We owe it to him after everything he did for us last year, not to mention the years he looked after Orion in the caves. We have to help."

"We are not going to Egypt," Melanie said. "We can barely afford to go to the seaside."

THE SEEKERS OF DUAT

"Maybe it's not in Egypt. Horace, show me your key fob." Horace took the set of keys out of his pocket and handed them to Olly. "This symbol for the Art of Darkness club, why is it triangular and what are these markings?"

"My father was obsessed with Egyptian history. The pyramid shape is obvious and I've already told you why the ankh is there. The other markings are of three gemstones which I know nothing about ... but I know someone who does."

"Who?"

"My father Leo, Archibald Griffin."

Olly snatched a glance at Leo and Melanie in bewilderment and then back at Horace. "Archibald? ... Your father? ... He's dead, yes?"

"Correct, young sir but you'll understand when we arrive."

"Where are we going?"

"I'm taking you all to Shrowton, a little village just out of town, where my father was born and where he's laid to rest."

CHAPTER 9

Melanie offered to drive to Shrowton, located three miles to the south of Brunswick. She felt more in control that way; she'd only known Horace for a few hours and trust hadn't grown yet. Horace squeezed his tall frame into the Beetle's passenger seat, his knee's inches away from the windscreen, level with his head. The boys in the back chuckled as Horace repeatedly poked his bony fingers forward to point out the direction they needed to take. Soon, they turned off the main road onto a single-track lane to enter the village. Similar to others, it had a post office, pub, cricket pitch on the green and a church surrounded by gravestones from centuries past.

"Park here," Horace told Melanie, indicating a spot. She manoeuvred the Beetle outside the lychgate of the church, whereupon Horace proceeded to uncoil himself from the car.

"Didn't think I'd be here today," Leo whispered to Olly.

"Me neither. There must be a good reason he brought us here, unless he's a serial killer who's going to chop us into hundreds of pieces."

"Shut up, idiot."

"Don't wind him up, Olly," Melanie said. "And Leo, stop it with your tantrums."

Sniggering, Olly held his hands up. "I'm joking. I'd trust Horace one hundred percent, seems a nice bloke."

"Well, let's see what he has to show us here first, and keep our wits about us," Melanie said.

Once out of the car, they strolled through the ten feet tall oak lychgate, decorated with carved roses up the sides and onto the arched roof. In the churchyard were hundreds of graves, standing like dominoes, each carved differently, some dating back centuries. Statues of angels, six-feet high and weathered stone crosses filled the space between, wildflowers hugging their moss-covered stems.

"They're impressive, aren't they?" Horace said, leading the way. "Now I'm back, I should visit here more often. Crisp winter mornings are best, when the stones have a dusting of frost, the low sun causing komorebi."

"What's that?" Leo asked.

"Scattered light that filters through trees. I learnt that on my travels to the Far East. A fascinating part of the world."

"Anyway," Olly said, trying to keep his focus. "Which one is your dad's grave?"

Horace stretched out an arm. "Around the side of the church. You'll both spot it easily."

The boys walked ahead, feeling strange meandering through and over gravestones. Leo said, "Do you think there's anything still under these?"

"I doubt it. The insects would've seen to that a long time ago."

"Cremation for me," Leo said, "No way am I ending up being a feast for the critters."

As they stepped around the corner of the church the boy's frivolity abruptly stopped, along with their footsteps. "No ... you're kidding me," Olly said.

"That's unreal. I've changed my mind. I want to be buried in one of those."

Prominent was a pyramid, five feet high and wide, its limestone angles reflecting the sun.

"That must be it!" Olly said, his voice decorated with delight. "The portal, that's the portal Stumpy told us about."

"Impressive, isn't it?" Horace said appearing from behind with Melanie. "My dad had it designed and made before he passed – except for date of death."

"It's beautiful," Melanie said. "I've never seen anything like it."

The Seekers of Duat

The boys rushed to the grave and wiped away the dirt that had built up over the years. On the facing side it read:

```
Archibald Joseph Griffin - Aged
81 years - Born 29th May 1895 -
Died 25th May 1977
```

"He had a long life," Olly said.

"An interesting life," Horace said, chortling to himself. "Take a look at the other sides. They're what I wanted you to see."

The boys glanced round and saw a phrase inscribed:

```
What flies you to hell

Will fly you to heaven
```

"What's that mean?" Leo said, scratching his head.

"I didn't know when I first saw it either – and I still haven't worked it out," Horace said. "I reckoned that your young, creative minds would be able to tell me. Take a look at the other sides too."

The next side showed the emblem of the Art of Darkness, the ankh painted in gold. The three *gem symbols* had coloured stones recessed into the limestone, dark blue, red, and green hues sparkling in the sunlight.

"This must have cost loads, Horace," Olly said. "Was your dad wealthy from his trips."

"He did well from his expeditions, yes, though his main income was from the shop and snooker hall."

"Here, take a look," Leo said, cleaning the surface of the last side. "Is that the throne you mentioned?"

"It certainly is," Horace replied.

Carved into the limestone was an engraving of the Iron Throne from Osiris' tomb that Archie had discovered, surrounded by hieroglyphics and foreign phrases. Next to the throne was a round plate containing three stones.

"Do you reckon those stones resemble the gems on the Art of Darkness sign?" Olly said.

Horace shrugged as he said, "Maybe, there are three of them."

"From this, it seems that the throne is linked to the gems and plate."

"Possibly, and I have suspected that but I don't have any gems and I don't know what gems they are. I've never seen a plate like that in his belongings."

"Well, what about the markings? Do they mean anything?" Melanie asked, gesturing towards Leo.

"It's ages since we learnt Egyptian at school and it's Olly who is studying ancient stuff in his GCSE's?"

"It's called Ancient History, but you were close … we haven't studied any hieroglyphics yet," Olly replied wiping away the grime to reveal another phrase – this time in English. He read it out: "The God awaits my beloved."

"It might as well be in Egyptian," Leo said. "I haven't clue what any of this means."

"Was he religious, your father?" Melanie asked Horace.

"Not especially, but the reference doesn't have to be to our God. Hundreds of gods are worshipped all over the world, in different regions. He was probably meaning Osiris, it would line up with the throne."

"Who's his beloved? His wife?" Leo said.

Horace chortled to himself, "He's unlikely to be talking about my mother … they split up when I was young."

The boys and Melanie stood by the grave as Horace walked towards a bench to sit for a rest. Olly knew that clues were staring at him, but his logical brain was malfunctioning. He placed his hands on the smooth limestone and tried to move it one way then another – nothing happened. Frustration was pulsing inside him. "This isn't right. Stumpy told us that this was a portal … a way to the Underworld to reach him. It seems to be no more than a lump of limestone adorned with symbols." He kicked the base in vexation, knocking a strip of dried mud from the stone.

Melanie put an arm around Olly to calm him down. "I was sceptical about this Egyptian nonsense but I think we're onto something here. Don't lose sight of what you're seeking. A clue might be right under your feet."

Olly stepped back. "Maybe Stumpy had it wrong? Perhaps the grave was a clue – one that leads us to the real portal?"

"Look," Leo said pointing to the floor. "Mum you were right, another clue."

The strip of mud Olly had disturbed revealed another phrase which Olly read. "Duat awaits the seekers."

Horace lifted his head on hearing Olly speak. "What did you say?"

"Duat awaits the seekers." Olly said, "Do you know what it means?"

"Duat is the Egyptian Underworld."

Olly glanced at Leo. "We're in the right place. We have to find the pieces to make the portal."

"The three gems and a plate?" Leo said.

"Exactly."

"Horace doesn't know what the gems are and as for the plate, that could be anywhere?" Melanie said rubbing her fingers over the jewels protruding from the limestone.

Olly shut his eyes in concentration. "Surely, there's some record of the graves construction?"

"There will be," Horace said, "But it will take me some time to sift through the paperwork. You saw how many boxes were in that room."

"You're right, we're going to need some help."

CHAPTER 10

Everyone decided to head back to the old club on Tower Lane with Melanie again parking in front of the sweet shop. Horace exited the vehicle first, giving Melanie an opportunity to speak to the boys. "Are you both okay with this?" she said. "Your experience last year had an impact on you – realise that when we step back into that building, you're going to be thrust into another adventure."

The two teenagers stared at her, smiling. "We're fine Mum," Leo said. "We like adventures – or would you rather we cause trouble on the streets like other kids?"

"This is a bit more than another adventure …"

Olly interrupted. "You believe in all of this?"

She paused, pondering for a moment. "Yes, I suppose I do. How can I not after witnessing what happened at the cemetery? I'm worried for you both – this could be life or death."

"We survived last time," Leo said, "and I developed slayer powers ... just like dad and they're sure to return. I've heard Stumpy's voice – that's something."

"Yeah," Olly said. "We need to do this for Stumpy and plus, you're helping this time."

Melanie knew that the boys had answers for all her questions so resigned herself to losing this battle, knowing there were bigger ones still to come. She turned to glance out of the windscreen and witnessed Horace waving them into the club. "Come on, let's find out about these gems."

As they jumped out, Olly turned to walk in the opposite direction.

"Where are you going?" Leo said.

"For some help. Like I told you, we need a few more sets of eyes."

"Who?" Melanie said.

"Katie and Claire, they're at the fair – Katie's mum told me. It's through that snicket to Brunswick common," Olly said, heading towards a one-way road dissecting a car park and a bowling alley. "I'll be back before you know it."

"I'm not sure," Melanie said, beckoning him back. "Lance and Marshall are still out there."

"If they've any sense, they'll be miles away by now. Anyway, the police might've caught them."

"What about Victor?"

"That ghost will stay well away from us whilst we have the cube." Olly said tapping his bag. "I'll be fine, promise."

"Can I go?" Leo said, dreaming of another meet up with Claire.

"No, you stay with me and Horace, we need you here," Melanie said before deciding to let Olly go. "Okay Olly, as quick as you can and come straight back."

"Thanks," Olly said doing a quick U-turn. "I'll nip in here first. It might help to have a bargaining tool with me."

Olly ran into *Sidney's Sweets* where he found himself surrounded by numerous multi-coloured jars brim full of every candy, chocolate, bubble-gum and lolly-pop anyone would want.

"Can I help you?" said a voice from behind the counter. Olly stepped forward towards a frail man seated in a rocking chair. Sidney had owned the shop for over sixty years and was a celebrity of Brunswick. In the Great war he'd been a flying ace, credited with over twenty aerial victories, earning him the Victoria Cross.

"Err, hi Sidney, how are you?"

"I'm very well, thank you for asking. What are you up to today young man?"

"A small adventure if I'm honest. The problem is, I don't know where we're starting, let alone where we'll end up."

"Those are the best missions," Sidney replied, slowly raising himself from the chair. "When I was your age, I was keen to explore the world, although I didn't realise that my wishes would come true so soon."

Olly had read articles about this war hero who had visited Olly's primary school to talk about his escapades. "Weren't you scared? ... y'know, when you were flying your plane?".

"Of course ... I was petrified, anyone would have been. I had no choice in the matter and I'll tell you this for nothing, I wouldn't change my life for anything. If bad is in the world, I would be the first in the queue to eradicate it."

Olly felt ten-foot tall after hearing the old man talk, realising that his own approach to life was the same. If someone needed him, he'd do his best to help.

"Now, what can I get you for your adventure?" Sidney asked.

Olly bought some fizzy cola bottles for himself, cherry bon-bons, black jacks and a packet of love hearts for Katie and Claire. As he left the shop, he watched Sidney return to his chair and said, "Thanks, see you later."

Back in the club, Horace was rummaging through box after box, searching for information about Archie's pyramid grave.

"Will this take long?" a frustrated Leo said, still annoyed that his mum hadn't let him go with Olly.

THE SEEKERS OF DUAT

"Patience, Leo," Melanie said, collecting up books on Egyptian history and myths. "Horace is going as fast as he can. If you want to help, try looking for a plate."

"What kind of plate?"

"I don't know, just look."

Leo reached up to pull a box from the top shelf, virtually dropping it – it was heavy.

"Be careful," Horace said hearing the thud. "It might seem like a load of old tosh in here, but some of this may be worth a fortune, and – if not – it's worth a lot to me."

Leo rolled his eyes as he lifted off the dusty lid.

"Any luck?" his mum said trying to peek inside.

Leo plucked a triangular container out and opened it. "No, just a set of snooker balls."

"Well, I never," Horace said, striding over. "These were my father's private set, I remember playing with them." Horace sensed that Leo was frustrated, especially knowing that Olly was at the fair, so he added, "I tell you what, why don't you go upstairs with your mum and have a game of snooker. Cues are under the tables, light switches behind the bar. I'll give you a shout if I find something."

Melanie winked at Horace, thankful for his interjection. "Come on Leo, let's see if you can beat your old mum at snooker."

"Easy," Leo said as they strolled from the room.

CHAPTER 11

Exiting the snicket from Tower Lane, Olly heard the sounds of the Brunswick Fair – mostly thrill screams and machinery whirring. The fair appeared twice a year, at Easter and again over the summer holidays. It was the place to be for a teenager in Brunswick as the town lacked anything exciting, except for shopping and admiring the flower beds – hardly major attractions.

Olly crossed the road and walked onto Brunswick common, an expanse of grass that horseshoed the centre of the town, suburbia evident on the far side. Olly's pace quickened as he closed in on the colourful spectacle, the smell of fried onions, hot dogs and burgers filling the air, luring him in. Hundreds of onlookers, mostly children begging their parents for more money, milled around, mesmerised by the attractions and noise of the rides. Feeling peckish, Olly failed to resist buying a burger. "Double cheeseburger with onions, please," he said to the young lady behind the steaming stove.

"Do you want bacon on that?" she asked wiping her brow.

"Yeah, why not." As Olly reached into his pocket for change, the burger being handed to him over the counter, his vision blackened as two hands reached from behind and covered his eyes.

"And where's mine?" came the voice.

"Bloody hell ... I nearly dropped that," Olly said, realising that he was being accosted by Katie. She released her hands and pecked him on his cheek. "I got you some of these instead." He pulled out a bag of sweets as he chomped into his burger.

"Aww thanks, that's thoughtful. Love hearts are my faves."

"Where's Claire?"

"She nipped to the toilet." Katie pointed to her, at the back of a long queue leading to the solitary green cubicle. "What are you doing here? Are you on your own? Were you looking for me?"

"Enough with the questions. Your mum told me you'd be here. Something has happened since we saw you yesterday." Olly took another bite of his bun.

"Like what?" Katie said waiting for him to empty his mouth.

Olly gulped, wiped a fried onion off his chin and said, "Victor's escaped."

"The ghost, Victor?"

"Yes. Do you know any others?"

Katie was unable to speak, a first for Olly. A scream from a nearby ride broke her contemplation. "How?"

"Don't know, someone must've read out the phrase – you know, the one that releases him."

"Shouldn't you be in hiding? Victor will want revenge," she said, grabbing his hand.

Olly shook his head and grinned. "Me and Leo scared him off, you know, with the cube, but there's something else. Remember that cave troll I told you about?"

"Stumpy?"

"Yeah, Leo had a vision … Stumpy's in trouble."

"So, where is this Stumpy? Is he nearby?"

"Not really, he's in *Duat* – what the Egyptians called their Underworld. If we're to save him, we need to find a portal."

Confused, Katie tried to understand, nodding her head though she had no clue what Olly was talking about. "Why have you come for me and Claire? What have we got to do with this?"

"We need help. The portal is identified by some gems and a plate and we need to find them, quick!"

"How do you know this stuff?"

"A guy called Horace; we met him at the book signing. He was left an old snooker club in his fathers will. It's over the road and Leo and his Mum are there now, looking. Will you help us?"

Katie pondered, but only a moment. "Course I will. I'd do anything to be involved in an adventure with you," she glanced over at Claire, still in the queue. "This might be inappropriate, but while we're waiting for Claire, do you fancy a few rides?"

"Well, we should get back to help, but … I suppose we are waiting for Claire … so, yeah."

"Great! How about this one?"

"Are you sure? You're ill on a car journey." Olly remembered one of their first dates as Katie had to exit his parents' car to be sick.

"That was when I was nervous. Anyway it's heights that make me ill."

Close by, the *Twister* was waiting, hoping to fill its remaining carriage. The assistant noticed Olly and Katie and waved them forward. He lifted the chromed metal bar, allowing Olly and Katie to sit before it closed over them. The loud music vibrating the floor was interrupted by the words **HERE WE GO**. Olly, pretending he wasn't scared, pointed to another ride, distracting Katie as his arm moved around her shoulders.

"Nice move," she shouted through the din. They leant towards each other and kissed as the ride began.

Olly grinned from ear to ear as every twist and turn slid the couple tighter together, Katie finally almost on his knee. They laughed hysterically as the ride accelerated. Feeling exhilarated, Olly wanted the ride to continue forever as Katie gripped his hand for support.

Inevitably, the ride did finish – as all things in life must. The arm holding the three seats of the attraction came to a halt, depositing them in the same place they'd started.

"So, there you are!" a voice drifted towards them. Claire stood facing them, dressed in black jeans and a padded brown coat with a furry hood hanging behind. Olly stood up from the ride as Claire said, "Oh, hi, didn't see you there." She scanned the area to see if Leo was in the vicinity. "Are you on your own?"

Jumping down onto the grass, Katie said "We're going to meet Leo now, they need our help with something."

Her blue eyes sparkled at the news, enhanced by the colourful reflections from nearby rides. Her cheeks lifted, invoking the hint of a smile. Trying not to act too keen, she said, "Shall we have one more ride? We might not be back again."

The sky had darkened, rain clouds looming over the trees, but the three teenagers decided for one more thrill. They scanned the spinning rides, hearing children scream and laugh while hanging on for dear life.

"What about that one?" Olly said pointing to the far end of the fair – the Ghost Train.

"I'm not sure?" Katie said. "Last time I went on one of those I wet myself."

The Seekers of Duat

Olly and Claire laughed at her misfortune.

"Don't worry, I'll keep you safe," Olly said, holding her hand.

On their way towards the ride, Olly and Katie told Claire about the opened cube, escaped convicts and, more importantly for Claire, that Leo was waiting in the Art of Darkness club on Tower Lane. Agreeing to assist, along with her cousin, Claire's excitement grew as she considered an adventure with Leo. The ghost train seemed more daunting as they neared the attraction, not helped by thunder rumbling across the skies. A giant white skull, laced with spider webs adorned the front of the ride. Its bright flashing eyes pierced through the dull light, children's screams sounding through the black swinging doors.

Katie grabbed Olly's hand, squeezing it so hard his knuckles turned white. "If you're that scared, we don't have to go." Olly said.

"She'll be fine," Claire said. "It's only a kiddies ride."

"I'm fine. Let's get on with it."

Olly handed the ride attendant a handful of coins. He pointed to an empty car sliding out of the exit doors. The carriage cranked forward; they were next. "Hold tight and keep ya' arms in," said the attendant.

Olly and Katie squashed themselves into the front while Claire, pulling up her hood, sat behind Katie. With a jolt, the creaking car sprang forward like a

81

greyhound chasing a rabbit, ramming itself through the black doors into darkness.

"This is horrible," Katie said, snuggling tight to Olly. "Aarrgghh!" She screamed as ghosts and monsters appeared from nooks and crannies. A fake spider web brushed over the top of their heads, making them want to quit the ride. A light appeared, becoming wider and brighter – a car heading straight for them.

"It's going to hit us," Katie screamed.

"Don't be silly, it's us, we're seeing ourselves in a mirror," Claire said, peering through her hood.

Their car came to an abrupt halt, when something strange happened – in their reflection, six ghosts were flying around them. "This is awesome," Olly said, captivated by the apparitions circling in the air.

"I don't like it, it looks real," Katie said, nestling her head into the back of Olly's.

Claire laughed. "They're in the mirror, it's a lighting trick … What's wrong?" she said, noticing a change in Katie's countenance.

Katie was mute, moving her eyes suggesting that Claire look to her side. Claire's peripheral vision was hindered by her hood but knew that something was wrong. She removed her hood, looked to her right and screamed

Olly shifted his focus from the light show and spun around, nearly knocking Katie from the car. "What do you want?" he said, recognising the face in the pale light.

Seated next to Claire was Lance, a gun pointing at her. "That's not very welcoming. A year in the slammer and that's what I get."

"What kind of welcome can someone like you expect?" Olly said, leaving the car, Katie in tow. "What do you want Lance?"

Claire trembled next to the escaped convict. "Don't you hurt her," Katie said. "She's done nothing wrong. Who are you anyway?"

Olly said, "The only time I've seen this person was in the dock, when he was tried and convicted of kidnapping and attempted murder. He's Marshall's Uncle, Victor's brother, Lance Golding."

"Why aren't you locked up?" Katie said.

"When you've a twin brother like mine, you can never be apart for too long," Lance said, a smirk decorating his face. The car moved along the track as Lance took hold of Claire's coat and dragged her from the ride.

"You won't get away with this," Katie yelled. "Another car will be along in a second."

Lance was already ahead of Katie. He'd bribed the attendant not to release another ride. "Money's a wonderful thing," he said waving a bundle of notes. "You can do anything you want with it."

"You can't get your brother back though, can you," said Olly.

A noise filled the dark room. "Mwahahahaha."

The sound was familiar to Olly, he'd heard it the previous morning at the exhibition halls – Victor's spirit. The ghost appeared from behind the mirror, illuminating the area.

"Oh my god, oh my god!" Katie said, shaking. "It's … a ghost, a real ghost."

Olly gripped his girlfriend's hand.

"I'm going to be kind to you, Oliver," the apparition said. "I'll not kill you and your friends immediately." Katie hugged Olly so tight that she could hear his heart thumping, while Claire was next to Lance, motionless with fear. Victor continued, "You have till tomorrow at midnight to discover the location of the portal or your friend will be no more,"

"No!" Claire said. "I'm nothing to do with this, I hardly know anyone involved in this." Lance took a cloth out of his pocket and forced it over Claire's mouth They watched as Claire struggled against her adversary until forced to acquiesce when the chloroform – or whatever it was – took control away from her. Her limp body fell to the ground as Olly moved Katie aside and ran towards Claire but was stopped by the sound of a gun cocking.

"One more step, Olly. I dare you." James Marshall stepped out of the shadows.

"Didn't think it'd be long till you showed up, Marshall," Olly said. "Wherever there's trouble you're not far away."

Marshall, wearing his prison uniform, had developed over the past year. His muscular physique and swept-back black hair was a menacing sight, reminiscent of his father, Victor. "Do what my father wants or she'll die." Marshall took a leaflet from his pocket and threw it at Olly. "This will tell you where to meet us, tomorrow at midnight. Oh, and don't be stupid enough to involve the police or she won't see the morning sunrise. Do I make myself clear?"

Olly and Katie nodded. Victor's ghost had seen enough. "Don't let me down." The phantom drifted around a corner and vanished.

Marshall, waving his gun erratically, ordered Olly and Katie to enter a passing ghost-train car. Through her tears, Katie watched Lance pick up the unconscious Claire, hoisting her over his shoulder like a sack of potatoes. Katie screamed louder than she'd ever done before, hoping that someone outside would hear. Her cries for help fell on deaf ears. Parents with children walked by, laughing at the noises from inside the ride, unaware of the perilous situation.

Olly and Katie peered over their shoulders, watching Marshall and Lance creep through a side opening with the lifeless body of Claire. The cart rose up an incline and dropped again at speed then spun around before barging through a set of black doors. They were outside again.

"Help!" Katie shouted.

Olly hugged her tight, before whispering in her ear, "We can't let anyone know. If the police find out, we will lose Claire forever."

Katie moved her head back and directed her sobbing eyes straight at Olly's. "We have to do something, my mum will kill me when she finds out."

"I'll think of a plan, we'll get her back … okay."

Katie couldn't speak any more, but a gentle nod answered Olly's plea.

"Where's the other one?" said the ride attendant looking confused.

"There were two of us," Olly said as the pair quit the ride as the heavens opened, an almighty crack of thunder and flash of lightening awaiting them. Hand in hand, they dashed through the fair across Brunswick common and to the Art of Darkness club.

CHAPTER 12

Leo leant over, his left palm stretched over the green baize of the snooker table. He needed to pot the final two balls to beat his mum. Pulling back his right arm, Leo stroked the cue ball, hit the pink and potted it into the middle pocket.

"Nice shot," Melanie said. "The black ball is all that's left."

Aiming to pot the black into one of the bottom pockets, he slid his arm back ready for the finale. A repeated thud on the club door interrupted Leo who miscued his shot, the cue tip slipping underneath the ball to launch the white into the air. It cleared the table to smash into the side of the bar area. With the knocking intensifying, Leo and his mum dropped their cues on the table and ran across the landing before rushing down the dim stairway. The sound of rain was interspersed with the insistent bangs on the door.

"Who is it?" Melanie shouted.

"It's me, Olly. Let us in."

Melanie snapped the catch open and leaned on the handle as Olly tugged the door hard from the other side. He and Katie fell in — both looking like drowned rats.

"Is it raining?"

"Leo, stop that sarcasm!" his mum said. The rain running down their faces didn't disguise the tears in Katie's eyes. "What's happened?"

Katie was struck speechless so Olly took over, offering her a seat on the stair. "You're not going to believe this."

"How many times have we heard that?"

Melanie raised her eyes at her son but continued to stare at Olly.

"It's Claire …"

"Where is Claire … didn't she want to help?"

"Will you be quiet for a minute Leo," Melanie said. "Can't you tell this is serious? Let Olly speak."

Leo looked forlorn; the tone of his mother's voice meant business.

"Claire … she's been taken."

"What? Where? You need to explain," Melanie said.

"On the Ghost train. Victor, Lance and Marshall appeared … and they took her away. They told us that we've till tomorrow at midnight to find them the portal."

The Seekers of Duat

Melanie was struggling to believe what she was hearing. "Didn't I tell you not to go on any rides?" she said shaking her head.

Olly hung his head in shame and spotted the slither of paper protruding from his jacket pocket. He pulled at the sodden leaflet. The drama of Claire's kidnapping had made him forget that Marshall had told him their whereabouts. He handed the slip of paper to Melanie with trembling hands. "This is where we have to meet them. St. Prion's Abbey, we had a history lesson there a few years ago."

"I went there with my old school … I think," Leo said.

"You did," Melanie said. "I went with you, helping out if I recall correctly. We have to call the police now, we don't have any choice now we know where they're holding Claire. We have to save her."

"No, no you can't," Olly said. "We have to find the portal for Victor, then they'll let her go. Call the police and they'll kill her."

Katie sobbed deeply as Olly spoke and opened a packet of love hearts for comfort. "My mum's going to go mad."

"I know, we'll tell Katie's mum that they're staying at mine for a few days. We were talking about doing that anyway. It'll give us time to sort this mess out. Will you do that?" Olly glanced at Melanie.

"I'm not lying to Katie's mum. She needs to know the truth."

Leo stared at his mother, his eyes displaying desperation. "She'll get the police involved mum. It's the only way. Victor might be watching us right now. If we call the police it could be curtains for Claire."

Melanie plonked herself down next to Katie on the step, wrapping her arm around Katie's wet shoulders. "It seems I have little choice but I swear, if anything else happens, the police will be involved. Okay?"

The youngsters agreed as a voice from the snooker hall interrupted them. "Leo, Melanie! Where are you?"

"We're down here," Leo, shouted.

Horace's footsteps could be heard as he left the snooker hall and made for the landing. A gangly figure leant around the corner of the staircase and greeted the new arrivals. "Hello Olly, and who do we have here?"

Katie wiped her face of any lingering tears and turned her head. "I'm Katie."

"We're in trouble," said Olly. Horace made his way down to the entrance hall where they told him the tale of Claire's kidnapping and urgency of finding the portal.

"You *can* help us ,... can't you?" Katie said.

"I can because I've found the receipt for the gravestone," Horace said, pulling a crinkled dirty-white piece of paper from his jacket. He straightened it out and passed it around.

The Seekers of Duat

Smith & Son Memorials

One 5ft x 5ft white marble pyramid gravestone.

All four sides engraved, including 3 gemstones resembling Lapis Lazuli, Turquoise and Carnelian.

Total price including VAT = £603.00 Paid in advance with thanks.

"That price doesn't seem much," Olly said.

"It was back then It would be thousands more in today's money."

"Well, we now know the gems we need to find. Is there a book describing them in the club?"

"We've still no idea where to find them, even if we know what they look like," Leo said, bursting their bubble.

Olly glanced at him in the dim light and a shallow smile drifted across his face. "Seem to remember we had that problem when we set off looking for your dad … yet we found him, right?"

"I'll give you that one."

Three of the party made their way up the stairs to the snooker hall, leaving Olly to comfort Katie. "We'll get Claire back, I promise you."

"Promise is a *big* word," she said sucking on a sweet. "If we don't find her, we'll be in massive bother, not only from my mum, but from the police too … we're holding back information about a kidnapping!"

Tears formed in Olly's eyes. "I know."

Katie passed him a love heart with the words DREAM BOY embossed on the sugary pink sweet. Olly blushed and leant forward, forgetting their problems for a moment. He moved Katie's wet hair stuck to her cheeks and kissed her. "And you're my dream girl," he said before releasing his lips and popping the sweet into his mouth. Crunching it, the moment was ruined.

"Come on guys!" Leo shouted from upstairs. "We've a portal to find."

Olly snatched another sweet from Katie's hand as they headed up to join the team. "This one says, MY BELOVED. Is that what I am to you?"

"Maybe ... Although my parents, Claire, and my grandma's ring are in the queue before you."

Katie dashed through into the snooker hall to meet the others and realised that Olly wasn't with her. She poked her head through the door onto the landing to witness Olly gazing at his hand. "Are you okay?"

Olly lifted his head. "BELOVED – it doesn't have to mean a person, it can be things you love as well."

"It ... can do, but to clarify, I did not use the L word just now."

Olly took Katie's hand and ran to the others. "Hey guys, I might have worked out one of the clues on the grave."

"Tell us more" Horace said.

"The phrase on the grave – about the god awaiting my beloved. BELOVED might not be a loved one ... it could be a loved thing. What did you tell us the first time we entered the club? About the three loves in Archie's life?"

"His shop, his cars and this snooker club."

"Exactly, he's hidden the three gems in his beloved places."

"You might be right, young Olly," Horace said.

"Well, let's get looking," said an eager Leo.

Everyone spread out, searching the snooker tables, even checking the pockets and light fittings.

"Where would they be?" Olly said, airing his thoughts. "Where would somebody hide a gem in here?"

"How do you even play this game?" Katie said. "My dad watches it a lot, but why do they keep knocking the balls into those bags, only for someone to take them out again?"

"It's called potting, not knocking, Katie," Horace said. "I'll teach you one day. I used to be a decent player when I was younger and it helped that my father owned a snooker club."

Melanie placed a box on one of the tables to gather up the balls. "Leo, find me the white ball, it's the only one missing."

It was the ball that had escaped the table during their game so Leo lowered himself to his hands and knees near the bar area to start the search. Under a green leather bench that occupied the side wall, Leo spotted the white, so reached under, grabbed it and stood, wiping away the dust from his knees. He rolled the ball from one end of the table to his mum at the far end. As the ball trickled over the green baize, a chunk came away.

"Well, I'll be damned!" Horace said, "I've never seen that happen."

"I'm sorry," Leo said. "I miscued it when Olly banged on the door. It probably cracked when it hit the wall."

"Blame me why don't you," Olly said, snatching the ball to investigate. "There's a good reason why Horace hasn't witnessed this happening before … because it never does." Everyone seemed confused, so Olly continued, "This isn't a normal ball."

"It seemed normal enough to me and my dad for the years we played snooker," Horace said.

Olly thrust the ball towards Horace, causing the old man to flinch. "Does this seem normal to you?" Olly said, exposing an orange glow radiating from inside the ball.

Horace examined it. "You're right, it doesn't seem normal. Can you find me some tools, Olly? Leo?"

"Do you think it's one of those gems?" Katie said.

"Not sure."

Olly rummaged in a cupboard behind the bar and retrieved a hammer and screwdriver. "Here, will these help?"

"Perfect," Horace said. Trying not to damage whatever was inside the ball, Horace chipped away at the exposed surface.

"Do you need any help?" Olly asked, watching the ball shoot away like a projectile across the oak boarded floor again.

"I'm fine, not easy hitting a globe. I need a good strike with the surface and … there it is," Horace said, delivering the decisive blow. Turning around he opened his hand, revealing a clouded, dark orange gemstone.

"Wow," Olly said.

"That's beautiful," Katie said. "I've never seen a gem that colour before."

"It's carnelian, one of three gems referenced in the grave invoice."

"Well, we've found one," Leo said. "Two to go, then we'll get Claire back."

"You like her, don't you? She likes you as well, told me after we'd dropped you off at Olly's house, Leo."

"Really?"

"Yes, really."

Melanie interrupted, not wanting to dwell on her son's love life, "Speaking of houses, we need to return home Leo. I don't like leaving your dad for too long. He's still not a hundred percent."

Leo shrugged his shoulders as only a teenager can. "Come on Mum, another hour, please? We need to find the other stones."

Melanie heard the anguish in her son's voice. "Half an hour, that's all. I need to call in to a shop on the way home too, I wasn't expecting a full house for dinner."

Olly took the carnelian stone from Horace, placing it in his pocket. "Right, that's the gem from the snooker hall. What next?"

Leo raised his arm, like he would at school. "I know! Archie's cars and his shop were his beloved items."

"Yes," said Horace, heading over to the secret stairwell. "The remnants of the shop are in storage downstairs."

The boys followed him into the darkness as Katie hesitated. Melanie took her hand. "It's okay, don't worry. Although it does look a bit scary down there, doesn't it?"

"It's not only that. I'm worried about Claire. I wish we'd never gone on that stupid ghost train. She must be terrified."

"We're doing everything we can to get your cousin back. Even if they have to go to hell and back, they'll sort this."

Melanie led Katie down the staircase to the Art of Darkness. Olly's torch light flickered around the rooms while Katie watched in wonderment. "What is all this stuff?"

Leo's face appeared in front of her as he pointed a torch under his chin, aiming to spook her. "Mainly dead things in jars." Unimpressed, Katie's eyes glistened with tears.

"Leo, you idiot," snapped Olly. "She's enough on her mind without you pulling your juvenile stunts." Olly handed Katie his torch and they strolled into an adjoining room containing oddities as Leo scurried off down the hall, trailed by his mum.

"Thanks," Katie said to Olly. "I'm emotional at the moment, I break down at anything."

"You've every reason to," Olly said. "You'll get used to Leo, he says stuff without thinking sometimes. Anyhow, these belongings and rooms were part of the Art of Darkness club, the origin of the Brunswick tunnel adventure."

Katie bent down to examine jars crammed onto the bottom shelf. "It's like something from a horror film. What are these?"

"Bat wings. There's lots of weird things in these rooms. Look, here are camel's eyes."

Katie declined Olly's offer to view them and rushed out of the room. "What were these people, warlocks?"

"Nope, just liked collecting strange things. Here, come on, let's find the others." Olly took Katie's hand and strolled past the remaining rooms, through the end door and into the meeting hall. "They'll have gone into the storage room, that's where the shop remains are."

Katie released Olly's hand and held the wall for support. "I'll wait here, I feel queasy."

"You do look pale," Olly said shining his torchlight into her face, making her scrunch up her eyes. "You don't mind if I help them, that gem must be in there somewhere?"

"Go to it, the sooner we find the gems, the sooner we're out of here. I only need a minute."

Olly sensed that she was scared. He pulled the cube from his rucksack. "Keep this next to you, it will keep the ghosts away."

"Thanks," she said, knowing that Olly was trying to help but the revelation made her more anxious. She pulled up a chair, plonking herself down next to the meeting table, before leaning forward to place her head on her arms. Thoughts raced through her mind, the most prominent one being the fate of her cousin and what the Goldings were doing with her.

CHAPTER 13

Waking up, Claire felt her face in contact with a coarse, gritty floor, cold to the touch. Were her eyes open? If they were, she saw nothing. She blinked and moved her stiff neck. *Was that a faint light coming from beneath a door?* Claire tried to move but her arms were tied behind her and fastened to something solid. Her legs were also bound by a rope. She tried to scream but a gag, tied tight around her head, prevented her from uttering a sound. The pale light brightened and she heard voices echo from down the corridor outside. It was dungeon-like and echoed like a stone castle.

"Do what I do and agree with what I say, okay?" Lance said, a smouldering cigar lodged in the corner of his mouth.

"Alright," Marshall replied. "But this is going too far. The plan was to escape and steal those gems, especially those that were ours. We'll take the rap for

THE SEEKERS OF DUAT

kidnapping now, another ten years added to my sentence when we get caught."

"*If* we get caught. Now brace yourself, your dad needs this plan to work." The creaking of the door intensified Claire's anxiety. "Look, sleeping beauty's awoke. Enjoy your sleep, did you?" Lance pointed his torch at her face.

Claire mumbled expletives, muffled by the muzzle.

"Think that was a yes, Unc," Marshall said as Claire's eyes widened, realising someone had spoken to her. "You were out for the count when I turned up in the ghost train. Let me introduce myself. James Marshall at your service madam."

He followed with an evil laugh and Claire wriggled but to no avail, she was bound tightly.

Lance walked over with a gun, blowing cigar smoke into her face. "Now listen here, you'd better be good for us because I've no reservations about using this if I have to."

"Time for her to talk maybe?" Marshall said.

"Yeah, nobody will hear her."

Marshall reached around the back of her head, untying the knot on the gag. Claire's piercing scream rang through the building.

"When you've quite finished," Lance said covering his ears. "Only the spiders will hear you down here."

"Where am I? What do you want of me?" Claire snapped, as she shuffled around to loosen her restraints.

"Shall I tell her?" Marshall said.

"She doesn't need to know where she is, except that she's miles from home," Lance said. "As for why we've kidnapped you. Don't you remember, or has this excitement emptied your little head?"

Claire cowered, trying to recall the events. Slowly, memories trickled back until she said, "Yes, now I remember … a portal, you want a portal."

"Well done and because we've got you in captivity, those two pests who had us locked up last year will do anything we ask of them."

"I don't know what you mean, I hardly know them."

"You better hope that they feel more about you than you do about them. If they don't do what we want … you're a gonner."

Claire gulped before she said. "You'll release me when they give you the portal, is that right?"

"Correct," Lance said, brushing the side of his gun up against her cheek. "Anything you'd like to share?"

Shivers reverberated through her spine as tears formed and trickled down her face, leaving trail marks in the dirt. "They'll be in the Art of Darkness club on Tower Lane. That's where they were going."

Lance took a long drag from the remainder of his cigar before throwing the nub onto the floor. "I remember going there as a child with my grandfather."

Alarmed, Claire realised she'd told them her friends' whereabouts. She had to think, so shuffled herself upright, wiping her eyes against her shoulders before fixing a stare on Marshall. "You're my age. Why are you helping this thug?" She sounded braver than she felt.

"He's my family. We stick together."

"And they helped us break out of prison," Lance said, laughing.

"That's how you escaped ... with Victor's help?"

"And with your friends' assistance, Victor will be reborn. They will discover the secret to opening a path into the underworld. Look, I've had enough of this, I'm off to find Victor and tell him the news; make sure she doesn't do anything stupid, okay?"

Marshall nodded as Lance strode off, footsteps echoing down the stone corridor.

"My wrists are hurting," Claire said. "Loosen the rope a bit."

"No ... no I won't, you'll be fine as you are," Marshall said, uneasy at being on his own with Claire. "One more day and you'll be out of here."

"What's wrong, afraid of your uncle? Will he tell you off? He seems to be in charge."

"Not at all ... I'm my own man, I do what I want."

Claire laughed. "You're not a man, you're a kid, just like I am. Why are you like this, wasting your life?"

"Things could have been different if all of that treasure had come to our family. Your parents will have loads of money. Now, imagine not living in a big house, nor regularly having a new car and no nice clothes?"

"My family had nothing when I was small," Claire snapped, "They worked hard, earned enough to give us a good life. They didn't steal from other people… or kidnap someone's daughter to further their own ends."

Marshall bowed his head and an uncomfortable silence ensued. Claire sensed an opportunity. "How was prison? I know I couldn't handle it. It's bad enough being cooped up in here for a short time, but years – you must be strong to deal with the adversities."

"It was a place for young offenders." Marshall said. "It was all right, shared my room with a petty thief – he was cool. He was released shortly before my escape and I need to thank him."

"Thank him, for what?"

"Yeah … I told him the phrase to open the cube. We owe him."

"So, you're the reason all of this has happened. Had Victor not escaped, I'd still be at home."

"Wrong place, wrong time, what else can I say," Marshall shrugged.

Claire knew he was right and it was in her best interests to stay on his side, "What happens if you're caught again?"

"I'll do the time. I can handle myself."

"It looks like you can."

Marshall glanced away for a moment; he felt awkward. A girl had never flirted with him before.

"You seem nice under that bravado. If you handed yourself in, tell the police that you were forced into this, you'd receive a reduced sentence. You've your life ahead, so don't make things worse for yourself."

"It's too late," he said. "Now, stop talking or I'll have to shut you up."

Claire paused for a couple of seconds. "It must have been hard for you. What about your mum, where's she now?"

"Moved away with a new fella, only got a suspended sentence, not even sure where she is," Claire noticed Marshall's eyes welling up in the torchlight.

"I'm sorry, a boy needs his mum. I'd hug you if I weren't tied up."

"Thanks."

"You're not all bad Marshall, been dealt a bad hand in life. I bet Lance has been constantly at you, exaggerating the family stories to make you angry, want revenge. You're a kid … it's not your fault."

"What's going on here?" Lance shouted after hearing the last exchange.

"Nothing Unc." Marshall wiped his eyes.

"Don't let her get under your skin. She wants one thing, and it's not you."

"I was only talking to him. He was upset," Claire said.

"Shut up," Lance said, replacing her muzzle. "Don't ever try anything like that again … do you understand!?"

Claire's eyes bulged in terror as Lance grabbed her hair and pointed the gun at her head. She nodded her head. She'd failed.

"Marshall come with me. Victor wants to show us something."

Leaving the room, Marshall turned around and mouthed "sorry" to her. Claire was once again left in darkness but was uplifted. Perhaps she hadn't failed.

CHAPTER 14

In the club, after half an hour of searching, Horace, Melanie, the two boys and Katie, who'd recovered from her nausea, had examined every box on every shelf in the storage room, to no avail. Frustrated, they called it a day.

Horace stretched to ease his aching body, yawned and said, "I'll pick you up in the morning and we'll have another look. We might be missing the wood and only seeing the trees. A night's sleep and fresh mind is what we each need."

"My thoughts exactly," Melanie said, guiding the three children into her Beetle before walking back to Horace, "Thanks for your help, it's appreciated. I was sceptical … and also about you if I'm brutally honest, but I think you have their best interests at heart – or at least I hope you do."

Horace was taken aback by her directness but recovered quickly. "I understand, especially with what you went through last year They're helping me as much as I'm helping them you know? We'll succeed tomorrow, I feel it in my old bones."

Horace wandered around the corner to his car as Melanie reached her Beetle to greet a car full of miserable teenagers. "Come on everyone, Horace is right. Tomorrow, I bet we find something straight away."

"You're right," Olly said from the back seat, his hand clasping Katie's. "There's always tomorrow."

Melanie started the engine and edged from the parking space.

"Watch out!" Leo shouted.

Narrowly avoiding them was a gleaming 1950's Bentley R-type which had pulled out, forcing Melanie to swerve. She blasted the horn and said, "What an idiot."

"Wow, look at that?" Olly said.

The Bentley moved over to the side and a gangly arm reached out of the window, offering an apologetic wave.

"Goodness, do you know who that is?" Leo said, "Horace!"

"I love the colour," Melanie said, her mood lifted by the revelation. "Aqua marine is my favourite."

"Turquoise, you mean turquoise" Katie said, showing interest.

"Yes, that's it."

"That is it!" Olly said. "Stop the car!"

Melanie slammed on the breaks, skidding to a halt, tyres screeching and parallel to the Bentley. "What is it?"

"Another clue."

Leo opened the passenger door to be catapulted out by an eager Olly, who'd pushed the seat forward from behind.

"I'm sorry about that," Horace said from the open window. "I'm still not familiar with this car."

Olly pushed aside Horace, sticking his head through the window to glance inside. "What's wrong? What are you doing?" Horace said.

Olly spun his head around, almost touching noses with Horace. "This car, who does it belong to?"

"Well, mine of course, who else?"

Olly stared at him, waiting for the penny to drop. "Okay, I'll ask another question. Who had this car before you?"

Horace's expression changed. "I see, yes. This was my father's car."

"I thought as much. Can we have a proper look."

"Of course." Horace exited to stand on the pavement while Olly and Leo leapt into the car.

"Whoa!" Leo said. "This is class."

"It sure is."

"Thanks," Horace said lurching forward. "It wasn't in the best of shape when he left it to me, but I know a few car enthusiasts who restored it to its former glory while I was away."

The Bentley was immaculate inside and out, seats upholstered in cream leather while the dashboard and interior panels were decorated in walnut veneer, matching the polished drop trays on the rear of the front seats that reflected the street lights amber glow into the car.

"What exactly does a Turquoise gem look like?" Olly said, searching the glove compartment. "Is it shiny, rough, smooth, different colours?"

"No idea," Leo said from his position, upside down in the back footwell.

"BEEP!"

"Ouch!" Olly said, smacking his head under the dashboard. He glanced up to spot Katie at the window, hand on the horn. "What are you doing? I banged my head."

"Leo's mum told me to come and get you both."

"She'll have to wait," Leo said. "We're searching for the gem."

"Do you know what Turquoise looks like?".

"Well yeah Olly, I've a turquoise bracelet at home." Katie pointed to the centre of the steering wheel. "It's like that."

"That's it, must be."

"What?" Leo said sticking his head between the two front headrests.

The Seekers of Duat

Olly shuffled himself into the driver's seat, holding the large Bakelite steering wheel in his hands. "It's here, the second gem."

In the centre of the wheel was a coloured disc, bluey-green colours distinctive against the surround.

"Well, I never. I thought that was coloured glass. Here use this." Horace pulled a screwdriver from his pocket. He'd used it to break open the cue ball earlier. Olly prized around the edge of the disc, trying not to scratch the Bakelite surface. The outer ring popped out, allowing Olly to retrieve the central stone.

"We've done it, we've found another one," Leo cheered. "Mum, look!"

"That's fantastic," she said, winding down the window of the Beetle "Well done, one more to go."

"And that plate thingamajig," Olly said.

"Both will be in the club somewhere," Horace said, "A good night's sleep and we'll find what we need."

"Right, now I insist," Melanie said, ushering the children back into the car. "I need to get back for your dad."

Olly, Leo and Katie bid farewell to Horace as he slid into his Bentley. Gliding away and shimmering under the street lamps, Horace shouted, "I'll see you all in the morning."

111

CHAPTER 15

The Beetle left and the children were smiling. The last twenty-four hours had been long, crazy and scary but they were hopeful of solving the puzzle of the portal and rescuing Claire the following day. Melanie, always thinking of her family, took a detour into town to pick up groceries for their evening meal. "Just wait here, I'll be ten minutes."

As his mum left, Leo turned up the radio. He loved music, especially indie and had hundreds of cassettes and vinyl records scattered around his bedroom with most of the cassette mixes given to him by Olly. He had every album or single – if Olly didn't have it, it wasn't worth listening to. His knowledge of music was legendary and he read the NME like a pastor studies the bible.

"Who's this?" Leo asked Olly as the radio burst into life.

"The Wedding Present – their latest single. They've a new album out today too."

"Really!"

Before Olly could stop him, Leo unbuckled his belt and dashed from the car.

"What's he doing?" Katie said.

"Off to the music store."

Across the road, sandwiched between a bakery and charity shop, was *Buzz Music*. It's red and yellow sign clashed with those of its neighbours which were more conservative. This was the place to be if you were young, retro and loved music.

As Olly pushed the front seat forward, Katie said, fearful of being left on her own, "And what are you doing?"

"If Leo can ignore his mum, so can I. Come on, we'll be back before she returns. Anyhow, it'll be shutting soon."

She followed Olly out of the car and across the road. They entered the store through an open door to be greeted by a wall of sound, one that brought a smile to Olly's face.

"Amazing, isn't it!?" Olly yelled at Katie, who had her fingers pressed tightly in her ears. She nodded to appease him and glanced over to the far corner where Leo was flicking through a box of 12" vinyl's. He lifted one, seeking Olly's approval – Leo received a thumbs up. Olly was in his element but knew he didn't have much time to find his next purchase. He wandered towards the new releases in the front window, Katie following.

"Oh no!" Katie said, spotting Melanie. "We need to go – now."

Olly whistled to Leo and waved.

"Will you shut that, lad," the shopkeeper yelled from behind the counter. Olly stared at him. "Yes, you. Shut the door. There's a cold breeze."

Raised eyebrows from his mum met Leo as he and Katie jumped into the car. "Where's Olly?"

"Not again," Katie said. "He was right behind me."

From the door window of Buzz Music, Olly waved.

"What's he doing?" Leo watched his friend open and shut the door numerous times.

"No idea."

Melanie was becoming frustrated; she wanted to return to her husband. "This is ridiculous. Go over and get him Katie. You stay with me Leo!"

Katie jogged over the road to see what Olly was messing about at.

"Will you stop playing with that door!" the shopkeeper yelled. "Shut it or I'll ban you."

Katie dashed in as the door closed.

"Thank you," said the shopkeeper, sarcasm dripping from his lips.

"What are you doing? Leo's mum's having a meltdown out there."

Olly leant close to Katie. At first she thought he was going to peck her on the cheek but instead, he whispered. "I think I've found the third gem."

"What!" Katie said.

"Shh. I think it's up there." He pointed to a dirty bell above the door.

"What are you talking about?"

"Don't you realise … this building was once owned by Archibald Griffin. Horace told us his father's shop is now a music shop and this is it. Every time the door opens it triggers the bell. I remember Horace telling us about the bell making a distinctive sound. There's a reason for that – look closely, you'll see a blue glimmer. That's the colour of Lapis Lazuli – it was in that book."

Katie strained her eyes upwards. "You're right." She was becoming interested. Hugging Olly, she emitted a scream of joy, attracting a curious look from other customers. "How do we get it? We can't just take it."

"We need to distract him." Olly gestured towards the shopkeeper. "I need your help, Katie."

Katie clapped as excitement built. "Okay, I'm ready. What do you want me to do?"

Olly's mind was ahead. "That far wall where the T-shirts are. Go over, shout to him and ask for help." Olly glanced at the old bell. "It shouldn't take much to knock it off the wall. Three screws are already missing."

Katie strode across the shop floor, drifting her fingers over some of the vinyl sleeves – pretending she knew the bands. As she reached the wall she shouted, "Excuse me, can you help, please."

The shopkeeper rolled his eyes and strolled over. "Yes, what can I do for you?"

"Err ..." Katie hesitated as she grabbed a Stone Roses T-shirt from a shelf. "Can I try this on please?" she said.

"Not really, you're not in a clothes shop. We sell music in here if you hadn't noticed and there aren't any changing rooms."

This was Katie's opportunity to use her skills. Her mother had enrolled her into a stage school when younger and this was the time to shine. She bellowed at the startled shopkeeper. "Well, that is not good enough!"

Olly smiled as the disagreement escalated and other customers watched the commotion.

"What do you want me to do?" the shopkeeper said, opening his arms wide. "Magically make a room appear with a beautiful red curtain."

"Now you're being stupid," Katie said as she pointed to a room with *staff* painted on it. "How about I go in there?"

"That's private."

"Look, I want to buy this T-shirt. Let me in there for two minutes and you might have a sale."

The Seekers of Duat

The shopkeeper, wanting to prevent further drama, shook his head and begrudgingly opened the door. "Right, give me a second to move some things out of the way." He entered the room and slammed the door behind him.

Katie turned to Olly and mouthed 'Now'. Olly reached up and pulled hard on the bell. With the bell ringing, the last remaining screw gave up its hold on the wooden door frame. Olly popped it in his pocket and nodded at Katie.

"Go on then, you can use it now," muttered the shopkeeper as he exited the staff room.

"Oh, it's fine, I've changed my mind."

Bewildered, the shopkeeper placed his hands on his hips, staring at Katie who was skipping over to Olly. "Let's get out of here."

Olly reckoned that the silence of the opening door would foil their plan so, while Katie pulled on the door handle, Olly shook the bell from behind his back. Katie smiled as he followed her out of the shop. The awaiting Beetle was revving loudly across the road, an impatient Melanie tapping the throttle with the beat of the radio. Leo stared ahead as his friends neared the car.

"Open it!" Katie said, banging on the window.

Leo jumped up and let his friends in.

"Right, let's go," Olly said, breathing heavily after his sprint from the shop. Melanie didn't hang about.

She floored the accelerator pedal leaving a cloud of fumes in her trail.

"Dare I ask what you've done?" Melanie said, clearing the condensation off the windscreen with a tattered cloth. "If you needed money for a new record, I'd have lent you it. You didn't have to steal."

"I didn't steal …" Olly said. "Well … not a record anyway."

"What did you steal?" Leo asked.

Olly held up the bell and rang it, surprising Leo and his mum who prevented the car swerving into a hedge.

Leo was confused and his scrunched-up face revealed his puzzlement. "Are you joking? What are we going to do with a bell? Are you going to summon a servant to rescue Claire?"

Olly rolled his eyes at his friend. "Pass me that cloth, will you?"

Leo threw the wet cloth behind and into Olly's face, causing Katie to snigger. Olly took the cloth and rubbed the clapper inside the bell.

"Is it what you thought it was?" Katie said.

Olly removed the cloth – now filthy – to reveal his discovery. "It is … Lapis Lazuli!"

Melanie brought the Beetle screeching to a halt. "Let me see." She turned her head around and Olly passed her the bell containing the blue gem. "You've done it, you've found the last gem. Oh my god, it's amazing."

The Seekers of Duat

Melanie passed the bell to Leo as she drove on to St. Prion. "Only the plate to find," Leo said. "We'll get Claire back then."

Olly had something else on his mind but didn't want to ruin the excitement of the moment. His mind was disturbed by Stumpy's predicament. His friend needed help and he it was up to Leo and he to save him.

"Hey!" Katie said, distracting Olly from his contemplation. "Isn't that where Claire's being held?"

On the grass verge a signpost signalled two miles to *St. Prion Abbey and Country Estate*.

The looked left in unison and the mood in the car changed, with a silence descending. Their thoughts were with Claire and what she was suffering.

St. Prion Abbey was halfway between Brunswick and St. Prion, in a vast country estate. It was home to an abundance of wildlife, especially deer that roamed through the many acres of luscious fields and woodland. The abbey and surrounding buildings had a long dark history. The abbey had been built over eight hundred years previously by Benedictine monks, who used the land for farming and lead mining until the Dissolution of the Monasteries by Henry VIII in 1539 bought an abrupt end to their life, leaving the abbey to lie in ruin for centuries.

The next chapter brought Lord and Lady Richmond to the estate in 1810. They renovated the gatehouse – which overlooked the ruined abbey – into a Georgian private house, transforming the gardens to form a

119

horticultural masterpiece containing fountains and a lake. Lord Richmond liked a game of Hazard and, within ten years, he'd gambled his entire fortune away.

The estate passed through several hands after that until the first world war commenced. The local army barracks were designated a high-risk area from Germany's bombing campaign, so the St. Prion estate was used as a training camp for soldiers. It's expanse of grass, wooded areas, deep valley sides and, combined with the abbey ruins and out-houses, made it ideal.

In recent history the abbey and its grounds have been taken over by a local trust, permitting thousands of visitors to explore the surroundings, the majestic gatehouse transformed into a café and tourist information site.

"Surely Claire would be found by staff there," Olly said.

"Not at the moment," Melanie said. "It's closed due to structural damage. Those storms last week damaged the abbey's tower and stronger storms are due over the next few days. No one is allowed in the place until the weather's better. That's what my friend told me – he works in the café." The car splashed through an enormous puddle before passing another sign which read: *5 miles to St. Prion*. "We're almost home, time to recharge our batteries."

CHAPTER 16

Darkness had descended like a comfortable blanket as the Beetle parked outside Leo's house. The curtains were open but no lights illuminated inside. The terraced house seemed deserted, until a dark figure appeared at the upstairs front window. Melanie waved and blew her husband a kiss as she hurried into the house with Leo, Olly and Katie dragging their heels behind.

"I'm nervous," Katie said, grabbing Olly's arm. "This is the first time I've met a proper dragon slayer!"

"Not any more he isn't," Olly whispered. "He's a shadow of the man I met in the tunnel. Then he had a six pack and the appearance of a Roman gladiator; he can hardly walk now."

"Come on guys," Leo said, waiting to shut the door.

"We're coming."

Melanie headed upstairs to check on her husband while Leo changed his clothes in his room, leaving Olly and Katie in the living room. "Hi darling," Melanie said. "I'm sorry for being so late but we've had a productive day. How are you feeling?" She walked over to her husband who was wearing only his pyjama bottoms, and hugged him tightly.

"I'm fine, thought I'd have an early night. Why was today productive?"

"You wouldn't believe it…" she paused.

"Well?"

Melanie spotted their reflection in the bedroom mirror; there was something peculiar on Orion's back. "What's that?"

"What?"

"That mark on your back, a red circle."

Orion twisted his head round but couldn't see the patch. "I've no idea."

"Does it hurt? Have you fallen on something?"

"No. I feel fine, well as good as I usually do."

"Mum! Dad!" Leo called from across the landing. "You should see this."

Melanie entered Leo's room and gasped. On her son's chest was an identical red mark. Orion walked towards Leo and placed his hands on his son's shoulders. "Are you alright? What's going on?"

"I'm okay Dad but I had a vision in the club. I saw through Stumpy's eyes and he is in trouble."

"Where was he?"

"Egypt, but not the real Egypt. He's in a parallel dimension called Duat. There was sand everywhere and strange creatures that appeared from a red mist."

"That name rings a bell," Orion said. "I remember Stumpy telling me about Duat while I was trapped in the tunnel caves with him."

Olly had heard the commotion and ventured upstairs. "Duat is the Egyptian underworld," he said, peering into the room. "Oh my god, look at you both. These marks must be telling us something. You are the last remaining slayers, yeah? I'd say he's trying to communicate with you. We have to help Stumpy after everything he did for us last year. The very least we can do is reach him."

Melanie was baffled. "What are you getting at? How do we help?"

Olly sat on the end of Leo's bed. "We don't tell Victor about the portal but use it ourselves to travel to the Egyptian underworld."

"Are you out of your mind?" Melanie said. "You expect me to let you go into some portal after what happened last year, or the previous eleven years for that matter, when Orion vanished from my life. You can think of another plan, Olly." Melanie stormed out, loud footsteps stomping down the stairs.

"She's right," Orion said, in a calming voice. "You have no idea what you're getting in to, don't even know if the portal will take you there. If you need my assistance in this adventure – think again. Look at the state of me. I can't walk five paces without losing breath."

Olly's plan had another negative and Leo was the first to raise it. "Hang on a second. What happens to Claire? If we don't tell Victor about the portal, she'll be left to die in a dungeon?"

Olly had been so transfixed on saving Stumpy that he hadn't seen the consequences of his suggestion. "Yeah, I suppose you're right, but maybe saving Stumpy could help Victor," he said but he was clutching at straws.

"Let's concentrate on saving Claire," Leo said, acting the older friend.

Olly gave a wry smile. Saving Stumpy was still his imperative.

Over the next hour everyone calmed down. Orion caught up on the day's events, including Claire's capture and the discovery of the Art of Darkness. They each knew they had to cooperate and rescue Claire; falling out would achieve nothing.

After making a wholesome beef stew, Melanie rang Katie's mum. She hated lying, especially when it involved the safety of a child. "Yes, they're all fine, I'll bring her home in a few days when they've finished camping," she said, finishing the conversation through gritted teeth, "Goodbye."

"Thanks Mum!" Leo shouted from the living room.

"Yes, thanks Mrs Hart," Katie said.

"Let's pray that our plan works. We need to find that plate in the club tomorrow – no fail," Melanie said, her voice drifting away as she went upstairs to make up the spare room.

"What kind of plate is it? Wooden? Metal? Like mum's dinner plate?" Leo asked.

"According to the picture on the grave," Olly said, "it will be metal, with three gaps where the gems fit."

Katie sat down and noticed a pile of books that Melanie had removed from the club. She plucked *Osiris versus Set – The War of Brothers* from the heap. Flicking through the pages, something caught her eye. "Will this help?" she said, revealing a picture of Osiris' tomb plus the iron throne. On the front of the throne was an indentation where something circular had been.

Olly examined the page. "That picture was taken when the tomb was discovered, I'd say. Horace's dad took the plate and gems, that's why there's a gap. Only he knew what it looked like."

"Oh, okay but judging by the picture, it's about twelve inches across. It could be anywhere. Are there any more clues?"

"Only the riddle on the side of the grave," Olly said, "*What flies you to hell, Will fly you to heaven.*"

"There must be some clues in another book." Leo said, fearing that time was running out for Claire. "It's tomorrow we need to rescue her. We *need* that plate."

"We'll find it in the club. Look, a couple of hours ago we had one gem, now there are three. Let's take a break and start again in the morning."

Leo huffed and puffed on the couch, before sloping off towards the kitchen, muttering.

The following day was to be a busy day so everybody took the opportunity to relax and watched an episode of *Harry and the Henderson's* on the TV.

"You think Bigfoot exists?" Orion said, "There's been a few sightings."

"Not sure," Olly said. "Someone might be dressed up as a big monkey."

"It's not you is it, Dad?" Leo said.

"Very funny, I might've put on a few pounds, but I'm not that big. Cheeky."

Olly ventured into the kitchen as the phone rang in the hallway, his heart skipping a beat at the sound.

"Get that would you, Olly?" Melanie shouted. "It's probably a miss-dial, not many people know our number."

"No worries." Olly said and picked up the phone. "Hello, who is it please? … Oh, hi Horace, is everything okay?"

"I am, now I'm home," Horace said, his voice tempo quicker than usual, seemingly agitated. "I returned to the club to sort through paperwork when I heard a clanking noise from the far side of the room."

"What was it?"

"The ankh, radiating a reddish glow. It jumped around on the floor. I had to stop it with my foot and I felt the heat through my shoe. It's now trapped under a box."

"What the hell?"

"You may be right about a connection with the underworld. Something strange is going on."

"Definitely. Red marks have appeared on Orion and Leo's skin too, resembling a dragon slayer symbol. What do you think we should do?"

"We'll be back at the club in the morning looking for the plate, let's decide then?"

Olly was worried; time wasn't on their side. "It might be too late. It needs to be put back in its box before then. It'll keep it safe from whatever is trying to connect with it."

"You're right ..." Horace hesitated. "I'll go back."

"We could come and help?" Olly said, sensing Horace's unease.

"Don't be silly, it won't take me long ... I'll see you in the morning."

"Okay, what time?"

"Nine o'clock prompt, and remember the gems."

"Don't worry, we'll have our bags with everything we need. Bye."

"Good night."

As Olly hung up the phone, the grandfather's clock struck ten. He strolled back into the living room.

"Right, we've eleven hours before Horace comes to pick us up."

The clock was ticking for Claire and the pressure was on. They had to find the components for the portal. Trepidation was in the air – Claire's life was on the line, she was depending on them.

"Come on, time for bed," Melanie said, rising to her feet. "Katie, I've made up the spare room for you. Olly, you'll have to make do on the couch again, I'll sort out a duvet."

"Thanks," Olly said.

"Thank you, Mrs Hart," Katie said as she reached over to give Olly a kiss. "See you in the morning."

Olly smiled. "Try to get some sleep. Don't worry, we'll get Claire back."

She nodded, tears forming in her eyes. Before she headed upstairs, she mouthed 'thank you' back to Olly. With the adrenalin coursing through his body, sleep evaded him. He grabbed a handful of books from the floor; he would learn more on Egyptian culture and history – it could help their cause. First, he examined *Osiris versus Set – the war of brothers*. It was an account of the battle between the two great gods of Egypt. Next, he reached for *The Egyptian book of Magic and Spells*. Inside were hieroglyphics plus verses in Arabic, with some translations jotted in pencil next to them. Perhaps, he could use the mysticism against the Goldings, he mused? How, he wasn't sure. He had no magic stick depicted in the illustrations. He whispered a few of the spells, half expecting something to move, freeze or vanish – but no such luck, much to his annoyance. *Maybe they worked only in the Egyptian underworld,* he pondered as words on the page blurred. He was tired so shut the book as sleep beckoned. Hopefully everything would be crystal clear the following morning.

Upstairs, Melanie and Orion were lying in bed, staring into each other's eyes, both aware of what the other was thinking.

"I know you want to help us," Melanie said.

"I do," Orion whispered. "I can't let you face the Goldings on your own. I don't trust them one bit."

"But you're too weak. If we needed to run, you'd be a danger to yourself and to us too. All we're doing is giving them access to the portal, then they'll hand Claire over, if we find the plate tomorrow."

"You think it'll be that easy?"

"If I sense a trap we'll drive away, promise." Melanie shuffled closer, moving her hand through Orion's hair. She knew Orion would have a bad night's sleep and the last thing he needed was the Golding family back in his life.

Orion sighed. "Okay, we'll discuss it in the morning. Good night." he said turning over.

Melanie kissed him on his shoulder. "Good night my love."

CHAPTER 17

The grandfather clock chimed, piercing through Olly's sleep into his consciousness until he was wide awake. It was irritating him – Olly was longing to return to his own house, wrapped in his duvet, listening to music with his dog Madison beside him for company. 'Get through today', he told himself, 'then this will be over, one way or another'.

Leo walked into the living room with steaming tea for them both. "A rough night last night, eh mate?"

Olly shot awake, remembering. "Oh my god, yes. Have you heard anything? Are you okay?"

Melanie had been right, Orion had a bad night. He'd been having sporadic nightmares and his mumblings became louder as she lie next to him, trying to wake him before the dream blackened. His screams percolated the house – it sounded like he was being attacked. Orion's flailing arms forced Melanie out of bed as he tried to battle with the creatures inside his head. Sweating, his heart pounded, visible in his chest.

Melanie needed help so left her husband, exiting the room to discover Leo outside, crying. "Mum, I'm scared."

"Don't worry, your dad won't remember any of this. He's having another episode," she said heading downstairs. "I'm going to call an ambulance … as a precaution. He's hyperventilating."

Twenty minutes the ambulance arrived and collected Orion, Melanie by his side.

"I'm fine," Leo said, gazing at the red mark on his chest. "Apart from the lack of sleep. Mum will update us soon."

Movement was heard upstairs, along with the sound of singing. "Katie seems happy," Olly said, hearing her skip down the stairs.

"Morning guys, how are you both?" she said "I've a great feeling about today. We're going to see Claire again!" She halted when she saw Olly and Leo. "What's wrong?"

"What's wrong? Didn't you hear anything last night?"

"No Leo, slept like a log. That bed was so comfy. Why … what happened?"

Olly stood. "Orion was taken to hospital last night."

"What?"

131

"He had a nightmare and was hyperventilating. Melanie phoned for an ambulance and she's still with him."

Katie seated herself beside Olly. "Oh, I feel so bad. I heard nothing." She glanced at Leo. "I'd have helped otherwise."

"Don't worry," Leo said. "There's nothing you could've done; he's had them before and he's in the best place."

The phone rang and Leo dashed to the hall, picking up the handset after a single ring, "Hello, who is it?"

"Leo, it's mum."

Leo took a deep breath before speaking. He'd known his dad for only one year and couldn't bear losing him again. "How's Dad?"

"He's doing well, even sat up in bed."

"That's brilliant, I've been worried sick … Tell him I love him."

"I will, but I think he already knows. You make him very proud, you know that don't you?"

"I guess."

"He says sorry by the way, he didn't want to scare you all. He's going for a few more tests this morning and hopefully be home this afternoon."

"That's great, but what about when Horace turns up? You were going to come with us."

"I have to stay with your father. I've been thinking about this during the night. I have to trust all of you to make the right decisions. Claire is waiting to be rescued. Find the plate and we can only hope that the Goldings keep up their end of the bargain."

"Thanks Mum, we'll get her back, promise."

"I know you will, son. I have to go now. A nurse has come to take another test. Love you lots and I'll see you soon."

"Love you, Mum. Bye."

With Horace due anytime, Olly, Leo and Katie packed bags for the day ahead. Leo raided the fridge for snacks, while Katie found a visitor's guide to St. Prion's abbey, plus torches, rope, penknife and a rusty screwdriver, in case things went awry. Olly gathered up the books on Egypt scattered across the floor, shoving them in his bag with the three gems they'd recovered.

"Something's missing," Olly said, confused. "What is it? What do we need?"

Katie and Leo stole a glance at each other and Leo said, "We need the plate."

"I know that stupid, something else … the cube, where is it?"

Katie held up her hand, knowing she'd messed up. "You gave it to me in the club, remember?"

"Of course. Did you put it back in the bag?"

"I forgot, it's still under the table … so I didn't lose it. I'm sorry."

"Don't worry, at least we know where it is. We'll get it when Horace takes us to the club."

The grandfather clock struck nine. "That's come around quick," Leo said.

"You know what they say, tempus fugit," Katie said.

"Who says that?" Leo said. "I've never heard it in my life."

"Everyone knows what tempus fugit means, don't they?"

"I do," Olly said, brushing past Leo into the hallway, glancing at the clock. "It can't be."

Katie wondered what was going on in Olly's head.

"Tempus fugit, it's written on this clock face."

"Can someone please tell me what tempus fugit means?" said Leo.

"Time flies," Olly said. "This clock … tell me about it? Where did your mum and dad get it? Do you know?"

"It was given to us by the Brunswick council when we moved here, don't know much else. Why?"

"Remember reading on Archibald Griffin's grave about what flies to heaven and hell." Leo stared at Olly blankly. "Time flies. It could be a clue."

"I think a lot of grandfather clocks have that written on them," Katie said, trying not to dampen Olly's spirit.

Olly pulled the clock forward from the wall. "But a lot of grandfather clocks won't have this." He pointed to a worn brown sticker, writing faded. He leant forward to read it, "To the Brunswick Railway

Corporation. May all of its passengers be on time. Signed by Archibald Griffin."

"What does it mean?" Katie said.

"This was the clock on the Brunswick station platform. Don't you remember Leo?"

Leo thought hard. "Yeah ... now that you mention it. It was dark, but I definitely remember a clock inside the waiting room, some pictures near it."

"It looks like Archie donated it to the tunnel, then Brunswick council gifted it to your parents."

"What's so special about it though?" Katie said.

Olly began taking it apart. "Let's see, shall we?"

"Hey, be careful. My parents will kill me if we break it?"

Olly, lifted off the top box, leaving the clock face and workings behind.

"I don't believe it," Katie said, peering from behind. "Look everyone."

Olly and Leo's eyes lit up. On the rear of the clock face were hieroglyphs with three perfectly spaced indentations – big enough for the three gems.

"We've found it!" Olly said. "The plate, we've found the plate. It's been here, under our noses all of the time, driving me crazy with its regular chimes. It's as if it was trying to get my attention."

"We can get Claire now," Katie said. "We've found the portal."

The boys stared at each other. "Are you thinking what I'm thinking?"

"You want to try it, don't you, Olly?"

"Yeah."

Katie shook her head disapprovingly but knew she couldn't stop them. Olly picked the three gems from his bag, each a different shape and detached the plate from the clock workings to place it on the floor.

"Are you really sure about this?" Katie said. "We haven't a clue what this thing is capable of. It could destroy the house?"

Leo stood back. He imagined his mum and dad shouting at him while the fire brigade put out the flames soaring from the roof. "Think she might be right, mate," he said.

"How about putting one gem on it – just to see if anything happens?"

Leo and Katie succumbed to his reasoning. Olly plucked the round turquoise stone and placed it into the right hole. Silence descended as the children stared at the plate.

"Did you see that?"

"Yeah Leo," Olly said.

"It's amazing," Katie said. Golden Egyptian scripture around the edge of the plate sparkled brightly, transforming the hallway into a kaleidoscope of reflecting symbols.

"Do you know what they mean?" Katie said, mesmerised by the light show.

"No idea," Olly said. "Do you know, Leo?"

"No, sorry."

"We now know that the plate works," Olly said, kicking the turquoise stone away from the plate, snuffing out the light show.

"I was enjoying that," Katie said.

"We have to be ready for Horace. He should be here soon."

"I was expecting him ages ago. Hope he's alright?" Leo said, peeking through the kitchen window.

Half an hour passed by, anxiety mounting because Horace hadn't appeared. They took it in turns to keep a look-out from the front bedroom window in case Horace had mislaid the address.

"I'm going to ring him," Olly said, remembering that Horace's business card was on the phone stand. Olly dialled the number, Katie and Leo close by, and waited – but nobody answered. After six tones the answering machine kicked in.

"This is Horace Griffin. Please leave a message after the tone."

"Hi Horace, it's Olly. Sorry to call you but we were wondering what time you're be picking us up. You told us nine o'clock and it's nearly ten. We'll set off on our own soon if we don't hear from you. By the way we've found the plate so we can go straight to St. Prion's Abbey. And another thing, can you nip to the club on your way and pick up the cube. Katie left it under the meeting table yesterday. Okay, well, hopefully we'll see you soon. Thanks. Bye." Olly replaced the receiver and breathed heavily.

"Are you alright?" Katie said, seated next to him on the stairs.

"Something's not right. Horace doesn't seem the type of person to be late for anything, especially something as important as this."

The children's nerves jangled. They walked back and forth into the kitchen to check on the wall clock and Olly, messing with his scruffy hair, made the tension tangible.

"Can you stop that for one minute?" Katie said. "It's driving me crazy. When this is over, I'm taking you to a barber."

"We need to go, we've waited long enough," Olly said.

"Without Horace and Leo's mum?"

"Have you a better suggestion?"

Katie knew Olly was right and her silence confirmed it.

"My mum will go crazy, she's already stressed out about my dad."

"What did she say to you over the phone. She trusts you to make the right decisions."

Leo sat at the kitchen table, grabbing an apple from the fruit bowl. Biting into it, the crunch broke the silence. "She did say that didn't she?"

"Yes ... yes, she did. Anyway, all we're doing is handing the portal to the Goldings and rescuing Claire. There's no adventure, not like last year."

"You're right as always," Leo said. "To be honest, I'm not sure all this Stumpy stuff is real. I had a nightmare and me and my dad have marks on us. Coincidence perhaps?"

Olly smiled but he knew it was a façade. Stumpy's call for help was real. "Is that a yes then, we go?"

"Okay ... let's do this." Leo said and threw the half-eaten apple into the bin.

"One more thing?" Katie said. "I don't want to spoil everyone's fun, but how are we meant to get there?"

Olly closed his eyes, waiting for a solution to pop into his mind.

"I know!" Leo said, surprising his friends. "By cycle. There are three bikes in the out-house around the back: mine, mums, and dads. We can cut through the fields. We'll be there in no time."

Olly looked at Katie. "Are you okay with that?"

"What are you trying to say? Course I am, I'll beat you in a bike race any day of the week."

Leo burst out laughing, "She's got you there, mate. Come on, let's get the bikes."

Olly and Katie followed Leo to the rear of the house where he removed a rusty padlock from a rotting door which creaked as he pulled it towards him.

"Perfect," Olly said, dragging out one of the mountain bikes for Katie. "I take it the BMX is yours?"

"Of course," Leo said and winked.

They checked the contents of their rucksacks – twice – before setting off on their mission to save Claire.

CHAPTER 18

"Wait for us, Katie," Olly yelled, watching his girlfriend leave a trail of dust down the country lane.

"Come on losers," she shouted. "Serves Leo right for having a BMX. We're in the nineties now."

"You don't even know which way to go," Leo said, out of breath and pedalling as fast as he could.

"He has a point!" Olly shouted as Katie glanced back to see the boy's detouring through a gap in a hedgerow.

"Oi!" she yelled, skidding her bike to a halt, turning and racing after them, the direction of their laughter guiding her.

The morning's heavy mist hugged the farmers' fields like a duvet. Bordering trees, once majestically upright, were bare and broken due to the storms over the previous couple of weeks. The children's

141

competing over, they rode side by side, Leo cursing his bike's absence of gears. Their mission was important – to save Claire. Leo figured that being Claire's knight in shining armour would raise his chances in the love stakes. Olly was apprehensive, not trusting the Goldings, especially after Marshall's nastiness. Stumpy's plight plagued him too and Leo's suggestion of a coincidence of circumstances didn't hold water to him.

After cycling up a steep incline, Katie spotted something in the distance. "Is that it?" Slowing, her brakes squeaked as her two team members pulled up alongside and gazed at the tower of the ruin on the horizon, partly obscured by the morning fog.

"That looks cool," Leo said.

"Cool doesn't do it justice, it's beautiful. I wish I had a camera with me. It looks so peaceful," Katie said.

"Hopefully it will be!" Olly said. "Come on, we've a job to do and it can't be far to the estate entrance?"

They set off, freewheeling down the hill into the mist.

"What shall we do when we're there?" Leo said, puffing and panting.

"Case the joint first," Olly said.

"Case the joint? Are you in the A-Team."

"Ha, ha Katie. I love it when a plan comes together."

"Can't believe you said that," Leo said, chortling along with Katie as they turned into the grounds of St. Prion Abbey, terrified of what the day held in its hands.

The sun rose through the trees burning off the mist, the rays striking the top of the ruined monastery. On both sides of the mile-long driveway, a herd of wild deer grazed the grassland, their breath visible in the vapour rising from the dew-covered grass.

"This is spooky, wouldn't like to be walking here on my own," Katie said.

"Especially at night, it'd be well creepy," Olly said. "Those deer seem to want to attack us at any moment."

"It's haunted, this place," Leo spouted. "I helped my neighbour clean the café a few months ago when he was short staffed. He told me later that there were always things falling off the shelves. I swore I wouldn't come back, yet here I am."

"Do we really need to know that? I told you that I'm scared," Katie said, riding closer to Olly.

"We'll look after you," Olly said. "We've seen worse than a few ghosts."

The driveway veered downhill, cutting its way through a grove of spreading oak trees. As the sun rose, a body of water appeared, several statues visible in the fading mist. Olly pointed. "There's the main entrance. Let's leave our bikes there."

The gates were twelve-foot-high made of twisted iron spindles, topped with spikes to deter intruders. To the right, a brick wall snaked into the distance around the vast estate. On the far side of the gate was the visitor centre and café.

"How are we meant to gain entry?" Katie said, peering up at the gates.

"Leave it to me," Leo said, vanishing off towards the café.

Olly glanced at Katie, the morning sun enhancing her face. "Can't wait for this to be over so that we can enjoy the rest of the holidays together," he said, leaning towards her.

"Me too," she said, their lips stroking.

"No time for that!" Leo said, chuckling.

"How did you get there?" Olly said, his friend now the other side of the iron bars.

"I'll come around and get you."

"If this involves climbing over walls, count me out."

Leo responded in a flash. "Trust me Katie, follow. I know this route from when I did the kitchen work." He guided Olly and Katie to the far side of the café where an opening led them to a yard, adorned with terracotta pots filled with pink fragrant roses. "They kept a key under that plant pot for the far gate and guess what? They still do."

"We don't have to go through the café?" Katie said, recalling Leo's mystical tale.

"No, through the yard and out through the back gate."

As she walked into the gravel courtyard, Katie shivered. "I feel like I've stepped on someone's grave. Anyone else feel the same?"

"Don't move," Olly said, pointing at one of the café windows. Katie and Leo turned their heads slowly towards where Olly indicated.

Through the glass was an apparition staring at them, wearing a Georgian maid outfit.

"Please tell me she's human and not a ghost?" Katie said.

Olly gulped, "If she is a human, she has translucent skin."

"That ... m m must be the ghost," Leo said.

"Oh my god, I've never seen a ghost. She's beautiful and is younger than me," Katie whispered.

The young girl in the window smiled, lifted her arm and beckoned the three children towards her. "What do we do?" Katie said, sounding braver than she felt.

Taking Katie's arm, Olly said, "We go over ... what have we got to lose?"

As they drifted forward, a door next to the window creaked open. Katie's breath quickened. She stuttered as she said, "We're going in, aren't we? Why did I agree to this? I could be at home watching TV now ..."

"Shh," Olly said, "We don't want to scare her."

"Scare her? What about me?"

The three children stepped into the café and grabbed a seat at the nearest table as the ghost floated towards them. "Good morning, please don't run from me," said the young maid, her voice ephemeral. "My name is Matilda, but my friends call me Tilly."

Fearless Olly spoke first, "Hello ... Tilly, it's nice to meet you. My name's Olly and this is Leo and Katie. How long have you been here?"

"Oh, an age. I worked for the Richmond family until I slipped off a chair and fell from the window, hitting my head. It's such a pretty place so I stayed rather than make for my home in Brunswick."

For once, Katie was speechless, staring open-mouthed.

"I live in Brunswick," Olly said, gesturing to Katie and Leo, "but these two live in St. Prion."

"I lived in St. Prion too," came a child's voice from behind.

"Aargh!" screamed Katie, glancing back. "This is becoming ridiculous."

Seated on his own on the next table was another ghost, this time a young boy dressed in a drab brown jacket with matching shorts and cap, socks up to his knees and heavy ankle boots.

"This is my friend, Arthur," Tilly said.

"Where in St. Prion do you live?" asked the frail boy.

"Near to ... Market Street," Katie said.

"On Fisherman's View," Leo said.

"I lived there, before I was shot," Arthur said. "Then I met Tilly and I've been here ever since."

"You were shot?" Olly said.

"When the army were training in the Great War, me and my friends would sneak in through the woods and watch. Tanks were blowing things up and hundreds of soldiers marched, learning to fight. One day I ventured too close to the gun range and was hit. Look." Arthur opened up his jacket revealing the wound.

"I feel ill," Katie said, turning away.

"Is there anything we can do to help you both?" Olly said, unsure why he asked.

"No, but thank you," Tilly said. "I spotted you heading towards the abbey and wanted to warn you."

"Why?"

"Arthur told me there's a lot of strange things going on near the abbey."

"What did you see?" Olly said, turning to Arthur.

"Bright colours – haven't seen them before – with screams and rumblings, like my tummy does sometimes," said Arthur, chuckling. "Bad things are coming from there. I'd have felt 'em in my bones ... if I had any, which I don't."

"But you're ghosts, you can't be scared?" Katie said, gaining confidence.

Tilly drifted over and joined Arthur. "There are good and bad spirits. Your soul, that dictates what you are – pleasant or evil – not your body."

"We're good spirits," Arthur said. "What I saw were bad 'uns."

"Are there any more good spirits here? We could do with help if things go wrong?" Olly said. "We're trying to rescue our friend, Claire. She's being held here by wicked people."

"There's plenty of good," Arthur said, pointing out of the window towards the lake. "Me and my friends play in the water at night."

"And hide and seek in the woods. Come and find me Arthur," Tilly said passing through the glass window.

"I'm coming," her ghostly friend replied before turning to Olly. "Good luck with your adventure."

"Okay… " Leo said, raising his eyebrows. "That was different."

"Amazing," Katie said. "Can you believe it but… I've spoken to two ghosts. This isn't a dream, is it? I *am* actually here?"

"I wish it was a dream," Olly said, "sadly we're really here."

The children made their way out of the café. "What did he mean about the bright colours and rumblings?" Katie said.

"Not sure, maybe he was referring to thunder and lightning? I hope we're not too late," Olly said.

Once through the courtyard, they entered the abbey's storm-battered gardens. "These have seen better days. I was looking forward to seeing the greenery," Katie said.

"We'll take a trip when it's been tidied up," Olly said.

"Can we all focus for a second? Lance and Marshall might see us, and god knows where Victor is."

"Sorry, Leo mate."

The once award winning gardens sat in a valley basin, around a meandering stream along the edge of acres of fields. It was littered with debris ripped from the surrounding pine and oak trees. The ruined abbey was distant, sunlight reflecting from its weathered Yorkshire stone, also damaged during the recent tempest. The steep valley sides, dense in woodland, were perfect to conceal their assault on the kidnapper's refuge.

Olly whispered, "Right, head towards the abbey. If you see anything, whistle but don't shout … You got that?"

"Yeah," Leo said.

"Okay boss," Katie said.

Sneaking along the valley, hidden by tall pine trees, they spotted something fluttering inside the main hall.

"Did we bring binoculars?" Katie said.

"Don't look at me," Leo shrugged.

"Can't believe this," Olly said. "We're not going to get much closer."

Leo tapped him on the shoulder. "I'll head down to the wall. If you see anything, whistle."

Before Olly had chance to stop him, Leo sprinted across the grass towards the abbey.

"Is he crazy?"

"Either that or he really likes Claire."

Leo stood, back to the abbey's wall, catching his breath. Something was fluttering, louder than a bird. Building up courage, he twisted his head to glance through the window. Inside a large hall, unglazed windows scattered light over a fire-scarred floor. Broken stone pillars lined its centre, while a solitary circular stone table had pride of place in the middle. At the far end was the source of the noise. Shuffling back away from the ruin, he frantically waved, trying to attract the attention of his friends in the woods.

"What's he doing?" Katie said. "Is he in trouble?"

"Think he wants us to join him. Are you okay with that?"

"Well, I'm not staying here on my own if that's what you think. It's scary enough being here with you, never mind witho …"

"This isn't the time to gabble on. This might be urgent," Olly said, setting off.

"Hey, wait for me."

Olly took Katie's hand as they ran down the valley slope on to the open grass towards Leo who had his finger against his mouth – indicating silence.

"Any sign of Claire?" Katie whispered.

"No, but you're not going to believe what's in there, Olly," Leo said, his voice carrying a serious edge.

Olly knew that whatever was in there – it wasn't good. He glanced around. "It can't be, we're not in the underworld."

Katie poked her head alongside Olly and whispered, "What in the name of creation is that thing?"

"It's a giabat – they were in the tunnel with us. But how ... how has it got here? And what's it doing?"

The giant bat-like creature, six feet tall, had the wingspan of a hang glider and the texture of black leather.

"It's eating something," Leo said, squinting his eyes as a ray of sun interfered with his vision.

"Let's get nearer while it's distracted," Olly said.

They continued along the outside of the abbey to the next window, hoping for a better view.

"It's eating someone, I can see an arm!" Katie said. "I think I'm going to puke."

Leo shone his torch, trying for a glimpse of the body.

"No!" Olly said but it was too late. The giabat was spooked by the torch light and stared towards the window, blood dripping from its mouth. It released a high pitch screech, flapped its wings, and flew high into the rafters.

"Probably too full to think about eating us," Leo said.

"Yeah, you're right. Come on, let's see whose body this is," Olly said, climbing into the ruin.

The three teenagers stepped closer, wafting away the numerous flies milling around, the smell of dead flesh pungent making Katie feel ill again. "I'm not sure I can do this."

"Don't worry, you stay near the side and keep a lookout for the giabat," Olly said, nearing the remains of the bat's meal.

The corpse was face down with lumps of fat and flesh torn from the legs and buttocks.

"It's no good Leo, it has to be done – we need to see the face. After three, roll it over."

"Okay," Leo said, taking a deep breath.

"One … two … three."

CHAPTER 19

"Oh my god, I don't believe it," Olly said, running back to the awaiting Katie who was resting against the inner wall.

His girlfriend welcomed him with a hug. Right then, he needed it. "Who is it?"

"It's Lance," Leo said, appearing as if by magic. "He's been shot!"

Katie paled as blood drained from her cheeks. Leaning from the window, she was sick; it was becoming too serious for her. She'd never seen a dead body before... let alone one being eaten by a creature from another dimension. She wiped her mouth with a tissue. "We talked to him at the fair yesterday ... my god, if someone's shot him, what about Claire? Claire!" her scream echoed through the building.

"Hush Katie, you're going to annoy the giabat," Olly said peering up.

"What the hell happened?"

"No idea Leo," Olly said, "but let's start by searching for Claire."

"Where?"

"Only one place I'd keep someone hostage around here Katie, the dungeons."

Katie and the boys ran along the stone corridors, down the steps and into the depths of the abbey.

"It's cold down here," Katie said, "she must be frozen."

"It's this door – trust me," Leo said, remembering his school trip to the abbey.

Olly grabbed the torch and ventured in, wafting the light from one side to the other. "She's not here."

"Look at that," Katie said, bending down. "Burnt rope, here on the floor. Do you think she might have escaped?"

"Where to?" Leo said, now concerned. "Someone's killed Lance, maybe she's …. "

"Stop – that gets us nowhere," Olly said. "You can't think like that. Back to the hall, there may be a clue near Lance's body."

When they reached the corpse, the giabat was nibbling Lance's left ankle again but disappeared at their appearance.

"I hope she's escaped into the woods?" Katie said.

"That's not what happened," The words came from a shadowy figure framed in the doorway at the far end of the hall.

"Who's there?" Olly said, unable to identify the person.

Walking forward through the rays of sunlight slicing into the large hall was Horace.

"Horace! You're here," Leo said.

Olly released a deep breath and relaxed. "It's good to see you. What happened? Did you get my phone message?"

Horace seemed agitated and the dark bags under his eyes suggested that he hadn't slept either. "Hello … it's good to see you. No, there was no message … I've been at the club."

Katie was confused. "How did you know we'd be here?"

After a pause, Olly said. "Well?"

"There's something I need to tell you," Horace said, "and I don't want you to react badly."

"Just tell us."

"It's okay, I'll tell them." Someone from behind interrupted Horace.

Olly recognised the voice but not wishing to believe it. He dashed forward, stretching his neck to glance around Horace, hoping he was wrong. But he wasn't. "Marshall!"

James Golding Marshall stepped forward until the sunlight hit his jet-black hair swept back off his pale face. He spoke with a cultured accent. "I guess you weren't expecting to see me with Horace?"

Olly and Leo continued to process events in real-time but Katie was having none of it. She ran to him and slapped his right cheek – hard – but Marshall hardly flinched. "Where is she? Where's Claire? What have you done with her? We have the portal for Victor, we met our side of the bargain – now where is she?"

Marshall stroked his reddening cheek but Horace intervened, staring at Olly, "It was late last night and I took your advice. I returned to the club to check on the ankh in the storage room and heard a knock on the club's door. This young man introduced himself as James Marshall and told me his story, that he'd been walking through the night and knew of the club's existence from speaking to Claire. He was shattered, physically and mentally. I've always liked to think of myself as intuitive – a good judge of character so I decided to help him."

"Help him?" Olly said. "Are you crazy? What's to say he won't turncoat on us again? He was only seconds from shooting us in the tunnel – remember that, Marshall?"

"Course I do," said Marshall." But my Uncle Lance forced me to do it, told me he'd kill me if I didn't go along with the plan."

"He ain't going to force you now," Leo said, pointing to his uncle's remains in the corner.

"I'm not grieving for him. I'd turn the clock back if I could, believe me."

"So, what happened?" Olly said. "And where's Claire?"

"I'll tell you, but first I need to say something."

"It had better be good," Katie said. "My cousin is missing and I want you to tell me what you've done to her."

A tired Marshall moved forward. "You must hate me, not want anything to do with me but... I'm sorry ... sorry for ruining your lives ... sorry for tricking you. I was brainwashed from childhood, told to *hate* those who killed my dad. I didn't know better. Claire made me realise the mess I was making of my life. I'm so sorry." He fell to the ground, sobbing.

"I'm not falling for the theatrics. Where is she?" Olly yelled.

Marshall wiped his face and stood, staring at his uncle's remains for a moment. "I was with Lance and my dad ..."

"Do you remember this, son?" Victor said, his voice resonating around the stones of the building.

"Yes," Marshall said. "That sword ... it was a dragon slayers. Stumpy mentioned that it was Bellafino's."

"Let me hold it," Lance said, pushing his nephew out of the way. He placed his gun down and gripped the sword with both hands – he managed to move it a couple of inches, even using every ounce of strength he possessed.

"Is it that heavy?" Marshall said.

"You could say that."

"Not to a dragon slayer," Victor said. "Leo and Orion must not find this weapon. Their powers could return at any time."

Marshall helped Lance with the weapon and succeeded to lift it aloft.

"No!" Victor bellowed.

Spinning around, Lance dropped the sword and went for his gun but it wasn't on the table – it was in Claire's hands.

"Surprise," she said, aiming the weapon at him. "You should be more careful where you drop your cigars Lance." Claire's clothes were dirty and torn, blonde hair a matted mess. Her hands shook, not with fear but with the adrenalin that coursed through her veins. "Put your hands where I can see them," she said, finger itching the trigger.

"Are you stupid?" Lance snarled and nodded to Marshall. "Get that gun off her. She won't shoot you, she's soft on you."

Marshall didn't move as he knew that Claire had been right. Lance had made a fool out of him all his life. This was the time to make a stand.

"What are you waiting for Marshall?"

"Not this time," Marshall said, stepping away from his uncle. "Too many times you've bullied me and too many times it's me who's ended up in trouble. You don't *love* me ... you use me."

"I've sacrificed much for you boy, raised you when your dad died. Is this how you repay me?"

"You raised me in your own image, not for me. You only cared about revenge."

"If you're not going to help, I know someone who will."

Victor's ghost materialised, piercing red eyes locked on his female target. He swooped towards Claire, anger burnishing his ephemeral presence.

Hands trembling, Claire struggled to track movements. "Stop or I'll shoot!" she shouted, but Victor continued his harassment.

Bang!

The gun released its projectile aimed towards the spirit but Victor swooped upwards with ease.

Claire screamed as the bullet came to an unintended halt, hitting Lance in the chest. With a gurgling, he collapsed to the ground, his heart the final target. "Help me." Were his last words.

"Oh my god ... oh my god, I didn't mean to hit him. It was the ghost I was aiming for."

"Shooting a ghost wouldn't have achieved anything," Marshall said, applying pressure to his uncle's wound.

"Will he live? ... Let me go and look for help. There must be a house nearby with a phone."

"Then what? Are you going to tell them you shot him?"

"I didn't mean to hurt him and anyway, it was self-defence."

Marshall took his hands away from his uncle's chest and bowed his head. Lance was dead.

"Oh my god, have I killed him."

Marshall stood and faced her. She seemed fragile and broken – all because of him and his family. He held her tenderly as he said, "It's okay. I know that you didn't mean to hurt Lance, how could you? You've never hurt anyone in your whole life I'd wager. You were in the wrong place at the wrong time."

Claire held Marshall tight, mascara-stained tears dribbling over Marshall's sweatshirt. For the first time in his life, Marshall felt needed but the moment was fleeting. A booming voice from above ended their tenderness.

"What have you done? My brother … my brother!"

Victor picked up the sword and flew towards Claire, his intention clear – to kill her. He caused the weapon to raise above his ghostly aura, ready to slice at Claire. Marshall knew he had to stop him. Stepping in front of Claire as a human shield, he yelled, "Stop this father! This isn't the plan."

The ghost hesitated and replied, "There is no plan now, my brother is dead."

The Seekers of Duat

"Lance could be saved if you retrieve the portal. If you kill her you'll both remain dead, forever."

Interested, Victor pondered until the ground shook and cracked open causing Claire and Marshall to be thrown in opposite directions. A fiery glow seeped from the chasm that now separated them.

"What's going on?" Claire shouted as the rumblings intensified.

"The underworld," Marshall said, unable to reach her. "I remember it ... it's coming back."

Victor grabbed his opportunity. This was an opening into the underworld and he no longer needed the portal. It mattered little what happened to Claire but revenge for his brother's death was still possible. The ghost commenced a further attack on the girl, who was trying to regain her footing as the floor split in two. Steam spurted high into the hall, forcing Victor's apparition into the rafters.

"Jump over to me!" Marshall shouted.

"I can't, the gap is too wide. Leap over to me?" she shouted as the floor opened another ten feet. A huge creature with dark wings like a pterodactyl appeared from the red mist, soaring high into the building. "What the hell is that?"

"It's a giabat ... this is definitely the underworld."

"Help me! I'm terrified!"

"I can't reach you," Marshall said, distracted by a white cloud rising from the molten lava.

161

Claire sprung to her feet, trying to find a way out of the mayhem when Victor grabbed her arm.

"You killed my brother," he roared. "I'm going to take you where no-one will ever find you."

The circle of cloud rose and a tall figure appeared, dressed in white, holding a mace. The visitation thrust out its arms, an electric charge darting from the staff, making for the sword like a limpet mine. Both the weapon and Claire were attracted towards the newcomer as Victor resisted the power used against him.

"That sword is a dragon slayer's. Release it!" boomed the mysterious figure.

"It is mine." Victor said.

A spray of magma flew upwards from the hellish depths, distracting Victor for a moment, causing his grip on Claire to loosen as she tried to pull away. Victor snatched her back with both arms, letting go of the sword in the process. The weapon flew like a missile straight into the mysterious beings' grasp. No sooner had the creature appeared than it vanished into the fiery pits of the underworld. Victor was certain that he'd witnessed the appearance of a deity of the underworld. He grabbed Claire and flew towards where the apparition was disappearing below.

"Help me," Claire shouted but her cries were in vain.

"I'll find you!" Marshall yelled as the light dimmed and the floor pulled together leaving a charred scar behind. A lone giabat remained, flying amongst the roof beams circling Lance's dead body while Marshall stared in silence.

CHAPTER 20

"And we're meant to believe that?" Leo said. "How do we know you haven't killed Claire?"

"It's the truth ... I promise," Marshall said, bravado replaced with something less tangible – gaunt, broken and apparently shamed by his past. "Sat on the cold floor, I remembered something Claire had told me. It was the Art of Darkness club on Tower Lane. The only way I could think of getting her back was with your help, so I went looking for you and that's when I found Horace ... I want to get Claire back."

Olly was unsure what to believe. He scanned the hall for clues to validate Marshall's story. The scorched crack, zigzagging across the centre of the room was a starting point; he hadn't remembered it on previous trips. *Who takes notice of a floor,* he thought, *It might have been there for hundreds of years.* He strolled to Lance's body to examine it. The bullet wound was as Marshall had described. *But who shot him? Was it Claire?* He glanced up at the giabat perched on a protruding stone watching them. *The underworld must have opened; how else could that creature be here?* Olly decided to dig deeper. "Leo's right, you could've killed her and she might be buried in the woods for all we know. Where's the gun she used?"

Marshall pulled the weapon from a back pocket of his trousers.

"Stop!" Olly yelled as memories of Marshall pointing a gun at them in the tunnel resurfaced. Leo ran for cover.

"I'm not going to use it," Marshall said raising his arms. "You wanted to see it." His possession of the weapon wasn't doing his cause any favours, so he threw the gun across the floor until it rested against the abbey wall.

Horace glanced at Olly and said, "I believe him. I've read much about the underworld and its deities. It seems true."

"Perhaps, but I still don't trust him," Leo said, now standing beside Olly.

"Look," Katie said, trying to calm the situation. "This isn't helping find Claire. Marshall, if you are sorry, how can you help us? The man in white, who was he?"

"I don't know who he was but I do know that he wanted the sword ... and he told us that it was a slayer's sword. His green hands grabbed it and then he was circled by light before he disappeared into the ground."

"He was green?" Horace said.

"Yes, his skin was. Didn't I mention that?"

"Olly … have you got those books with you?"

"Yeah, in my rucksack."

"Can you look for a picture of Osiris."

Scrambling through his bag, he plucked out the book on Osiris and Set. On the first page was a drawing of Osiris, tall and proud wearing white robes and headpiece decorated with plumage. The god was holding a crook and flail and – he was green.

Olly showed the picture to Marshall. "Is this who you saw?"

"That's him … that's who appeared."

Olly suspected that Marshall *was* telling the truth – he couldn't have known the god's skin was green, unless he *had* seen him.

"He wanted it for Stumpy," Leo said. "That was his sword. Stumpy must be alive."

"The circle, where did it come from?" Katie asked. "Isn't the underworld like hell, fire and devils?"

"It comes in many shapes," Horace said. "If it was Osiris who took the sword, then he used a portal of his own making. The hell we recognise as the underworld, is a gateway, that's all."

"The portal," Olly said.

"Oh yeah, that was a waste of time," Katie said. There was no chance now of swapping the portal for the safe return of her cousin.

"No, it's not a waste of time. That's how we're going to save her."

Katie and Leo stared at each other, unsure what was going through Olly's mind.

"Don't you see," Olly said. "*We'll* use the portal to take us to the underworld and rescue Claire."

"Are you joking?" Leo said, unable to control his laughter. "You believe a few gems and a plate will transport us to the underworld – and back?"

"I do," Katie said, "I know what you went through last year and most people don't believe you. But it happened ... didn't it? You, of all people should believe in the impossible. Let's give it a try, yes?"

"Archie's grave – remember – Duat awaits the seekers. Don't you see?"

"What?" Leo said to Olly.

"We are the seekers. We are the seekers of Duat. We've found the portal to Duat, the Egyptian underworld."

They held hands, confidence renewed. "To the seekers!" Horace said.

"The seekers!" everyone yelled, arms in the air.

"Will we end up in the same place with this portal?" Leo said, now supporting Olly's plan.

"My father's pyramid grave implied that it will take us to the Iron Throne, that of Osiris," Horace replied.

"What do we think then?" Olly said. "Shall we give it a go?"

Katie was first to agree, sticking her hand straight into the air but Leo was unsure. He'd already entered the abbey without his parent's consent and was on the brink of transcending a portal to another dimension. Olly sensed his anguish. "It's okay to be scared mate, because I am. I know you want to rescue Claire but think about it, your slayer powers could return."

"What about my parents?"

"They trust you to make the right decision, remember," Olly said.

"I don't believe this but … okay I'm in – but this had better work or we're in serious trouble."

Olly high-fived his friend before turning to Marshall. "I don't know what to believe, but I can't risk you coming with us. If you are truly sorry, you must wait here and guard the portal while we are gone. Do you understand?"

"Yes, I'll do that. I won't let you down."

"I'd like to help," Horace said. "I'll go with you."

"That's not a good idea," Olly said. "I don't mean to be rude but aren't you too old for this sort of thing?"

Horace chuckled, "I think it was Mark Twain who said that age is an issue of mind over matter. If you don't mind, it doesn't matter – and I certainly don't mind."

"Who's Mark Twain?" Leo said.

"It doesn't matter," Olly said, shaking his head.

"With age comes wisdom. My knowledge of Egyptian myths will be handy, I'm sure."

"That's okay with me," Leo said.

"And me," Katie said. "The more the merrier. In fact, we'll need all the help we can get. Will this portal work? Also, how do we get back? I'm getting nervous now."

"I can tell." Olly said, holding her hand. "I'm unsure about returning but Archie must have done it. After all, clues about the portal were on his gravestone?"

"A good point," Horace said, "but there is one more thing you should know."

"Now what?" Leo said.

"When I went to check the ankh last night, well …"

"Well, what?" Olly said.

"It wasn't there. All that remained was a charcoaled crack in the floor – like that one," Horace said, pointing to the fracture in the abbey's floor.

"Was it taken?" Katie said.

"Sounds like it," Olly said. "But by something from under the ground."

"Maybe Set?" Leo said. "He's a god. He could've opened a portal, like Osiris did."

"I don't know," Horace said. "Whoever's taken it, it must be important to them. It's time, I think – the portal Olly?"

Olly removed the gems and plate from his bag, placing them on the floor. Everyone retired, not knowing what to expect.

"Are we ready?" Olly said. "We'll hold hands when it appears – we go in together. If anyone doesn't want to do this, now is the time to say."

"I'm in," Leo said.

"Count me in," Katie said. "My cousin's down there and I want her back."

Horace handed Marshall an envelope. "Look after this, just in case," he said. Marshall shoved it into his pocket. "Right, everyone, I'm ready."

Olly positioned the turquoise stone onto the plate, causing symbols on the plate to glow. Next was the carnelian gem, highlighting different hieroglyphics. Olly looked up – everyone was transfixed by the plate. "This is it … good luck everyone," he said, adding the lapis lazuli gemstone.

He stepped back as the complete plate pulsed and then …

NOTHING.

"What's wrong with it?" said Leo.

"Don't know," Olly said. "Have I put them in the wrong order?"

Horace said, "I told you that I'd be of some use." Examining the glowing Egyptian scripture, Horace crawled his memory to recall an incantation. "The god of Duat will await your soul, at the temple of the iron throne."

"Yes!" Olly said, "The plate's moving."

The plate span clockwise causing dust from the floor to be disturbed. The increasing speed caused the glowing symbols to merge into a golden ring. Everyone stepped back, watching as the circle expanded and rose from the plate. Like a tornado it stretched towards the hall's roof. The giabat, resting on an exposed beam was sucked into the vortex. Olly, Leo, Katie and Horace circled the portal, joining hands.

"On three, we all step forward," Olly said.

"Good luck everyone," Marshall said. "I'll be waiting."

Olly gave a nod, enough for Marshall to know that there was a chance that he'd been forgiven.

"Let's go seekers! 1 ... 2 ... 3."

They moved half a step, enough for the vortex to take hold of them, sucking their bodies forward until they vanished from the abbey hall. Marshall was alone, only the remains of his uncle's body for company. Relentlessly, the portal continued to spin.

CHAPTER 21

A scream bellowed from Katie as she witnessed ghosts and mythical creatures flicker past the four seekers. The kaleidoscopic portal twisted into another dimension, the adventurer's helpless as they were ferried to an unknown destination.

"Hold on tight!" Horace shouted, as the end to the light show neared.

The three children closed in on each other until darkness descended like a blanket. "What's happening?" Leo said.

Olly spotted a distant light growing in intensity. "Something's coming nearer. I think we're …"

"Aargh!" came the collective cry as each tumbled down onto a gritty surface, their skin scraping the floor as a dust cloud bellowed to conceal their surroundings.

As the visibility improved, they scanned around in awe. Close by, standing to attention like soldiers, rows of limestone columns filled the room – each thirty feet tall. "Whoa!" Leo said, glancing at the carved stone spiral they had somehow appeared from. "That was awesome."

"You okay, Horace?" Olly asked, seeing his friend confused.

"I think so," he said, brushing the dirt off his smart trousers. "I seem to have banged my head."

"Where are we?" Katie said, rising to her feet. "Is it a temple?"

"Exactly right, Katie," Horace said. "The temple of Osiris."

"It worked, we're actually here? It doesn't seem like the underworld," Olly said, feeling the hieroglyphics inscribed in the pillars with his fingers.

"Like I said … the underworld has many guises," Horace said. "The portal has taken us to the iron throne, somewhere in the temple."

Katie, eager to find the throne, examined one of the many aisles. "What … are they?" she said, pointing at two ghostly figures drifting between the stone pillars.

Olly joined her. "They seem normal, except they're translucent," he said.

"We're in another dimension, separate from our world," Horace said. "You're seeing tourists visiting the temple but *they* can only see what's in their world."

"That's cool," Leo said, running up to them and waving his arms. "You're right … they can't see a thing."

"How do you know this stuff?" Katie asked.

"I'm not sure, probably read it in a book," Horace said.

Horace and the three seekers searched the building, meandering through the stone columns and hidden rooms.

"Is this it!?" came a distant shout from Katie.

They made their way to a small chamber at the far end of the temple. Inside was a four-pillared monument, within which was a majestic throne.

"Are you sure it's the right one?" Leo said.

"Positive," Horace said, kneeling to study its markings. "Yes, this is the iron throne of Osiris."

"Well done Katie," Olly said. "And well-done Horace too. It must be all of those books again."

"No, not the books," Horace said, standing, rubbing the back of his head. "I remember now … it's coming back to me."

Katie seemed confused. "Have I missed something? I don't understand."

Olly and Leo shrugged at her, neither none the wiser as Horace froze, jaw hanging loose, eyes staring at the throne. Olly waved a hand in front of the old man's eyes, breathing a sigh of relief when Horace blinked. "What is it? What happened?"

"It was all true," Horace said, in a low voice. "All of it, true."

"What was true? What's going on?" Leo's voice became high-pitched betraying his anxiety.

Horace's eyelids fluttered as he realised that he had to tell his tale. "Archie, my father, told me a story when I was a boy. I believed it to be a bed-time tale he'd made up and I remember it giving me nightmares. Seeing the throne has made me remember …" His words tailed away as Horace seemed unable to continue.

"You're scaring me," Katie said, her voice higher than Leo's. "What do you remember? What's happening?"

Horace looked away from the throne, channelling his attention to the children, gesturing them to move nearer. Olly, Leo, and Katie removed their backpacks and seated themselves on the stone floor, staring up at him like eager pupils listening to a teacher.

Horace continued, "At the age of two, I … I died of diphtheria."

"What?" came the startled response.

"It was a common disease in 1939. My father was devastated but remembered something Gamal, the historian he knew from Egypt, had mentioned to him. He'd spoken of the Egyptian belief in rebirth and reincarnation – and that items they'd taken from the tomb were capable of transporting someone to the iron throne where their fate could be decided by the god

175

Osiris. My father had nothing to lose so he did as Gamal explained and spoke the incantation etched into the plate."

"You knew this when we were at the abbey, didn't you? You didn't have to decipher the hieroglyphics," Olly said.

"The words appeared in my head but I didn't expect it to work … let's return to my story. The plate rotated, sucking my father into the portal whilst he held my lifeless body. He told me later of flashing lights and colours he'd never seen and about falling into a temple. He told me that he panicked, unsure of where he was, until he heard a resonating voice that filled the space. *Who dares enter my temple? Who dares?* My father introduced himself and told the deity that he needed help from the God of resurrection because his son Joseph had died."

"I'm lost," Katie said. "Who's Joseph?"

"I am … I was Joseph."

"Sorry, one more thing – didn't Archie find the throne in an underground tomb? Not a temple?"

Olly said, "The throne was moved from the tomb back to Osiris' temple in Abydos, to allow visitors to appreciate it. The portal is connected to the throne."

"Yeah, something like that," Leo said.

Horace smiled at Olly before continuing with his story, "*I am the mighty Osiris; God of the underworld and the resurrection,* the voice had boomed. My father witnessed, like us today, the four-pillared temple, the throne within. Unlike today, Osiris was on the throne. From the carvings and paintings he'd unearthed with the tomb, he knew it was Osiris. The god was dressed in a vibrant white gown, a matching-coloured crown draped in peacock feathers on his head. His green skin was unmistakable.

"My father walked towards him, carrying my body begging the god to resurrect me. *What do you offer me in return for this miracle?* Osiris had said. My father offered his soul – he had nothing else to offer.

"Did Osiris accept the deal?" Olly said.

"No, he told my father his soul wasn't pure enough."

"What happened?" Katie said. "Some deal must have been agreed, otherwise you wouldn't be here today unless you're a ghost. Are you? Not sure I could deal with more surprises …" Olly tapped her leg, suggesting she be quiet.

"Osiris asked my father for my soul. You see to the god, a child's soul hadn't yet been subject to the evils of the human race. The god told my father that he would return me to life and name me after his own son Horus, who'd died in a battle. He would ensure that the child lived a true and pure life.

"My father agreed of course – he had no choice. He placed my limp body in front of Osiris on a stone table. The god stood, raised his green arms and chanted in an strange language. Claps of thunder intertwined with flashes of lightning, crashed against the great temple. A single bolt of fork lightning penetrated my body and my father was forced backwards. Petrified and mute on the floor, probably where you're seated now, he watched as Osiris picked up my body and kissed my chest. My dad then heard the sound of my crying and ran over, grabbing me from Osiris' arms. Holding me tight, he told Osiris that he'd saved his life as well as his son's. He knew that he'd be forever in Osiris' debt.

"The god instructed my father to return to our world and to educate the world about Egyptian culture and the gods. Osiris warned my father that, if his brother Set were to return to Egypt, then I must also return."

"Does Osiris think you can defeat Set?" Olly said. "You must have powers?"

"Wow, you have powers like me," Leo said. "What can you do?"

Horace shook his head. "I haven't any that I know of."

"Maybe when you're closer to Set, you'll find some?" Olly said. "Like Leo does next to a dragon."

"How did you and your dad return?" Katie said.

"I don't remember of course, and my father never mentioned it. Osiris must have found a way."

Leo dashed into the columned hall to examine the stone spiral they'd materialised from. He ran his fingers around the chiselled grooves, hoping to dislodge a stone to a passage that led home. Nothing transpired. A dejected Leo turned his back to the wall and slid down to the floor.

"That's a great story Horace. Or should that be Horus?" Olly said, back in the throne room.

Horace chuckled as he said, "My dad changed it – children can be nasty about names."

"What do we do now?" Katie said. "Wait until Osiris decides to show up?"

Horace was about to reply when a crumb of rock dropped from above, falling into Olly's lap, causing them to glance upwards.

CHAPTER 22

"Did anyone else feel that?" Katie said, leaping to her feet.

Leo ran back into the throne room "I felt the room move!"

"Yeah, I did too," Olly said as a block of limestone landed on the floor in front of him. "Come on, let's get out of here."

They made their move, speed increasing with every step. The room was visibly wobbling like a jelly when a giant column collapsed, smashing into the room where the iron throne stood.

"What's happening?" Katie shouted.

"Just keep running, let's get out of here," Olly yelled, grabbing her arm.

They dodged the falling pillars, slid by the ghostly figures from the real world as Leo heard a familiar voice in his head.

You will find what you need at the necropolis of Giza.

Stumpy is that you? Leo thought back.

Yes, came the reply.

"We need to find a necropolis in Giza," Leo shouted through the chaos.

"What's a necropolis?" Katie said.

"A large cemetery laden with tombs," Horace shouted through the falling debris.

"Great! It couldn't have been a nice garden with a waterfall, could it?"

"Where's Giza?" Olly yelled.

"I don't know," Katie replied.

"Don't look at me," Leo said, running from the crumbling temple into the Egyptian heat.

"I wasn't asking either of you! I was asking Horace. Where is Horace?"

The youngsters glanced around, hoping for a glimpse of their friend.

"Thought he was behind us," Leo said.

"He was a second ago, I heard him," Katie said.

The seekers stepped back, watching the temple collapsing.

"What do we do now?" Leo said.

"I'm going back," Olly said, shrugging off Katie's attempt to prevent him for going. Through the mayhem of smashed limestone rocks and falling columns, Olly called out for Horace, wafting away the dusty air that stung his eyes. He glimpsed a figure crouched against the side wall, rays of sunlight struggling through the grime.

"Is that you Horace? ... Horace? ... can you hear me?" Olly shouted.

All he could hear was a scream, like somebody being eviscerated. "Olly! LEAVE before the temple collapses," he said, agonising pain evident in his expression.

"I won't leave you," Olly said, as another column slammed down, smashing into a thousand pieces.

"I'll be okay, trust me. LEAVE!" said a voice, deepening as he spoke.

Olly had little option but to retreat. He dashed to the exit, crossing a sandy track to join Leo and Katie. Together they watched the temple crash to the floor creating a cloud of dust that shrouded everything it touched.

"Did you find him?" Katie said, her breathing deepening as the temperature rose. "He's our only hope."

"Yes ... he was in there, but I couldn't get to him. I had to leave him, he told me to go."

The dust cloud gradually dispersed, allowing the sun's powerful rays to illuminate the damage. Leo spotted something. "Look! That's the outline of the temple – it's still standing."

Horace had mentioned that the real world was tenuously visible. undisturbed by the underworld.

Even the tourists remained, oblivious to the chaos of their surroundings. Forced to shield their eyes and ears, the seekers witnessed a powerful beam of light penetrate the rubble of Osiris' temple, triggering something bizarre – a screeching sound, similar to the call of an eagle, echoing from the debris.

"What is that?" Leo said, peering through the cracks between his fingers to screen his eyes from the intense light.

"I don't know," Katie said. "But we need to get away from here, more buildings are collapsing."

"What about Horace?" Olly said. "We can't leave him to die."

Katie put her arms around him. "It's too late. I'm sorry." Olly cradled his head on her shoulder and cried.

"It isn't fair, he was a good man. He only came to help us and now he's … dead."

"We should keep moving," Leo said. "We need to find this necropolis place."

"How can we do that without Horace?" Katie said. "He was the only one with any knowledge of this place."

Olly wiped his tears and reached into his rucksack. "Horace told me that a lot of our questions would be answered in these books. Let's see if he's right."

Seated cross-legged on the dusty warm ground, they flicked through the volumes.

"Hey, I might have found something here," Katie said. "A map of Abydos. That's the city we're in, or so Horace told us."

"There are many, many temples," Olly said. "Plus a river with an island in the middle of it. It must be the Nile."

"So, where's Giza?" Leo said.

Katie flicked through more pages seeking a larger map. "Here, I've found it."

Olly held his head. "It seems close on the map but judging by the scale, it's around three hundred miles away."

"What?" Leo said. "How are we going to get there?"

"I've no idea – hitch a lift from someone? Ride on a boat? The Nile goes straight there."

"That'll take forever."

"He's right," Katie said. "Is there a quicker way."

"Don't think we have many options. We need to get there," Olly said. "If Stumpy told us to go, then we go."

A thud sounded close to the children, vibrating the ground as stones fell from nearby buildings. Seconds later there was another, then another, and another.

"What's happening now?" Katie said, holding on to Olly.

Scanning the stretch of road, they spotted the origin of the noise. Through the sandy haze, a pair of figures strode towards them.

"What or who are they?" Olly said.

"Don't know," Leo said.

Katie remembered seeing something similar in one of the books. She rifled through the pages of one and said, "They look like this." The image on the open page was of the Colossi of Memnon.

"They're stone statues in the book!" Leo said. "These are alive?"

"Horace was correct – the underworld comes in many shapes," Olly said, beads of sweat trickling down his forehead in the heat.

"Why are they pursuing us?" Katie said.

"I don't know. Maybe Set knows we're here?" Olly said.

The statues in the book depicted pharaohs and they loomed twenty metres in height. Impossibly, the limestone feet of the moving effigies pounded the ground and made for the three teenagers.

"Run!" Olly said.

They sprinted down the road, the statues closing the gap with every step.

"They're gaining on us, what do we do?" Katie said.

"Don't know," Leo said.

"Head for the river, swim to that island," Olly said. "Hopefully, they won't follow us into the water."

They each entered the Nile with a splash and swam as fast as they could. Olly was the strongest swimmer and led the way, reaching what he thought was the safety of a sandy knoll protruding from the glistening waters. Glancing back at Katie and Leo, he spotted a shape in the water – making a beeline for his friends. "CROCODILE! Swim quicker."

Leo and Katie didn't need much encouragement – they struck out their legs and propelled themselves forward with their arms.

"Come on, nearly there," Olly roared, treading into the water to grab them as they reached the shore. "Got you."

Leo and Katie collapsed onto the sand, panting, too exhausted to speak. The crocodile, deciding it was outnumbered, circled the island before heading to shore. Olly's relief was to be short lived.

CHAPTER 23

The stone giants reached the water's edge but instead of retreating, their thirty-tonne mass stomped into the water, causing a strong wave that thundered towards the island. Olly grabbed Katie and Leo to stop them being buttressed by a flurry of waves heading their way.

"Can't take much more of this," Katie gasped. "I can't catch my breath."

"You still managed to speak though."

"Okay, stop it you two," Olly said as he turned to the shore, he cupped his ear, "Listen, that noise again."

Leo and Katie emptied their ears of water and were silent. Piercing screeches echoed from the ruins of the temple, temporarily halting the stone giants' progress. In the distance, fallen columns began to move.

"Can you see it? Something is trying to get out," Olly said.

A sound like an explosion turned out to be two columns being launched into the air before crashing down again. From the temple's ruins a winged creature broke free of its stone prison, soaring towards the cloudless azure sky.

"What *is* that?" Leo said as the creature flew across the sun's path.

Katie reached into her bag and dragged out a book, dripping from the swim. "The pages are falling apart."

"I've an idea what it is," Olly said.

"What?"

"It's Horus."

"You mean that's Horace?" Leo said. "How can that be?"

"It is in the books – I read it the other day. Horus is the *sky god*, takes the form of a falcon. Horace told us that Osiris needed him back when Set returned to seek revenge. Osiris has transformed our Horace into this Horus."

The flying deity's muscular body was adorned with blue and gold jewellery. A golden pleated fabric skirt wrapped around his waist. Falcon-shaped with a six-metre wingspan, he soared on the warm thermals of the desert sand.

"He's making a bee line for us," Katie said.

They waved their arms frantically, hoping Horus would see them on the sandy isle in the Nile. The stone giants, intent on catching the adventurers, strode towards the children with increased urgency. Horus swooped down from the sky, gliding inches above the water's surface. His wings stretched out horizontal, feathers brushing the waves as he approached the stone giants from their rear.

"What's he doing?" Katie said.

"I'm not sure," Olly said.

With a clean swoop, Horus darted between the giants, slicing their stone legs in two using his tough wings. The statues collapsed into the river, their stone legs protruding from the water like four towers.

Olly, Leo, and Katie jumped and punched the air in unbounded delight.

"He did it, he saved us!" Leo shouted.

The winged god flew up to them, manoeuvring its giant wings to descend beside them.

"Horace, is that you?"

The muscular beast released a jubilant screech and spoke, "It is, my friend Olly. I am here to help you rid this world of Set and prevent the evil he will bring."

"He's turned into Superman with a bird's head … and look at the jewellery he's wearing," Katie said.

Olly strolled forward and spoke. "Will you help us? We need to get to the necropolis in Giza. Can you take us there? It's too far for us to walk."

Horus lowered himself to his knees, spreading out his wings. "Of course. Climb on to my back."

"Are you joking?" Katie said. "I hate heights."

"So do I," Leo said. "But we need to reach Giza and find Stumpy if we've any chance of rescuing Claire – unless you'd rather walk or swim with the crocodiles?"

Realising they had little option, they stepped onto Horus' wings and slid up his body. Olly was at the front, a reluctant Katie behind and Leo at the rear. As they held on tightly, Horus's wings fluttered. Katie slammed her eyes shut in fear. The downdraught whirled the sand into a gritty storm.

"Hang on everyone!" Olly shouted. "We're ready for take-off."

Horus straightened his legs and propelled himself into the air.

"Whooaayeeaahh! Open your eyes Katie, you've got to see this."

Katie's face was burrowed into Olly's back and he wasn't going to change her mind. Leo braved a peek through Katie's long hair that billowed in his face. "This is amazing!"

Horus flew high into the warm sky, gliding like an eagle over the endless river Nile snaking its way through the vast desert.

"I thought we'd lost you," Olly shouted to Horus over the wind.

"The underworld brings many surprises, even to me." Horus said. "Next time it might help *you*."

Olly hugged Horus, for safety and to say thank you. Without this falcon god, their quest would have failed.

Olly had no idea what to expect when they arrived at Giza, but what he did know was that Stumpy needed them there and he'd vowed that he wouldn't let his friend down.

CHAPTER 24

In St. Prion's Abbey the sun was setting and Marshall was asleep, leaning against the central stone table, metres from his uncle's corpse. The last couple of days had taken its toll on the young Marshall. Numerous emotions taunted him, not only those of a typical teenager, but anger, hurt, loss and loneliness. His encounter with Claire in the dungeon told him he had to change – fight the demons of his mind, those that had led him down the road to evil.

A pebble struck him on his leg, disturbing his slumber "What's that? Who's there?" he said, raising himself, scanning around for anything amiss. "Oh no."

The portal had stopped working, the remaining plate holding the three gems a far cry from the operating gateway.

"Hehehehehe." The sound came from the giggles of children.

"Who's there? Show yourself," Marshall said, shuffling around, trying to pinpoint the intruders until his peripheral vision spotted movement. Through the far window, two spirits appeared holding hands. Marshall rubbed his eyes to make sure he was awake – and he was.

"Don't be scared, we mean you no harm," said the girl.

"I'm not," Marshall said, after all his father was a ghost.

"My name's Tilly. Me and my friend Arthur were playing hide and seek when we saw you lying there. We weren't sure if you were dead or alive."

"So we threw a stone at you," Arthur said, chuckling.

"Well, I'm alive … I think. Did you mess around with that?" Marshall said pointing to the portal.

"Not us, sir," Tilly said. "We did see the magic tunnel stop spinning, a shame, because it was so pretty."

Marshall seemed lost. He'd promised he'd look after the portal for Olly but instead he'd fallen asleep – and for the majority of the day. They'd be stuck in the underworld. "I have to fix this, somehow," he said. "My friends are depending on me."

"Your friends, who are they?" Tilly said.

"Two boys and a girl – well two actually but one of the girls went first. Oh, and a man named Horace. I hardly know the girls, but one helped me see what a fool I'd been – she's the one who left before the others."

"We've seen em," Arthur said. "They were in the café with us."

"Yes," Tilly said. "They mentioned someone called Claire. They were looking for her."

"Then you know I'm telling the truth … don't you?" Marshall said, aware that he was speaking to ghosts.

"Let us help you," Tilly said.

"Erm … well, I'm not too sure if you could. Unless you can reach the underworld and fight the creatures of the afterlife?"

Arthur shook his head, apparently angry. "No, we're the good spirits, no need for us to go down there."

"Exactly," Tilly said. "When we were alive we were righteous so we stay up here, along with all our friends."

"Friends?" Marshall said, puzzled.

"Yes. They don't want to be visible like me and Arthur, but they're still here."

Marshall twisted his head like a startled owl as Tilly and Arthur giggled. "Don't worry, we're the only two here. It's at night when they come alive."

Marshall pondered for a moment. If Tilly, Arthur and their friends couldn't travel to the underworld, could the underworld come to them? "Have you ever fought creatures from the underworld?"

Tilly and Arthur glanced at each other but it was Arthur who spoke. "No, but the monks did."

"Monks?"

Tilly floated towards a window over-looking the expanse of grass next to the meandering stream. "That's where a thousand monks fought the dragons from the underworld over seven hundred years ago."

"Did they win?"

"No, the dragons burnt everything down," Arthur said.

"According to legend there were five dragons that escaped from the underworld. The monks tried to protect the abbey and nearly succeeded. They made maces and swords from lead they'd mined and tried their best to defeat the dragons, but warriors they were not. Hundreds of monks were burnt alive by the fire breathing monsters with four dragons slain. Finally, one dragon faced fifty men. The monks tried to surround it, wounding the remaining beast using arrows and swords – slashing it with their weapons. The dragon was too strong and a large fire ball caused the death of the last monks. After the battle it returned to the underworld."

"Hornbeam," Marshall said, more to himself. "It couldn't be."

"Who?" Arthur said.

"Doesn't matter. Have you seen these monks? Did they rise from the dead?"

"I've seen a few pop up and say hello," Tilly said. "If anyone wants revenge over the underworld, it's them."

Marshall was confident that he'd have the help he needed to fight anything the underworld threw at him. He still didn't know how to tempt the underworld into the abbey. Marshall sat musing as Tilly and Arthur chased each other through the stone walls and across the fractured abbey floor.

"That's it!" Marshall said.

"What is?" Arthur replied.

Marshall stood, vigour returning. "I need a bike."

"The ones your friends used, they're near the gate," Tilly said.

"I have a plan and I need your help," he said, a glint in his eye.

CHAPTER 25

Marshall propped the borrowed bicycle against the rear wall of the Art of Darkness club. "Now, listen carefully," he said whispering to Tilly and Arthur. "I need you both to go through this door and open it from the inside. When Horace was here, I remember seeing a spare key hung up on the wall. Can you do that for me?"

"Yes," Tilly replied. "This is very exciting. We never leave the abbey."

Marshall watched his ghostly accomplices float through the wooden door. Within seconds the door handle moved, synchronised with the sound of a key turning in the lock.

"Well done ghouls … I mean guys. You know what I mean," Marshall said.

"I do," Tilly said.

Marshall picked up a torch from a nearby shelf. "I'll need this."

"Or you could stay close to us?" Arthur said, giggling and emitting a white glow.

"What are we doing here?"

"When I was here early this morning Tilly, Horace checked a storeroom looking for an ankh. It was in a metal box and he told us that it gave off bad vibes."

"Was it?" Arthur said.

"Well … no – because it wasn't there. All that was left was a burnt floor, similar to that in the abbey. I think the ankh was taken by creatures of the underworld, like the time Osiris came through the floor and collected the slayer's sword."

Tilly and Arthur glanced at each other, bemused but it was Tilly who spoke, "If the ankh is already gone, why are we here?"

Marshall walked into the storeroom, scanning around for something. "Horace told me about a box his father had acquired. The box needs to stay locked; he was adamant … this must be it," he said, shining the light on a metal case.

Tilly and Arthur floated over to see what the fuss was about as Marshall twisted the catches, allowing him to lift the creaking lid. "Just as I thought."

"What?" Tilly said.

Marshall reached in and grabbed a long rolled up rug. "I knew there'd be something else in here. Don't you see? Whoever needed the ankh so badly, will also need what's wrapped up in this."

Marshall placed the carpet on the floor and allowed it to roll away from him, revealing an ornate tapestry design.

"Wow, it's beautiful," Tilly said.

"That'd be worth a fortune," Arthur said.

Inside the rug was a staff, a head of a dog-like creature at one end and a double-pronged fork at the other; it was four-foot in length and made from iron. Marshall plucked it from the floor; it was warm to the touch. "We need to take this back to the abbey quickly," he said. "Arthur! Tilly! Where are you?"

Laughter drifted from the corridors – Marshall decided to investigate. In the old meeting room he shone the torch around. He'd not seen this part of the club before. "Well, I never!"

Underneath the meeting table was the cube that Katie had left there. Triggered by seeing the cube, Marshall remembered releasing George Bumble's ghost on Brunswick station. *I'm a different person to him now*, he thought, but he still had to prove himself. He picked up the cube, hoping its power would help, and walked through the far door to where he could hear the laughter. From the left-hand room, he spotted a white glow.

"Come on you two, stop fooling about," Marshall said, poking his head around the doorway. "Aargh!"

"Hehehehe." Arthur and Tilly giggled.

"Oh, very funny," Marshall said and sighed as a collection of bones danced in the room. "We've no time for fun and games. We need to return to the abbey."

"We're sorry," Tilly said.

Arthur lifted a skull off the shelf and moved its mouth, "Yes, we're sorry."

"Okay, stop it," Marshall said, grabbing the skull and placing it back on the shelf. "Hey, what's this?"

Next to the skull was an array of objects in labelled jars, including a preserved pixie, a two-headed foetus and the heart of a werewolf. One label dominated: Dragon's claw.

"It can't be … can it?" Marshall said.

"Can't be what?" Arthur said.

"Hornbeam's claw. My uncle told me this is how my great grandfather made Orion into a dragon slayer. A drop of blood from this claw was given to Orion when he was born."

"Who's Orion? Could he help?" Tilly said.

"He's Leo's father, one of the children stuck in the underworld. I don't know where he lives, or even if he's a slayer now."

"I know!" Arthur said.

"How do you know?"

"Leo told me, the same street where I lived."

With no time to lose, Marshall grabbed a bag for the jar and cube and plucked the staff from the floor where he'd left it. Back on the bike, he journeyed to St. Prion, the ghosts flying close, guiding the way.

CHAPTER 26

"Look, It's the pyramids, Leo," Olly shouted, flying high above the Nile on their magic carpet. "The necropolis is near to them."

"That's what the map showed. What do you reckon, Katie?" Leo said.

A muffled voice murmured from Olly's back, "I'm sure you're both right. Can we get down – quickly?"

Olly and Leo laughed, until Horus dipped his wings and dive bombed. "Aargh!"

"Steady Horus," Olly said, pulling the feathers on Horus's neck.

Horus swooped, soaring past the pyramids towards a group of giant ruins where he landed next to two enormous boulders.

"Thank goodness for that," Katie said, climbing off Horus' back, legs trembling. "Hold me Olly until I gain my balance? … Olly!"

Horus had flown off leaving Olly and Leo perplexed at the sight of giant rocks littering the ground. Olly didn't hear Katie's request. "Why has Horus dropped us here? We need to find Stumpy and Osiris?"

"OLLY!" Motion sickness had kicked in and Katie fell in front of the boulders as Olly and Leo ran towards her.

"Wait," Katie said, lifting her head to prevent her surroundings from spinning. "Look through the gaps in the rocks – I can see something."

Olly illuminated his torch and pointed it through into the boulders. "Steps, they're steps … I think we've found a tomb."

"Err excuse me. I think you'll find that it was *me* who found the tomb," Katie said, starting to feel better. She gripped Olly's arm and pulled herself up – brushing sand off her jeans.

"Yeah, and like finding the first gem, it was complete luck," Leo said.

"Well, fortune favours the brave," she said, scrunching her face up into a false smile.

"Shut up and give me a hand with this," Olly said, trying to move a three-tonne rock.

Katie tried to push one. "You are joking? These rocks have been here for thousands of years, and you expect us to shove them out of the way."

Olly ignored Katie – he was no fan of her negativity – and continued trying to dislodge the boulders, pushing them with his back, panting with exertion. "Whenever you're ready Leo."

Leo dashed over, a spring in his step, something he'd not felt for a long time. Placing his hands on a stone he straightened his arms and the boulder slid across the sand like a curling rock on ice. Olly and Katie watched in amazement.

"How did you do that?" Katie said.

Olly's eyes bulged with delight. "He's got his powers back! Leo! You have your powers."

"Oh my god, how? There's no dragon near us … is there?" Leo said, doing a celebratory somersault.

"COME HERE CHILDREN!" said a voice seeping through the new opening.

Olly, Katie, and Leo, stared at each other, unsure what had happened.

"Well, what do we do?" Katie said, whispering.

"We go in. This is where Stumpy told us to go," Leo said.

"Yeah, we don't have anything else to go on. Anyway, seems there's a storm brewing," Olly said, as a red sandy mist drifted over the pyramids.

Katie sighed before saying, "Why did I know you were going to say that?"

Olly led the way, stepping onto the steep carved stairway descending into darkness. "You'll need your torches here. One slip and we're done for; it's very narrow," he said.

Katie followed Olly, with Leo the last to venture down into the tomb. A room with six doorways was ahead with a steeper stairway continuing down through the masoned limestone.

"Leo?" Olly said.

"Yeah,"

"This place reminds me of somewhere,"

"We definitely not been here before, mate," Leo said scanning his torch around.

"No, I know that, but we've heard about it. Remember that story Horace told us about his dad stealing from a tomb after losing a card game? I think this is it."

Leo entered a room. "You might be right."

"And if I am, then this is Osiris' tomb."

"PLEASE HURRY," said the voice.

"Who is that?" Katie said, her arm interlocked with Olly's.

"Only one way to find out," Leo said, his head disappearing as he descended the other staircase, Olly and Katie close behind. Nearing the bottom they witnessed a white light shining upwards, sporadically dimmed by a shadow.

"Did you see that?" Katie said.

"I did," Olly said. "Keep going … trust me."

Leo reached the lower tomb first, covering his eyes from the glare of the beam of light at the centre of the room. Katie, face snuggled into Olly's chest, joined Leo.

"Who's there?" Olly said, sounding braver than he felt. "Show yourself."

CHAPTER 27

Gradually, the intense light from the lower sanctuary faded, allowing the children to see a tall, white gowned figure with flaky green skin, standing proud in front of them.

"Marshall was right," Leo said. "This is who took Stumpy's sword."

"Osiris?" Olly said.

"I am he. Bellafino summoned you to help my world."

"Bellafino?" Katie said.

"Stumpy's real name," Leo said. "Where is he? Is he okay?"

The god stepped to one side, revealing their old friend lying on a Persian rug. He was covered in blood.

"Stumpy!" Olly shouted, dashing over to him. "What's happened to you?"

The frail cave troll's eyes twitched open and a weak smile drifted across his face. "I remember that voice … but I don't have much time left."

"What do you mean?"

"Talking is painful. Leo will enlighten you."

Leo instinctively knew what Stumpy meant. He shut his eyes and concentrated hard.

"What's going on?" Katie said.

"They're using telepathy – a slayer power. Stumpy's letting Leo see what he's witnessed."

Leo's head twitched as the communications began. Crouching down against the tomb wall, holding his head, he said, "I can see fire and a red mist surrounding me, there's a burning lake. There … seems to be a …"

"A what?"

"An island is in the distance … a tall square tower in the centre." Leo stopped, shaking his head to dislodge beads of sweat that had formed on his face – not from the scorching heat outside for the tomb was cold. The warmth was from fear. "No! No!"

"What is it?" Katie said.

"A scream … I can hear a scream," Leo said, tears forming in his closed eyes. "A girl's scream."

"Claire! It must be Claire."

Olly comforted Katie as he glanced towards Osiris. "Where is this place?"

"Qarun Lake."

Leo's voice broke through the tension. "A red fog is blowing across the sands and I see a temple across from the burning lake."

"Set's temple, where Bellafino and I were attacked," Osiris said, "Set's spirit has been released and my brother has returned to enact his revenge on our world."

Leo fell back, gingerly awaking from his trance.

"Are you okay?" Katie said. "You look like you've seen a room full of monsters."

"I did …" Leo said, standing unsteadily. With dazed eyes remembering the horrors from the telepathy, he held onto the wall and faced Osiris. "What did I see through Stumpy's eyes? What attacked you?"

"They were Serpopards, one of the many types of creatures beckoned to help Set."

Katie's anxiety grew – she was concerned for her cousin. "What did they look like?"

Leo's skin became paler as he slid down to the floor. "They were massive." Leo stretched his arms to represent the size of the creatures. "Each with the body of a leopard and head of a snake. They breathed fire from their mouths – one came right at me. Poor Stumpy, he didn't stand a chance."

Osiris drifted across the tomb as if floating, white robe fluttering in the breeze that channelled through the stairwell. "We can expect more atrocities now that Set's spirit has been set free. We must be careful."

Olly and Leo stared at each other. "We know who freed Set," Olly said. "Our friend Horace who … who has now turned into Horus, opened up an old casket. He told us that a red mist escaped."

"Is that the Horus I saved many seasons ago?"

"Yes, but he didn't realise he was releasing the deity. He was ignorant of his past until he arrived here."

The god reached out to the teenagers, "Thank you for coming. Bellafino told me that you were the last dragon slayers."

"Oh, sorry," Katie said, pointing at Olly as she said, "I'm not a slayer and neither is he. Only Leo has that gift. We're here to save my cousin who was taken here by a ghost. We need to rescue her."

The god seemed confused so Olly stepped forward. "What Katie is saying is that we have another reason to be here. An evil spirit named Victor escaped – we'd previously captured him in a cubed prison. He discovered that we knew of a portal to the underworld – that's from our previous adventure with Stumpy – and he threatened to kill our friend if we didn't disclose its whereabouts," Olly took a deep breath before continuing. "When we searched for the portal, Leo became aware of Stumpy crying for help – we knew he was in trouble. When you visited our world to recover Stumpy's sword, our friend was dragged into the Egyptian underworld by Victor. We used the portal we unearthed to follow them to Duat. We want to find our friend *and* to help Stumpy."

Osiris moved his long green fingers over his chin, removing dying skin from his face in the process. "When I took Bellafino's sword, a spectre followed me, it's true. He asked me to resurrect him in human form but his soul was impure so I could not oblige him. He left with a girl, heading for Set's temple."

"Victor!" Leo said.

"And Claire," Katie said.

Olly put his arm around her. "We'll rescue her, I promise."

"My faithful slayer and I visited Set's temple to offer our peace, but it was not to be. The red mist of Set has risen over Egypt … the creatures of the underworld have turned against me. The serpopards attacked both Bellafino and myself, knocking my flail from my grasp. I brought Bellafino back to the safety of my tomb here and Bellafino begged me to connect with his slayer sword in your world. It was the only weapon that could protect us.

"Aren't your powers strong enough to kill the serpopards?" Katie said.

"Not without my flail. These objects enable my powers and without them, I weaken. When Set finds his ankh and staff, his powers will be unstoppable."

"Set has the ankh. It was removed from our world before we arrived," Leo said.

"Then we are doomed. I could open the portal with my dwindling powers and the help of Bellafino – you see I own his soul. Set has opened the doorway using only his ankh but he hasn't obtained his staff – the final piece to the jigsaw."

"You are surprised that Set can open the portal?" Olly said.

"Set is absorbing powers from his worshippers – an adored deity brings with it energy. He has used that to open his portal."

Olly's mind was doing cartwheels. He'd witnessed so much in the last few days, it was difficult for a Sherlock Holmes wannabe like himself to link the events – until… "I think I know why he connected with the ankh. His soul and the ankh were together in the same box. There was also an object which remained in the lead box and maybe that metal is preventing him from connecting with it."

Osiris nodded.

"Have you any powers left?" Leo said to the god.

Osiris held out his crook. "Yes, but I am becoming weaker. I will be reunited with my flail one day. I can sense that it is close."

"Set doesn't like you, does he?" Olly said to the god, whose skin was deteriorating, green flakes littering the limestone floor. "The books we read told us that he killed you. Is that true?"

"The god of the underworld offered balance and stability to Egypt. I decided who went to heaven and to hell. Set was jealous of my position among the people of Egypt, and yes, he defeated me … until I was resurrected. With the help of my son Horus, we fought Set for decades, until we reasoned that he'd perished but I was mistaken. He is too powerful for me at this moment, in his powers and also his mind. He controls creatures and the forces of nature. The sandstorms of Stumpy's vision were created by him and the serpopards are one of the many beasts he'll pit against you, if you try to fight him."

"What about Stumpy? We can't leave him to die," Olly said, crouching down next to his old friend.

"I cannot help him now. I have saved his soul once."

"Show Stumpy your mark," Olly said.

Leo lifted up his top revealing the scar, identical to Stumpy's wound. "But why do I have this? You're not going to die …" he said, kneeling.

Stumpy turned his head towards Leo. "My time is coming to an end," his frail voice said. "You and your friends are the only ones who can save this land now."

"No! There must be something I can do?" Leo said. "My dad saved me with healing powers in the tunnel. I can do that to you!"

"You are kind, but my wounds are too deep."

Stumpy's life was fading away. Olly interrupted, "How can we save this world? There's only Leo who seems to have his powers back. Katie and I are … well, we're just human."

"Everything you need is here," he said, breathing deeply before closing his eyelids. After exhaling, an arm fell loosely to the floor, brushing Olly's foot.

"No, no. Stumpy!" Olly said, moving his face near the cave troll, hoping to detect Stumpy's breathing, but there was nothing. He glanced at Leo with mournful eyes.

"Stumpy!" Leo said. "No!"

Stumpy's hairy body was silent on the rug. Tears streaming down his face, Leo placed his hands on Stumpy's chest, trying to encourage his father's slayer magic to appear – but to no avail, nothing happened.

"Why doesn't it work," Leo screamed, the sound echoing through the chambers. "I wish my dad was here. He'd have saved him."

"You tried your best." Katie said, trying to calm the young slayer but he was inconsolable. He placed his head on Stumpy's body, trying to connect with him one last time until he was distracted by the long green fingers that draped over his shoulder.

"Stand back my child," the god said.

Leo rose to his feet, wiped away his tears and joined Olly and Katie at the wall.

"What's he doing?" Katie said.

"Is he going to try and save him?" Olly said.

Osiris bowed his head and prayed, the children looking on with tears in their eyes.

"I don't believe this," Leo said. "Everything he did for my dad in the tunnel and I couldn't save him."

Osiris turned his head. "You did save him, young slayer," he said. "You saved him from the perils of war. He's going to a good place now. I'll make sure of that."

With those words, an apparition of Stumpy floated from Osiris' body.

"Stumpy's soul," Leo said as the pale phantom rose.

"Of course! Stumpy told us his soul belonged to Osiris. He's sent him to heaven," Olly said, holding Katie tight, suddenly unable to speak.

Leo watched the last remnants of Stumpy's soul disappear into the limestone ceiling. "No more fighting for you little man, you've done your bit."

CHAPTER 28

A stillness blanketed the area where Stumpy's body lie in peace. One of the reasons they came to Duat had come to a tragic end. Olly and Leo leaned against a limestone wall, lost without the cave troll's guidance.

Katie bear-hugged Leo and Olly. "We owe it to Stumpy to help Osiris."

"How?" Leo said, wiping his face. "Like Olly told Stumpy, only I have powers. I can't defeat Set on my own."

"Stumpy told us that everything we need is here … so let's start looking. Any ideas Osiris?"

"Without my flail and a slayers soul inside me, my powers are weak. I can help you find new powers."

They were confused as the god glided over to Stumpy's lifeless body and knelt down. His green hands unclasped Stumpy's wrinkly hand and removed his walking stick. "This is for you."

Katie wasn't sure what to make of his gesture. "A walking stick? What do I want with a bashed up walking stick? I'm not old and I'm good at walking."

"Unless you've been drinking champagne," said Olly, receiving a rib dig in return from Katie.

"Use this wisely," Osiris said as a shard of light left the god's green hand to be absorbed by the stick.

Hesitantly, she took the pole from the god and lifted it, finally understanding. "A wand, it's a wand, isn't it? But I don't know any magic."

"Magic is in us all," Osiris said. "We simply have to find the spells."

Olly was two steps ahead of Katie and was scrambling through his bag. "Here, now you have the spells." He passed Katie the book of Egyptian spells they'd found in the club. "I couldn't use it back home, but something tells me they'll work for you here."

Katie flicked through the Nile-soaked book. "It's damaged, but I can read some phrases."

"You're a witch," Leo said.

"Excuse me, I'm not a witch … I'm a sorceress," she said wafting her new wand.

"Careful!" Olly shouted, avoiding the sparks shooting out from the stick's end.

"I'm going to have so much fun with this. You two better not annoy me anymore," she said.

Osiris walked into a side room and spoke from within, his voice reverberating, "This is yours, Leo." The god returned, holding the same sword Leo had slayed Hornbeam the dragon with the previous year.

"How have I got slayer powers again? I need to be close to a dragon?" Leo said.

Osiris strode towards them, lifting the sword high above his crowned head. "You've been closer than you realised." Like an executioner, his arms dropped, to land a decisive blow on Stumpy.

The three seekers yelled in unison, before realising what the god had done. Osiris had chopped off the bottom part of Stumpy's wooden leg, revealing something odd.

"That's not wood," Olly said. "It's bone. Stumpy painted it to look like wood?"

"That's gross," Katie said. "Imagine having someone else's bone attached to you."

"It isn't someone's bone," Osiris said.

"What is it then?" Leo said.

"A part of Hornbeam the dragon."

Olly's eyes widened. "It's his horn … isn't it?"

Osiris nodded. "Bellafino took the dragon's horn and carved his leg. After all, the dragon took his."

"That's why I have powers, because I'm near Stumpy."

Osiris reached down and plucked up the sliced tip of bone. "Keep this close and you will always be a slayer."

Leo picked up the slayer's sword, swinging it around in delight – just missing Olly.

"Watch it mate, you nearly gave me a haircut," Olly said, waiting expectantly for a power of his own.

Osiris placed his green hands upon Olly's shoulders. *This was it*. Olly had always wanted a special power of his own. *Maybe invisibility or the ability to fly?*

"Stumpy told me great things about you: your intelligence, loyalty, courage, calmness under pressure and dexterity. You already have gifts that many do not. You have everything you need."

Disappointed, Olly wasn't sure whether to laugh or cry as Osiris departed. "What the heck? Is he joking? I need something to help you guys, even that telepathy stuff would do."

Katie hugged him. "Maybe Osiris is right. We could have all the strength and magic in the world but without you, we're nothing. You keep us calm, make the decisions, solve the puzzles …"

"She's right, I wouldn't have found my dad if it weren't for you, and I'm the slayer."

Olly tried to put on a brave face. "I'm jealous, Leo. I wanted to do magic, have a superpower and fight creatures with my bare hands."

"You're perfect the way you are," Katie said, pecking him on the cheek.

"Thanks, it means a lot," Olly said, distracted by a noise above. "Who's there?" Heavy footsteps bounded around the tomb, heading down the steep steps.

"It is me, Horus." said the winged god as he entered the chamber.

Osiris heard the fellow god enter. "You have returned."

Horus, seeing the deity who'd saved his life as a child, knelt down in adulation. "Osiris, my God, how can I ever thank you?"

"You must do what is right for this world. I gave you my son's name as a child, now I have given you his powers as a man. Help these children of Earth."

"I will rid this land of Set once and for all. You, my god will have your kingdom returned."

Osiris nodded.

"I have news of Set. I flew over his temple and with my eagle-like hearing, overheard him talk to his henchmen."

"What did he say?"

"Set has connected with his staff in the real world. He plans to open another portal and collect it."

"You must stop this from happening!" Osiris said, his voice booming. "With his staff, this world will be destroyed. War and chaos will prevail."

"This is our chance!" Olly said.

"What, our chance to die?" Leo said.

"No … our chance to return to our world. We need to enter Set's portal."

"You're right," Katie said. "See, we told you that you didn't need special powers."

"What about Claire?" Leo said. "We can't leave her."

"We'll rescue her, then escape together," Olly said.

Up above they heard gales blowing across the desert, a giant sandstorm engulfing the necropolis.

"Act now," Osiris said. "Set is becoming stronger."

"Aren't you helping too?" said Leo.

"I must stay safe; I cannot risk perishing. If I die … so does Egypt. The mighty Horus will help you."

Olly thought for a few moments. *How could they save Claire and find the portal in the quickest time?* "Horus, we need you to fly us to the tower on Qarun Lake."

"I will."

"And then what?" Katie said.

"It's a work in progress," Olly said. "First we rescue Claire, then we head to the temple."

"Be careful," Osiris said. "The land is populated by Set's creatures. They will inflict grave suffering on those who try to stop him."

"We'll be careful. Anyway, I've a dragon slayer and a sorceress with me … what could possibly go wrong?"

CHAPTER 29

Horus was first to climb up the steep stairway towards the tempest outside. With Stumpy's death fresh in their minds, the seekers interrupted their grief with laughter as the winged god struggled to squeeze through the chiselled limestone.

"Humour is a good medicine for sadness," Horus shouted, "Never feel guilty about being happy … but please help me."

Olly needed to renew their focus – rescuing Claire and finding a way home. They followed the god up, freeing Horus' wings and shoving him from behind. At the top, Horus stood, supported by the boulders, wings flapping frantically in the storm.

Olly following closely, poked his head out into the wind, shielding his face from the stinging sand. Horus awaited but was thwarted by another winged creature brushing Olly's head before attacking Horus. Olly watched the stronger beast with the body of a lion and head of a bird wrestle Horus out of the sky. Sand danced like a tornado around the beasts in the intensive winds, tossing the creatures around like whirling dervishes. Olly was helpless, watching glimpses of the god's wings consumed by the cyclonic winds sucking the fighting duo into the tempest.

"Horus!" Olly shouted but the only response that could be heard were their screams. "Get back down!" he shouted to Leo and Katie below. "Horus has been attacked."

Osiris met them at the bottom of the staircase. "What happened? Where is Horus?"

Taking a few recovering breaths, Olly said, "Something attacked him, a giant bird-like creature, bigger than Horus. It swooped in and before I knew it, they were gone."

"That can't be!"

"What? What was it?" Katie said.

"Shirdal, the protector," Osiris said. "A griffin in your world."

"A griffin?" Leo said. "Aren't they make believe?"

Olly stared at him with raised eyebrows. "Tell me you're joking. After everything you've seen in the last year, you're questioning whether a griffin is real or not?"

"You might have a point."

Osiris interjected, "Shirdal had been the protector of treasures in the underworld but had succumbed to a pack of hell goblins. Set has resurrected him."

Katie couldn't believe it. "What do we do about saving Claire? She'll be terrified. I hate to think of the state she'll be in."

Olly glanced towards Stumpy's body. "I know what we need to do."

Katie and Leo stared at each other.

"How is Stumpy going to save us?" Katie said.

"Not Stumpy but what he's lying on," Olly said, pointing to the patterned crimson Persian rug. "Use your powers to make it fly!"

Katie smiled, realising this was the moment to try out her wizardry. Grabbing the spell book from her backpack, she flicked through it and said, "Yeah, I've found one, a flying spell."

"Hang on a second, let's do this first." Olly knelt down next to Stumpy, carefully rolling the cave troll's body off the rug over toward the side wall. "There you are my old friend. When this is all over, Osiris will give you the burial you deserve."

"I will," Osiris said, bowing.

Olly nodded at Katie, suggesting she proceed. She studied a page in the book, pointed her wand and chanted, "Yatir! Yatir! Yatir!" Sparks flew from the rod and engulfed the rug as everyone watched.

"Erm," Leo said, now doubting Katie's powers.

"There!" Olly said. "Did you see that?"

"No."

"A corner twitched. There's another and another. And the other."

The Seekers of Duat

The carpet lifted from the stone floor as Katie stared in wonder.

"You did it!" Olly said. "I knew you could."

"Thanks," she said, still in shock.

Leo walked over and seated himself on the mat. "So, it works. Now, how do you steer one of these?"

"No idea," Olly said. "You're the strongest, you tilt it?"

"How are we even going to get out of here? That griffin creature might be waiting for us at the entrance."

"I'll go first Katie, and beat it up," Leo said, pumping his fists.

Olly stood, shook his head and said, "If Horus vanished up there, so could you. That griffin is powerful and it can fly." Olly paused for a moment. "Osiris, in the real world your tomb was waterlogged. Do you know where the drainage pipes are?"

Katie peered at him. "What are you on about?"

"Don't you remember, Leo? The story Horace told us about his father stealing from this very tomb. It was full of water until Archie moved a keystone, causing the water to spurt out through different outlets into the desert."

"Now you mention it, it rings a bell," Leo said.

"Well, if we can find out how the water escaped, that's how we'll escape too."

Osiris followed Olly to another room and pointed to a waste pipe in the corner. "This will take you to the desert. I wish you success in your journey."

"Thank you for your help, we'll do our best." Olly said, waving over his fellow adventurers.

Leo jumped off the rug, rolled it up and tucked it under his arm. Katie grabbed her rucksack, keeping tight hold of her wand. One at a time they squeezed into the hole, bidding farewell to Osiris.

"This is a bit tight," Katie said, squeezing in last. "It doesn't get any smaller, does it?"

Olly was at the front with a torch. "No, doesn't seem to."

"Couldn't you just make yourself smaller?" Leo said, chuckling.

"I'll make you smaller than an ant if you don't shut up," Katie said.

"We'll need your magic for something else, Katie … this way's blocked."

"There's no way I can get to the spell book in here. I'm like a sardine in a tin."

"Hang on, I hear something on the other side," Olly said, moving closer. "There's a howling noise, hope it's not the griffin."

"Only one way to find out," Leo said, thrusting his sword past Olly's head, breaking through the blockage.

"Are you crazy?"

"You think too much," Leo said, "That noise was simply the wind."

They each popped out into the desert, scanning around like meerkats defending their burrow. The sandstorm showed no signs of relenting.

"Unravel the rug, Leo," Olly said, protecting his face, "Let's get out of here."

CHAPTER 30

Unfurling the magic carpet in the strong winds turned out to be easy. Leo, as designated driver, hopped to the front while a fretful Katie sandwiched herself between the boys. Although scared of another flight, Katie felt safe with Olly's arms and legs cocooning her.

"Now what?" Leo yelled through the sound of sand blasting against the Egyptian tombs.

"No idea," Olly said. "Try moving it about."

Leo grabbed the front tassels and leant forward.

"We're moving!" Katie said. Her thrill that the spell worked overrode the fact that she was rising in the air. "It's working!"

Gradually, Leo steered across the sands, his strength needed to adjust the speed and direction of the carpet. "Think I've got it. Which way are we heading?"

Olly leaned over while still holding onto Katie's waist. "Up," he said. "Out of this storm."

Leo pulled his arms back to make the carpet ascend, forcing Katie to cling to him like a baby monkey does to its mother. Within seconds they were above the storm, gliding in tranquil azure skies. Below them twisters caused chaos in the Egyptian underworld.

Olly rested his chin on Katie's shoulder and whispered in her ear, "We're through the worst."

Katie braved a sneaky peek downwards, her long hair fluttering in the breeze. "Wow, can't believe we're doing this. We're ... so high up."

"Best not to look down. Look into the distance."

Katie glanced left. Through the heat shimmer she noticed familiar objects. "Are they ..."

Olly interrupted, "Yes, they're the pyramids of Giza. Look Leo, to your left."

The three pyramids stood resolute as they had for thousands of years, unconcerned by the trouble surrounding them.

"They're class!" Leo shouted. "Want to go nearer?"

"We're not sight-seeing," Olly said and turned to peer in the opposite direction until something else caught his eye. He pointed to the right and said, "There, look! Can you see black smoke in the distance? I think it's coming from the lake of fire – that's where Claire's being held. Head towards that."

"I hope she's alright," Katie said.

"We need to be prepared for everything. If you can, check your spell book for any help it can give."

"I'll try." Katie rolled her eyes. It was hard enough for her to stay on the carpet without reading from a book. She let go of Leo's waist and reached for her rucksack. Much to her surprise, she stayed upright, thanks to Olly tightening his grip from behind – which she didn't mind at all.

While Katie rummaged in her bag, Olly shouted to Leo, "How are you doing mate? You still feeling strong?"

"I feel great. Let's find Claire and get the heck out of here," Leo said gripping to the carpet like a clam on a rock.

"I know what you mean. Can't believe we're in this situation again, especially after last year. We'll be fine though. Fingers crossed we find the portal and get home."

"Wish my dad was here to help. He'd soon sort Set out."

"True, but he's not. You're the only slayer here now and you'll do Orion proud."

Olly browsed over Katie's shoulder, wanting to help with her magic, but something in the distant skies caught his eye. "Don't want to alarm either of you, but we're not alone."

Katie scanned the sky, "What is that?"

"It's the creature that attacked Horus – Shirdal!"

Skimming over the white clouds gaining on the adventurers, was the griffin. The half-eagle, half-lion beast soared through the sky, its golden plumage from its colossal wingspan shimmering in the sunlight.

"What do we do?" Leo shouted.

"Keep heading towards the smoke … leave this to us," Olly said.

Olly knew they were in trouble but he had to be strong. He stared into Katie's eyes and said, "Don't be scared but we need your help. We need your magic."

Katie's heartbeat intensified. Nervous about flying, she was unsure whether she could use her magic on the approaching mythical creature. "Okay, I'm fine."

"What spells can you use?"

Katie grabbed her wand and turned to face the incoming griffin. With a wave of her wand, she yelled, "Sedjetraca!" Three balls of fire flew from its tip.

"Point it at the griffin!" Olly screamed, seeing the projectiles skew away from the creature.

Grasping the wand with both hands as her boyfriend held her tight, she regained control. "Have some of this … Sedjetraca!"

"Great shot!" Olly said.

Loud screeches filled the air as the shots found their mark, forcing the griffin to descend.

"Did you kill it?" Leo asked.

Not sure but it's vanished," she said, catching her breath.

"Oh no!" Olly said, leaning over the edge of the carpet. "A shadow in the cloud, it's coming our way. Steady with the wand again."

Circling in the air, the seekers braced themselves for the attack. The silhouette darkened as it ascended, breaking through the water vapour.

Katie was preparing her spell when Olly shouted, "No! Stop! It's Horus."

The eagle-headed god soared in front of them, muscular torso bloodied with claw marks. "Shirdal is close by but I will protect you. Keep going."

"We thought you'd …"

"Died Olly? Death is not an option for me at the moment, my friend."

"How can we help?" Leo said.

"Keep using your magic, Sorceress of Egypt," he said, pointing at Katie. "Shirdal's weakness is fire. Once you arrive at Qarun Lake, the fires will shield you from him."

"Sorceress of Egypt! I could get used to that," Katie said as the boys shook their heads in embarrassment.

"Stick with Katie," Olly said.

"What's wrong?" Leo said, noticing Horus staring below them.

"Hold on!" Horus shouted as the griffin appeared from the clouds, flying towards the carpet. Before Leo had time to adjust his course, Shirdal smashed into them, ripping the carpet with its talons. Screams of panic filled the skies as Horus dived onto the griffin, pulling it away.

"Leo, we're falling! Do something!" Olly screamed.

"I'm trying … but … there's a hole in it," the young slayer said trying to halt their descent with all his strength.

"Use your wand, Katie."

The Sorceress of Egypt found her confidence. With one hand gripping Olly, she waved the wand at the duelling beasts. "Sedjetraca!" Balls of fire made a bee line towards the intertwined Horus and Shirdal, hurtling through the air like meteors. Horus' beak locked on to a leg of the griffin, who retaliated by stabbing its talons into Horus' stomach. Screams signified the agonising pain, until a burst of light filled the sky as the fireballs hit their target.

"What happened?" Leo said, trying to focus on keeping them airborne.

"I hit them," Katie said.

"Both of them?" Olly said.

"Not sure, they were spinning together in the sky."

The carpet entered the clouds as it lost altitude. "We can't see anything now. I hope Horus is okay," Olly said.

Katie welled up as she said, "What if I've killed him?"

Olly snuggled Katie tight. "Don't be silly, you had no choice and anyway, I told you to do it."

233

"Hey guys, these clouds are getting darker," Leo said.

"I can smell burning," Katie said.

The magic carpet fell below the clouds to be met by the heat of a furnace.

"It's the lake of fire," Olly said. "Claire must be close."

Underneath them, the inferno was devouring every molecule of oxygen it could consume. The flames rose as Leo struggled to control the damaged rug.

"Try to land over there," Olly said, pointing.

In the distance was a solitary island in the flaming lake containing a tower looming ten stories high. Approaching the tower and the fire below, Katie noticed something. Her voice took on an edge of panic as she said, "Err … Leo, you might want to speed up."

"I'm going as fast as I can."

"What's wrong?" Olly said.

"The corner of carpet … it's on fire!"

The tassels around the edge were burning and flames were spreading across the carpet.

"Extinguish it!" Leo shouted.

"I can't, it's too fierce."

"Use magic!" Olly said but it was too late. They were riding a lacerated magic carpet which was ablaze, disintegrating before their eyes.

"We're nearly there," Leo said. "We'll have to jump."

"Jump?" Katie said.

"Yes," Olly said as the island approached, flames intensifying. Olly stood, pulling Katie up with him. "When I go, you go."

Leo jumped to his feet as the island approached. "Are we ready? Right, let's do this."

Holding hands, they leapt from the burning carpet onto a sandy bank on the island. They tumbled and somersaulted as the remaining burning fibres of the carpet floated away in the air thermals.

Olly, Katie and Leo stared at the reddened sky as they gathered their breath.

"That was close," Leo said. "We were nearly burnt alive."

"Too close," Olly said, checking himself over for injuries. "We've been lucky."

Katie sat up and felt her hair. "Lucky? My hair is ruined ... look at it. It looks like it's been blow-dried by a jumbo jet engine!"

Olly and Leo glanced at each other, neither able to keep a straight face.

"Stop it, I'm serious," she said as the boys laughed.

"Sorry," said Olly. "But we can either laugh or cry at our predicament. We're on an island surrounded by fire, searching for our kidnapped friend, with no idea if we can make it home or not, and you're moaning about your hair!"

"You have a point Olly," she said, joining in the laughter.

CHAPTER 31

The three seekers composed themselves after their descent. Even without the god Horus by their side, they knew their focus had to be on the next challenge – saving Claire. They peered at the nearby tower dominating the small island. They were hoping that Claire was both in there and alive.

"Did you hear that?" Leo said. "It's the scream I heard through Stumpy's vision."

Katie's eyes widened. "I heard it … it's Claire – she's still alive!" She scrambled to her feet as Olly reached over and grabbed her ankle, causing her to fall down in the dry sand. "What are you doing? We need to save her."

As flames danced around them, Olly kept his calm, giving a reassuring look at Katie. "We *will* save her but something's not right."

"What do you mean? It was her, I'd know her voice anywhere. She's in trouble."

"Exactly, that's my point. Someone or something else is in there with her; we need to be careful."

"So, what do you suggest?"

Olly thought for a moment. He knew that *he* couldn't help on his own, he had no powers. He couldn't stomach losing Katie as well as her cousin, even though she knew magic spells. That left one option. "Leo... this is your moment. You and your slayer powers will rescue Claire."

"They will?"

"Alone. Me and Katie need to stay here for when Horus appears, or if Shirdal turns up. We're stronger if we're together. Are you up for it?"

Leo stood as adrenalin took over. "Yeah, I think so, just need to keep reminding myself I've these powers." He pulled the sword from his belt and swung it around his head.

"Good luck," said Olly, embracing his friend.

"Bring her back," said Katie.

"I will." Leo turned and made for the centre of the island to the tower stretching high into the sky, leaving Olly and Katie hand in hand.

Onwards, Leo stomped, feeling stronger with each step. He swung his sword while perfecting his technique, like his father had shown him in the tunnel the previous year. Before he knew it, he'd arrived at his destination, confronted at the entrance of the crumbling tower by a pair of hardwood doors.

From above, Leo heard a tortured scream. He glanced upwards. Unglazed windows decorated the tall structure. Leo knew he couldn't hang around so took a deep breath. He twisted the iron loop handle, easing the squeaking door open. Scarab beetles and a lizard scurried out, searching for warmth and giving Leo a start. The only route was up a spiral stone staircase. With his sword ready for action, he ascended.

"Help!"

Quickening his step, Leo scaled the heights passing empty alcoves until he reached the top where a padlocked door greeted him. Pressing his ear against the grubby surface he heard sobbing. After checking the staircase for a pursuant, he broke into the room. Holding the padlock in his hand he clenched his fist, crushing the mechanism with his slayer strength. With a shoulder barge the door left its hinges and collapsed into the room.

It was mostly dark with shards of sunlight trickling through the windows. In the far corner a solitary figure was seated on the stone floor, fingers interlocking to hug their legs in a tight embrace. Long blonde hair scattered the light as the person rocked back and forth. The sound of crying echoed around the room.

"Claire! … it's me, Leo … I've come to rescue you," he said, closing in on the forlorn figure. "You're safe now."

The crying morphed into a cackling laugh, forcing Leo to step back. He glanced around, expecting an assailant. "Are you okay?"

"I'm fine." A croaky voice said. "But *you* won't be!"

Leo recalled in shock as a wrinkly old woman wearing a wig stared at him, eyes whiter than snow. "Where's Claire? What have you done with her?"

"Do you think our master would let you stroll in here and steal his prized possession?" the old hag said. "She is imprisoned in Set's temple. You and your friends ... will soon perish."

Leo ran to the window, checking on his friends – they were where he'd left them, to his relief. He spotted something rising and falling as it approached in the distant flames.

"You can see Bihellasaur," the witch cackled.

"What's that?" Leo said.

"The two-headed beast from the depths of the underworld. It's here for you. Killing a dragon slayer will give it new life."

Leo stuck his head out through the opening and shouted, "Olly! . . Katie! ... Get away from the edge! It's a trap!"

"Your mistake was coming to our world," said the witch revealing her string-like, grey hair.

Leo lifted his sword in defiance, swinging it at the witch. "Slayers don't make mistakes."

"You foolish boy." As she waved her wand and shouted the word. "Jumudaca!" she cast a spell to release a stream charge that left Leo's body paralysed. His sword fell to the floor, leaving him helpless.

"What did he say?" Katie said, flicking through more of her spell book. "I couldn't hear for the gale."

Olly sensed danger. "I'm not sure but it sounded important. Can you hear that?"

Katie closed her eyes and concentrated. "Yes, a crashing noise. Let's move higher, towards the tower. We'll have a better view."

They scampered up the hill and turned to face the lake.

"What's that?" Katie said.

"What?"

"Something rose through the flames ... there it is again."

Olly stared, open-mouthed as he watched both of Bihellasaur's heads rise above the fire, followed by its muscular body. Dark red scales adorned with black markings lined its back. At the top of its long necks were two heads, each with sharp horns tapering down to their napes.

"Olly ... Olly!" Katie said nudging him. "A dragon! What do we do?"

"Err ... I don't know. We need Leo, he's the dragon slayer."

Katie pointed towards the tower. "He's busy at the moment. Any other ideas?"

"Use your wand. Shoot fire balls at it."

Katie waved her wand and shouted the spell, "Sedjetraca!" Fireballs rocketed from the wand, across the sands and towards the gigantic beast. Olly and Katie's hopes of victory evaporated as fireballs crashed ineffectively into the dragon.

"What on earth are we thinking," Olly said. "It's over a lake of fire. It likes fire! Pick something else from the book?"

With the dragon approaching fast, Katie remembered another spell. She flicked her wand towards the lake of fire. "He's a raca!" she shouted – nothing happened.

"He's a raca?" Olly said. "Are you sure you're saying that right?"

"Well … I don't know," Katie snapped. "I'm not a proper sorceress. How else should I pronounce it?"

"Say it as one word."

Katie held the wand out and shouted the spell with added fervour, "Hesaraca!" Katie's hand shook as the wand reacted to the spell. "You need to help me?" Olly held her tightly.

A white mist shot from the stick, transforming part of the lake into an ice rink. In the distance, the two heads of the dragon roared – its body trapped under the frozen lake.

"You did it! You actually did it," Olly said, giving Katie a peck which transformed into a full-on smooch.

"Not without your help," Katie said. With their lips locking again they sensed an unwanted sound. They turned to witness the dragon pummelling the ice with one of its heads, the other melting the ice with its fiery breath.

"We're in trouble," Olly said. "It'll be free soon."

"Where's Leo?" Katie said. "We need him to help. He should be back by now."

"Leo! Leo!" they shouted towards the top window but there was no reply.

"Mwhahahaha, your friends are calling you," said the witch. "All you can do is watch them die … one by one."

Leo closed his eyes as Bihellasaur smashed through the ice. Leo wanted to help his friends but all that moved in his body were tears trickling down his motionless face, dripping onto the stone floor.

CHAPTER 32

With a resounding crack, Bihellasaur, the red two-headed dragon, broke clear of its ice prison and headed towards the island.

"I don't know how we're going to stop it," Olly said to Katie. "Leo's the dragon slayer and he's up there. Can you find any more spells? Any without fire and ice?"

Katie rolled her eyes. "I am trying my best you know. I've no idea what's going to come out of this stick."

"Sorry, I didn't mean it like that. Let's go through the book together, it'll be quicker that way."

"There's no point," she said, plonking herself onto the sand. "The water's damaged it, most of the book's unreadable."

Olly thumped the stone wall of the tower in anger. Olly was known for his problem solving but – this time – the skill evaded him. He sat beside Katie as the giant dragon came closer. "We have to get through this. A lot of people are counting on us."

"I don't know how?" Katie said, tossing a stone into the air.

Olly followed the stones trajectory as it traced a perfect parabola until he was distracted by something in the distance. "It can't be?"

"What?"

"Look! It's Horus." Olly and Katie jumped to their feet, waving their arms like maniacs vying for his attention.

"He's alive! I didn't kill him, thank goodness," Katie said.

The bird god spotted his friends and landed next to them on the sand. His once perfect gold and blue attire was ripped and splattered with blood.

"Where's the griffin?" Olly asked.

"Shirdal gave up the fight and fled towards Set's temple." Horus said. "We need to go there. Time is running out."

"We can't. We have to rescue Claire, and Leo's in there as well," Katie said glancing up at the tower.

"And not forgetting that thing!" Olly said, signalling at the approaching monster. "Any suggestions?"

The two-headed beast had reached the island. It thudded its clawed feet deep into the sand, simultaneously releasing an earth-shattering roar.

"Olly, go inside the tower and wait, you'll be safe there," Horus said, "Katie, divert its attention with magic – any magic. I'll fight it."

"I can't leave Katie," Olly said. "And you want me to go in there … where Leo's disappeared?"

Before Horus replied, Katie spoke, "Do what he says. Remember what you told me, people are counting on us. Anyway, where would you prefer to be? Out here with a dragon or in that tower."

"I don't want to lose you."

"You won't," she said gazing deep into his eyes. "I'm the one with the magic Olly. There's nothing you can do here and you might find Leo in there."

"It's a dragon, Katie!"

"I promise I'll keep out of its way and anyhow … Horus will be doing the fighting."

Reluctantly, Olly agreed and pecked Katie on the cheek before entering the tower's doors. Katie kept to her word and hid behind one of the corners of the tower.

"Sorceress of Egypt," Horus said. "Are you ready?"

Katie stuck her head out and gave a thumbs up as Horus nodded back in acknowledgement and leapt from the sand, soaring high above the dragon.

As Horus signalled to her, Katie enacted the spell, "Hesaraca!" The ice-spell was ejected from Stumpy's walking stick like horizontal forked lightning, zigzagging its way towards the beast. The dragon, cognisant of Katie's powers, dodged the onslaught, retaliating with a tirade of fire aimed at the tower's base. Katie dashed back behind the structure and watched the firebombs pass. Taking advantage of the distraction, Horus spread his wings and rocketed towards the dragon, aiming his talons for one of its necks.

Katie caught her breath from her vantage point and realised something – the fire balls had stopped. A thunderous roar prompted her to poke her head around the corner. She watched in awe: Horus had decapitated one of Bihellasaur's heads.

"Woohoo!" Katie shouted into the sky. "You did it!"

Horus knew the fight was unfinished. In pain, the injured dragon span in circles on the sand, spitting fireballs sporadically.

"Move!" Horus shouted to the young sorceress. The dragon was closing in on the tower. Horus dived again, but this time Bihellasaur spotted him. The disorientated beast raised a claw which sliced through Horus' chest, like a warm knife through butter. The falcon god dropped like a rock until he hit the sand with a thud and a blood curdling scream.

Katie was now terrified – her and a terrifying dragon were the only combatants left. She had to put distance between herself and the dragon, and quickly. She ran to the far shore of the island until she was at the edge of the fiery lake. She glanced back at the spinning dragon, fire belching from its remaining mouth. If she used magic she might damage the tower – and that was where her friends were hiding. Then the unbelievable happened.

The dragon's jagged tail whipped rapidly, striking the centre of the tower.

"NO!" Katie screamed.

The top of the tower started to shake. Leo was still under the witch's influence so was unable to move. His eyes watched as the bricks fell around him, dislodging the mortar holding others. He glanced at the witch, willing her to set him free,

"This is where I leave you to die."

Thanks, thought Leo but, with the tower crumbling, Leo suspected that his time was coming to an end. He shut his eyes intending to pray but opened them again when he heard the witch scream. A wooden roof joist crashed onto the old hag and continued through the floor.

Her bony fingers tried to grip the floorboard but the gesture was futile. The next wave of destruction caused her to tumble with the rubble, as did Leo's sword. The slayer's sword ricocheted off the debris as it followed the witch to the floor below. With a thud the witch hit the ground, her neck broken. To finish her demise, the sword, gliding like a javelin, finished its journey embedded in her chest. The witch was no more and Leo's spell was broken.

He fell to the ground as the tower fell apart around him but his slayer powers saved him. Like a fly avoiding being swatted, Leo dodged boulders crashing around him. He kicked away debris, somersaulted through the air and landed next to the witch. He grabbed his sword, yanking it from her chest. The hag's body shrivelled into a ball of dead skin.

Stepping out onto the sand, Leo spotted the injured Bihellasaur. Blood oozed from its wound, but it was still able to attack. Leo dodged the fiery cascade escaping from the dragon's remaining head and countered using the skills his dad had taught him. He somersaulted, landing on the dragon's back, sliced into the beast's armour until he was alerted by a flash of white light flying past him.

"Katie?" Leo shouted with relief as the creature's head was encased in ice.

"Thought you might need a hand," she said. "Now finish it off!"

Leo thrust his sword firmly into the dragon's heart through its exposed chest. It squeezed out its final roar before falling in defeat. Bihellasaur was no more.

The two seekers ran towards each other and locked in a tight embrace. "Why are you crying? Where's Olly?" Leo said.

"He was in there, hiding," she said, her shaking hand pointing to the remnants of the tower.

"What about Horus?" Leo said.

"He came to help but the dragon saw him off too. Where's Claire? Why isn't she here… where is she?"

"She wasn't there, they set a trap to kill us all. Claire's being held in Set's temple."

"She's still alive? Please tell me she's still alive."

"Yes, that's what I think." Leo replied. "Let's hope the same can be said for Olly. Come on, let's find him."

With all his slayer's strength, Leo removed boulders from the rubble as Katie repeatedly shouted Olly's name.

"Try under there."

Leo lifted the heavy doors. "Got him!"

Olly was lying flat on the floor, not moving.

"Is he alright? Oh my god, oh my god. I don't think he's breathing."

They dragged him onto the sand where Katie leant forward and gave him mouth to mouth resuscitation. She pumped his chest again and again, but to no avail.

"He can't die! We need him. I need him."

"He's not going to die."

"He's not bloody breathing, Leo. We've lost him."

"Let me try," Leo said, rubbing his hands.

"What are you doing?"

"My father used this to save me. Now it's my chance to save someone."

Leo's palms glowed orange as he placed them on his friend's head and waited. With Katie holding Olly's hand and praying, they searched for signs of life in their friend.

"He's moving!" Katie said, feeling his fingers twitch just as Leo's hopes were fading.

Olly's eyelids fluttered open as a stream of sunlight, broken by two shadowy figures, caused him to scrunch up his eyes. "Oww, my head. Where am I?"

As Olly rose to sit, Katie hugged him. "You're with your friends, the best place you can possibly be."

As Olly recovered, Katie explained what had happened and Leo told them about his encounter with the witch.

"So, where's Horus?" Olly said. "What's happened to him?"

Leo and Katie walked arm in arm with Olly to the far shore where Horus had fallen from the sky. The falcon god was no longer lying there in his blue and golden regalia. Instead, the deceased body of Horace replaced him, battered by the claw that had sliced his chest in two.

"No!" Olly said. "He can't be dead. It's not fair."

"He was a great bloke. I'm going to miss him," Leo said.

"He was a brave man," Katie said. "Without him, we wouldn't be here."

"It wasn't his battle to fight. He should have been at home, enjoying his life," Olly said. "Can't you bring him back Leo?"

Leo shook his head, tears dripping from his cheek onto the sand, "No mate, his injuries are too severe. I don't have those powers."

The Seekers of Duat

They buried Horace in the sand and used a stone from the fallen tower as a grave marker. Heads bowed, they stood over him in silence.

CHAPTER 33

Losing their friend Horace was a blow. Everything they did from now on was for him. He'd continually given them hope and imparted his knowledge. What a better way to remember him, than to complete the adventure in his name.

"First, we need to leave this island and head to Set's temple," Olly said.

"It was in that direction," Leo said and pointed. "I remember seeing it from the tower window."

Katie suspected that she knew what to do. She waved her wand and cast the ice-spell. A frozen walkway appeared across the fiery lake in the direction of Set's temple – a blurry object visible on the distant horizon.

"There it is guys. That's where Claire is."

"It's miles away Olly," Leo said. "Are we all up for this?"

"Definitely ... I can't wait." Katie said.

Treading tentatively on the iced walkway, they headed towards the temple. On dry land, they scanned around. The formidable giant pyramids of Giza seemed to stand on attentive guard.

"They're spectacular," Olly said. "I always wanted to visit Egypt."

"Yeah, me too," Katie said. "Maybe not in this manner."

"Definitely not!"

"We'll find Claire ... won't we?"

"I'll make sure of it. We've lost Horace and Stumpy, two loyal friends who risked everything for us. It's our time to repay their valour."

Katie gave Olly a kiss.

Walking towards the temple, Leo practised his swordsmanship while Katie turned the pages of her spell book, searching for one she could use against Set and his army of monsters. Olly strolled along, arms swaying as if he was on a stroll, listening to music. "Can't wait to get home. I'd do anything to be walking my dog."

"And I'll join you," Katie said.

"That'd be nice."

Leo cartwheeled past them with his spinning sword, interrupting his friends' moment. "Hope we find this portal."

"We will. If not, your dad will come after us for sure," Olly said.

"He'll have to lose a few pounds first," Katie said. "When I saw him, Orion could hardly walk never mind do a somersault ... oh and don't tell him I said that!"

The three exploded into short-lived laughter, until they realised that they'd almost reached their destination. Half a mile ahead was Set's Temple. It didn't sparkle in the sunlight because this one was constructed of black limestone that sucked daylight from the sky, leaving a dark cloud that released lightning, continually peppering the ground.

"This is intimidating," Olly said, noticing the creatures guarding its boundaries. "They're not going to welcome us in with open arms."

"They're the creatures that attacked Stumpy – I saw them in my visions," Leo said.

"They're Serpopard's, shoot fire from their serpent's heads. We need to be careful ... Katie! What are you doing?"

Katie wasn't in the mood to be careful. She ventured nearer until the creatures spotted her.

"Err Katie!" Olly yelled. "Get back!"

Katie stood her ground as three creatures approached, stalking her like cats on the Serengeti.

"We need to help her," Olly said.

"I'm ready."

Katie made the first move. "Hesaraca!" The wand released its spell, turning the serpopards into ice sculptures.

Katie glanced at her friends. "Finish them off, Leo."

Like a majorette spinning a baton, Leo strolled over as he rotated his sword, smashing the creatures to smithereens. "That felt great."

"What now?" Katie said.

"Steady on Boadicea," Olly said.

"Boada who?" Leo said.

"It doesn't matter mate. Let's not get carried away, okay."

Katie noticed an entrance was partially open. "We can't simply walk through the front door ... can we?"

Olly stood and pondered. "We'll be noticed. We're public enemy number one in these parts. Could we climb up the side? There are openings at the top."

"I could, but not carrying both of you ... no offence."

"I'll pretend I didn't hear that Leo," Katie said. "We're not that heavy."

"I meant that you might lose your grip and fall."

"He's right," Olly said, "It's too dangerous. What about magic?"

"I could try blasting my way through?" Katie said.

"Too noisy. We don't know what else is in there. We need to be quiet. Hey, I remember a vanishing spell near the back of that book. I tried it out at Leo's house but nothing happened. Try that?"

Katie took Olly's advice and opened the back pages. An illustration of someone disappearing caught her eye. "Found it!"

Katie mumbled the spell under her breath, trying to pronounce the Arabic phrase correctly, when Leo had a thought. "Hang on. You're going to make us all vanish? How long does it last? … a minute? … forever?"

"You've a point but what are the options? Risk fighting? Falling off the side of the temple? Or sneaking in unseen? The spell might not last too long so we need to be on our guard if we become visible again."

"Okay," said Leo, finally.

"Tatalasharaca!" Katie said. White dust exploded from the wand into the air, creating a cloud in the slight breeze. It covered them from head to foot.

"Anyone feel owt?" Leo said, without moving his lips.

"Feels a bit strange," Olly said holding out his arm. "Something's definitely happening."

"I'm feeling okay," Katie said, turning to Olly for reassurance. "Olly! Where are you?"

"It's worked. I can't see you either … or Leo."

"Of all the weird stuff that's happened, this is the craziest," Leo said, holding his arms out to touch his friends. "Who's that?"

"Ow! It's me," Katie said. "And if you touch me there again, you'll regret it."

"Sorry, not my fault."

Olly bought things under control suggesting they stretch out their arms and clasp hands before heading towards the temple.

CHAPTER 34

A steep flight of stone steps led to the doorway of the truncated square pyramid, guarded by two colossal statues of Set. Cloaked by the spell, Olly, Katie and Leo walked hand in hand, dwarfed by the stone monuments.

"He really loves himself, doesn't he?" Katie said, stretching her head back to see the top of the effigies.

"A god can do whatever he wants, I suppose," Olly said.

In the temple, translucent people passed them as a chanting noise boomed throughout the building.

"They're the tourists from our world again. Horace told us about them."

"Well as long as we're not seen, I don't care who they are Olly," Leo said, dragging his friends through them. "Hey, look at this."

Olly and Katie peered at Leo's discovery – a 3-D model of the temple in the vestibule.

"Of course," Olly said. "It's from the real world for visitors to see. That's why it's transparent."

The model showed a circular room awaiting them through connecting doors, ten hallways leading off. They appeared to wind deep underground.

"This isn't going to be easy," Katie said. "It's like a rabbit warren."

A tourist touched part of the map, highlighting what it was used for.

"The big room is a preaching hall to Set," Olly said.

"Come on, time is against us."

"Patience Leo, Claire will be somewhere else. The tourists can help us find her."

Leo rolled his eyes though nobody could see his facial expression – the invisibility spell saw to that. A river of tourists highlighted different parts of the model with chambers explained. It wasn't long until the seekers were better informed about their destination.

"Right," Olly said. "We know where the dungeon is. I say we head straight there."

"Let's do this," Leo said.

As they approached the next room, the chanting increased. Still invisible, they opened the double doors causing a creaking sound to echo throughout the building. The chamber was populated with every creature imaginable. As the beasts turned, the children stood silently, hoping that the spell was active. Two hell goblins hobbled past them. The small red creatures dashed up the centre aisle before jumping onto a vacant bench.

"Quick, walk forward," Olly said. "They'll think it was the goblins that opened the door."

The congregation of creatures carried on with their worship, the teenagers undetected.

The circular room was swarming with monstrosities ranging from king cobra snakes, giant birds, mummies and people with crocodile heads. In front of the beasts stood an altar bearing a bust of Set, his ankh and other treasures beside it. The followers shared a common belief; they were worshipping a god. Fire pits around the circumference of the inner sanctum had Egyptian slaves – mute from fear – dangled above them, ready to participate in reincarnations.

"This is crazy," Katie said. "At least Claire's not over one of them pits."

"Not yet," Leo said. "Where's Set?"

"Don't know, but he won't be far away," Olly said.

The congregation rose from their seats. Those who harnessed magical powers stretched out their limbs to release a burst of energy at the altar. Charged particles streamed over the shrine onto a circular metal frame positioned on the back wall.

"Look!" Katie said. "That's a portal?"

The metal frame consumed the magical power to create a spinning silver vortex.

"It has to be," Olly said. "Let's get to the dungeons and find Claire. Who knows how long the portal will be open?"

Continuing to hold hands, they moved into one of the dark tunnels adjoining the central room. The racket of the crowd faded as they went further and deeper, Olly remembering the route from the map in the foyer.

"Can you hear that?" Katie said.

"Chanting?" Leo said.

"No, something else, from down there to the left."

They listened. Two voices were echoing up the corridor. Quietly, the invisible threesome continued until they reached a door.

"They're in there," Olly said. "Let's listen."

"Shirdal, you wanted to speak to me?" said a deep voice.

"You promised me resurrection, oh great one. You told me that I would be free to walk Earth's soil again. Everything you wanted, I've given you – even the human girl," Shirdal said.

"Soon I will regain what is mine. Once the ankh and staff are in my possession, nothing will stop me. Until then, you remain Shirdal."

"Yes master."

"Oh my god," Olly said, unable to keep calm.

"What?" Leo said.

"Shirdal – it's Victor. Set reincarnated him into the griffin."

"They're about to enter the portal," Katie said.

Finding Claire was now more urgent. He switched on his torch to help them in the darkness but was horrified by what he saw.

"Who'd you expect to see?" Leo said, not understanding his dilemma.

"Think about it … I … can … see … you," Olly said.

"You can see me?… I can see you … and you … oh goodness, the spell has broken."

"Try the spell again Katie," Olly said. "We'll not survive if we're caught in this place."

Katie frantically waved her wand, "Tatalasharaca!" Nothing happened. "Tatalasharaca!" Nothing. Not one single spark of light appeared from the wand.

"What's wrong?" Leo said.

"I don't know! Maybe it's run out of magic?" the sorceress said. "Maybe I've lost my powers?"

"You haven't lost your powers," Olly said. "The wand has." Katie and Leo stared at him blankly. "Osiris told us that Set uses his minions to open the portals by draining their magic from them – remember. That's what will have happened. The magic was sucked from the wand when we were in the hall."

"Great!" Leo said. "I'm the only one with powers now."

Disappointed, Katie waved Stumpy's stick around one more time before conceding defeat.

"I'm sure the magic will come back when we get out of here," Olly said.

With nothing else to lose they rushed along the winding tunnel.

"Who goes there?" a voice said, unable to recognise them through the glare of the torchlight.

Olly had to think and act, fast. "We are here for the girl. Our master Set wants her."

The guard scratched his bald head before extracting a lump of wax from one of his long ears. "Point the light towards you, let me see your faces."

Olly winked at Leo before turning the torch around. Before the guard had chance to blow his horn, Leo thumped him squarely in the face. He was knocked out cold.

"Shall I smash the door down?" Leo said.

"No, let's take his keys," Olly said. "If Claire's in here, the guard can replace her."

Olly opened the wooden door, scanning the torch around the eerie cave. Blonde hair was visible in the flashlight.

"Hang on," Leo said. "I've fallen for this before. Let me go first." Olly handed Leo the torch who hesitantly walked towards the figure. "Claire, is that you?"

The figure twitched, arms and legs manacled together, a black tie covering their eyes and mouth, words muffled as a result.

"Take off the gag," Katie said. "Let her see us."

Reaching down, Leo untied the cloth.

"Aargh! Leave me alone."

"Claire, it's us," Katie said moving nearer. "We're here to rescue you."

Claire remained curled up like an alarmed hedgehog on the stone floor, shaking with fear.

"It'll take time for her senses to return," Olly said. "She won't be able to see or hear for the moment."

Leo ripped apart her binding chains, freeing her from her nightmare. Holding her hand to the bright torchlight she said, voice barely registering, "Is it really you?"

"It is," Katie said. "Everything's going to be okay."

Claire collapsed, crying – tears of joy joined the blood and dirt spread across the floor. Katie knelt, hugging her cousin as Leo dragged the unconscious guard into the dungeon.

"Can you stand?" Olly said; time wasn't on their side.

"I think so," Claire said, her body was weak, but her will strong. Her friends were risking their lives to save her and it was her turn to show courage. "I'm okay. The blood needs to circulate again, then I'll be fine."

"Good," Olly said. "There's a way home open, but we have to be quick."

"What about those creatures?" Claire said, hearing the chanting echoing down the tunnel.

"Leo's slayer powers will help, but Katie's lost her magic."

"What?"

"Don't ask, well not for now," Leo said.

"I'm the sorceress of Egypt," Katie said.

"I've missed something, tell me all..."

"Later," said Katie.

Exiting the dungeon, Olly and Leo steadied Claire, while Katie locked the guard in behind them. Meandering up the tunnel, they exchanged stories. Claire described how she had befriended Marshall, while Olly told of Stumpy's death.

"Wonder what Marshall's doing?" Leo said.

"Waiting at the abbey for us ... that's what Olly told him to do," Katie said.

"That was before the first portal was destroyed. That plate will have stopped spinning," Olly said.

The noise from the beasts increased in volume as they neared the hall.

"What are we going to do, Olly?" Claire said.

"Depends on how you feel."

"The feeling is back in my legs, if that's what you're asking?"

"I was. We might have to make a run for it, catch those creatures off guard."

"Run where?"

"Into a portal. Set has opened it to retrieve his staff from our world ... it's our way back – temporarily."

Reaching the rear of the temple, they hid behind a wicker screen. Peeking through the frayed covering, they spotted the spinning vortex.

"It's ready to be used," Olly said.

As he spoke a visually fragmented figure with an animal's head crossed in front of the altar. The congregation cheered.

"What's happening? I can't see a thing. Who is it?" Leo said.

"Sssshhh!" Katie said.

Acknowledging his followers with raised arms, the figure spoke, "Your powers have created this portal for me. Once I have my staff, I will be complete and all of Duat will be mine."

Another cheer erupted, followed by a chant, "Set, Set, Set …"

"Does that answer your question?" Olly said.

"Yeah."

"Osiris was right," Katie said. "His body formation is nearly complete."

"We have to make sure he doesn't retrieve his staff."

"How do we get past him without being caught? A griffin is next to him," Claire said.

"That griffin is Victor – reincarnated," Olly said.

"It's his fault I'm here – he dragged me here. It's also why you're here."

Leo put his arm around her. "You've been through a lot but we'll soon be back home … I promise." Claire turned to hug him but was stopped by a blaring noise filling the temple.

Olly stared at Leo. "Please tell me you took away the guard's horn before chucking him in the cell?"

Leo scrunched up his face. "Erm ... I'm not sure ... I can't remember."

"I think we can safely say he didn't," Katie said, shaking her head.

"Well, you were the one who locked the door. Don't blame me."

"Okay," Olly said. "It's too late to change things now. Anyway, it might work in our favour."

"You think?"

The congregation fell quiet, realising something was amiss. Set and Shirdal knew exactly what was happening and darted along the central aisle towards the dungeon. The children peered at each other – this was their only chance of escape. They leapt from their hiding place and ran for their lives. The creatures watched them whizz by in a flash, too slow to act except for a few hell goblins who spontaneously exploded, causing the hall to vibrate.

"No!" The roar boomed out of the tunnel, followed by a flapping noise. Shirdal was in hot pursuit.

"Quick," Olly shouted. "Set knows we have Claire. Over the altar, slide, make it quick."

Katie was right behind Olly. She flung herself over the shrine, displacing Set's bust. Close behind were Leo and Claire. He helped Claire over the altar when he noticed something.

"Shall I take this!?" he yelled.

"Yes!" Olly said, as Shirdal rocketed up the passageway.

Leo grabbed Set's ankh.

"Go! Go! Go!" Olly pushed his friends one by one into the spiralling vortex. Something else caught his eye, lying on the altar – a flail. *Could it be Osiris'* he thought. With no time to consider, he took the treasure and followed his friends through the rotating circle.

The monsters were left in their wake.

CHAPTER 35

Over an hour later, Marshall made it to Fisherman's View in St. Prion – despite Arthur's wayward directions.

"Half of these roads weren't here when I were alive," Arthur said.

"Yes, it's been a hundred years since he lived here," Tilly said, defending her friend.

Marshall took a few deep breaths. "It's okay, we're here now. Which house is it? … Well?"

"Well, I lived in that one," Arthur said, pointing to the end house. "Not sure about Leo's home."

"That's just great, what are we meant to do? Knock on every door – in the middle of the night – to see if a dragon slayer lives there?"

Tilly whispered to Arthur before they both drifted towards the row of terraced houses. Marshall didn't have time to question them, but hoped they'd be quick. He was still an escaped convict and didn't want the police to be called. He leant the bike and staff against a stone wall and watched the ghosts enter a property. Rooms illuminated dimly as the spirits flew around, exiting through the walls, flowing seamlessly into the next. Six houses later they dashed back to Marshall.

"It's that one, there," Arthur said, pointing. "Next to where I lived."

"Are you certain?" Marshall said.

"There are photos of Leo in there. Easy really," Tilly said.

Marshall smiled. "Well done. I'd give you a hug … if I could."

Marshall and the ghouls strolled into Melanie's well-kept garden.

"Float up to those bedroom windows and tell me if they're in?" Marshall said.

Orion had recently paid a call to the bathroom and was walking back to the bedroom to join Melanie. "The moon must be bright tonight Mel, I didn't have to put a light on."

Melanie pulled the duvet off her face and, squinting, she gazed at Orion at the end of the bed – something seemed odd. "Dear, that's not the moon? How could it move like that?"

He strolled to the window to investigate – as Tilly came into view.

"Aargh!"

"Think she's found 'em," Arthur said from outside of the house.

"What's wrong?" Melanie said, now wide awake.

"Come here. You won't believe me otherwise."

Melanie joined Orion at the window to witness Tilly floating outside peering back at them. Melanie froze, open mouthed.

"Are you okay love," Orion said.

Melanie remembered Victor's ghost – but this was different. "She's ... beautiful. Who is she? What does she want?"

"She's pointing down. I think she wants us to go downstairs."

Leaning closer to the window, Melanie glanced down at her garden. "I don't believe it!"

"What?"

"There's another ghost down there and ... it seems that Marshall's stood next to it."

"You're right it's him."

"What's he doing here? Has something happened to Leo?"

Orion headed for the bedroom door. "I'm going down."

"Be careful love, you're not as agile as you were last year. Marshall is nearly as tall as you are, and probably stronger."

Melanie's words fell on deaf ears. Orion had gained a few stones and lost his slayer powers but when it came to Leo's safety, he wasn't someone to mess with. "Don't worry, I'll find out what's going on, even if I have to beat it out of him."

Orion plodded down the stairs, through the kitchen and out of the back door. Without hesitation he grabbed Marshall by his collar, forcing him against the wall. "What have you done to Leo? Where is he, you waste of oxygen?"

Marshall's face reddened as Orion's grip tightened.

"Let him go," Tilly said, floating next to them. "He's come to ask you for help."

Melanie appeared at Orion's side. "This boy tried to kill my family. You're asking us to trust him?"

"Let him speak, he'll tell you."

Orion released Marshall and watched him slide down the wall. "You've five minutes to convince me before I call the police!"

Marshall stared at Orion towering over him, eyes like a submissive puppy. He knew he had to spill the beans if he was to regain his trust. He told of Claire's kidnapping to the Egyptian underworld and that Leo and his friends had used the portal to find her, only for the portal to stop operating. Orion could see that Marshall was upset, tears forming in his eyes. He seemed repentant for the pain his family had afflicted on Orion's and promised to make amends, whatever the cost to him. Orion and Melanie had little choice but to believe him – especially knowing that the plate had been found in their clock.

Marshall rose to his feet. "I need your help?"

"I can't help you, I'm not a slayer any more. Look at me ... how could I fight an Egyptian god? I struggle to get out of bed in the morning."

"He's right," Melanie said, placing her arm around his extended waistline. "He's lost his powers."

"I can help with that," Marshall said, reaching into his bag to pull out the jar. He handed it to Orion.

"Well, I never. Dragon's claw."

"Is that Hornbeam's?" Melanie said.

"It was in Archibald Griffin's old club. Drake must've given it to him after extracting the blood," Marshall said. "If you open it, your powers should return."

Orion was silent. The unwanted attention he had received during the last year had been tough on them. Did he want to thrust himself into the limelight again? Frustrated at not being able to help his son, he now had a chance to rectify that. He would do what was needed if it helped Leo.

They watched as Orion gripped the lid and try to turn it, but his hand slipped. Melanie felt his frustration and said, "Pass it to me."

"I must've loosened it for you," Orion said as he watched the lid come unloose under Melanie's grip.

"Yes dear," she said, raising her eyebrows. Melanie passed the jar back to her husband who continued to loosen the lid.

"Can you feel anything?" Marshall asked.

"Give it chance," Orion said, opening the jar. He rattled the claw out of the container, grabbing it with his other hand. The jar shattered.

"What happened?" Melanie said.

"Nothing, I gripped it … Aargh!"

Melanie ushered the ghosts closer to make use of their glow to illuminate the area. "Oh my god! What's wrong, what's happening to you?"

Orion was rolling on the ground, his torso in spasm. "My body … it feels like … I'm being … crushed."

He twisted, screamed and thumped the grass in pain. Fearful, Melanie intended to run inside and phone an ambulance but she stopped – something was happening to her husband. His features were changing, rounded face becoming chiselled, muscles bulging, weight reducing and pudginess disappearing. He stretched his newfound athletic body and stood tall. "I feel fantastic!"

Melanie and Marshall stared at Orion in awe, they couldn't believe what they'd witnessed – especially Melanie who had never seen her husband as a dragon slayer. Her overweight, lifeless husband was now an Adonis and flush with vitality.

"Keep the noise down," bellowed an awoken angry neighbour.

Melanie ushered everyone inside, especially the ghosts. There was enough going on without her neighbours becoming involved.

"What's the plan?" Orion said. He brimmed with confidence and the sparkle had returned to his eyes.

"Can I have a minute with Orion?" Melanie said, asking Marshall and the spirits to wait in the living room.

"Are you alright my dear?"

"Not really, not after hearing Marshall tell us about Leo. This isn't like last year – he was in our world then. What about you? The trauma you went through in the last year. Can you go through it again when you return? I love you so much and … yes, you look great," she said looking her husband up and down, "but your pain hurts me too."

Orion put his muscular hands on her hips and captured her eyes. "I understand, but I have this claw now. As long as it is near me, I won't change back."

"You shouldn't have to depend on that to simply be you. I don't care about what your body looks like. It's your state of mind that I care about."

"I'd forgotten who me was, Mel. I was a slayer for eleven years in that tunnel. Being a slayer makes me happy, gives me a sense of worth. I need to rescue Leo and the others."

"I don't want you in the underworld again. Let Marshall and the ghosts go. Tell them what to do, anything, but don't go. I don't want to lose you!"

"It's okay, he won't," Marshall said as Tilly and Arthur followed him into the kitchen.

"What do you mean he won't? How on earth is he meant to rescue them?" Melanie said.

"We're not going to the underworld. The underworld is coming to us."

Marshall dashed outside to grab the staff. A crack had appeared on the path where the staff had stood. The staff was hot so he rushed back inside. "We need to move quickly. The underworld is connecting with the staff."

"I don't understand," Melanie said.

"This staff is what we're going to use to tempt the underworld into our world. It's happened twice before: with an ankh at the Art of Darkness club and with a slayer sword at the abbey. It's our only chance. When the floor opens up, the Egyptian underworld will appear and Leo and his friends can escape. We need to keep the gateway to the underworld open as long as we can if we're to succeed."

"Is there any way I can help?" Melanie said.

"You could drive us to the abbey? I'm not sure I can peddle any more."

"Definitely," Orion said. "I'm not getting on a bike."

CHAPTER 36

Melanie tapped the steering wheel nervously – eager to help her son.

"Put the staff in the back!" Orion shouted to Marshall. "I'll be back in a minute."

"Now what's he doing?" Melanie asked Marshall, plonking himself behind her, the staff sticking out of the window.

Marshall strained his neck. "He's saying something to the ghosts. It's okay, he's coming back."

Melanie, keen to leave, started the engine as Orion opened the passenger door, waving at the ghosts flying into the night sky.

"Where have they gone? We need them to help us," Marshall said.

"They won't be long. They're doing a job for me," Orion said squeezing into the car.

"Are we ready ?" Melanie said.

"Yes," Orion said. "Let's get our son back."

Melanie sped off like a racing driver, spinning wheels and scorching rubber – to the annoyance of their neighbour behind the twitching curtain.

"So Orion, where have the ghosts gone?" Marshall said, buffeted around in the back.

Orion still wasn't sure about Marshall and decided to play it cool. He was watching Marshall's every move. "I may have the strength of a dragon slayer but without weapons, I'm as vulnerable as you."

"Have you sent them for your bow and arrows?"

Orion nodded. "Plus my slayer sword. If it was good enough to kill Hornbeam, it's good enough for this mission."

"I hope my plan works."

"It had better?" Melanie said, skidding around another corner.

Orion turned around to face Marshall. "What is it you want me to do?"

"Keep this staff close to you. If the underworld opens up, you can fend the creatures off with it. But don't fall into the crevice or you may never return."

"I'll be ready."

Another corner of tarmac benefited from a layer of rubber as Melanie screeched into St. Prion Abbey's estate, Marshall sliding across the backseat. "That was fun," he said with a snigger.

"There's nothing fun about this," Melanie said. "My son has vanished and I'm at my wits end."

"Sorry, I wasn't laughing at the situation, I just slid."

Orion broke the seconds of silence, "Let's concentrate on finding Leo, we need to work together."

Melanie eased off the accelerator, driving along an avenue of oak trees leading along the edge of the lake, eventually ending outside the iron gates.

"Look, their bikes," Orion said. "Which way now?"

"Through the gates. The abbey's a quarter of a mile through the valley."

Marshall exited the beetle and passed the staff to Orion.

"You have the claw, yes?" Melanie said.

"It's safe." Orion tapped his coat pocket.

Melanie stepped up to the gates and tried to open them. The padlocks held them secure.

"It's okay, go through the café courtyard," Marshall said.

"Or I could do this!" Orion walked up to the gate, grabbed the chain with both hands and pulled it apart. The padlock fell to the ground with a clunk sound.

Marshall's mouth dropped open in surprise and Melanie had never seen such strength from her husband. She stared at him. There was new life in Orion – he was comfortable in this skin. She kissed him and said, "I see now, you need to be a slayer – and I need a slayer to save our son. Come on, let's find him."

Marshall led the way along the stream. Cutting across the grass, he told Leo's parents about the fallen monks that Tilly and Arthur had said were buried underneath the ground where they walked.

"And the monks are going to help us?" Melanie said, treading gingerly.

"Yes."

"They will," Orion said. "I saw many crazy things when I was trapped in that tunnel. Everything you've told us rings true."

Melanie glanced at her husband when something distracted her. "Look at the staff!" Orion held it aloft – pulses of red light were darting from the carved animal head at the top of the iron rod.

"That's so cool," Marshall said.

"Cool isn't the word I'd use," Orion said, swapping the staff to his other hand. "This thing's becoming hot."

"The underworld is connecting with the staff. We need to be prepared."

Melanie shrugged. "How prepared can we be? I have no weapons."

"Let's get into the abbey first," Marshall said. "The underworld can certainly open a gateway in there."

The night was clear, the moon illuminating the abbey, casting a shadow over the expanse of grass. Before they entered, something in the sky attracted Melanie's attention. "Look! The stars … they're becoming bigger."

Orion and Marshall glanced up to witness two shimmering lights drifting through the night sky.

"They're not stars," Orion said. "That's Tilly and Arthur."

The ghosts flew over the café towards the abbey and floated down next to their friends, each carrying a bag.

"That building was huge," Arthur said. "Like a giant workhouse."

"There were so many things … but we think we've everything you wanted," Tilly said.

"How can you hold things?" Melanie said. "Victor's ghost could do it too."

"It's in the mind," Arthur said, poking his finger through his head. "We don't have muscles … or anything really."

"It took me a while to learn," Tilly said. "Now it comes naturally."

Orion passed the staff to Marshall before reaching inside a bag to pull out his sword and bow and arrows. He ran his hands over them. "My old friends, it's been a long time. Now I am a slayer!"

"That's fine for you. How am I meant to keep safe?" Melanie said.

"By letting me deal with everything. You need to stay as far away from here as you can."

"I'm not leaving, knowing my son is in danger."

"Okay, but please stay in the wooded area … it'll be safer there."

Melanie turned and walked towards the valley side but was stopped by Tilly saying, "We have something for you!"

Melanie turned. "For me?"

"We wanted to help get your boy back," Arthur said.

Tilly pulled out a weapon. "Oh my!" Melanie gasped.

"That looks familiar," Marshall said.

In Tilly's hand was a gun, the same gun that Marshall used in the Brunswick tunnel aiming to kill everyone.

"You can't use that!" Orion said. "You've never even held a gun before, never mind pulled a trigger. You'll kill someone."

"Isn't that the idea?" Melanie said. "I'm taking it. It might keep me safe. That's what you wanted … wasn't it?"

Orion didn't have a winning argument so ushered his wife to a densely wooded area on the bank. "Promise me you'll keep hidden. I've no idea what will appear from the underworld."

"I promise."

"Only use the weapon if you have to. I love you."

Marshall spotted the tip of the staff – the red glow was intensifying. "We better get ready."

"Here, put the staff through my belt," Orion said gesturing to his back. "You realise it's in our interest not to give you a weapon … don't you?"

"I understand," Marshall said securing the staff. "There is something that will help us though." He reached into his bag to reveal the cube.

"Where did you find that?"

"Lying on the floor in the club. It might come in handy."

"It will." Orion said, "Put it back in your bag and hide. At some point we'll need you to open it. Do you know the phrase?"

"Yes, my uncle told me, he's dead you know." Marshall looked over towards the abbey where Lance's bloodied remains lay on the stone floor.

Orion placed a comforting hand on Marshall's shoulder. Orion realised that Marshall had been dealt a tough hand in life.

"Okay, I'm going to wait in the abbey's hall," Orion said. "Tilly and Arthur, I've been told you know some ghostly monks that can help. Can you summon them?"

Arthur and Tilly held each other's hands as they flew to the middle of the expanse of grass as a rumbling emanated from the abbey. Orion and Marshall ran over and peered through an unglazed window.

"It's happening again," Marshall said, breathing heavily. The crack reopened, gradually expanding as a mist seeped into the empty hall from the depths below.

"Hide Marshall, hide!" Orion shouted.

Marshall ran towards the safest place he could think of – the dungeon where Claire had been a prisoner.

CHAPTER 37

Orion watched the floor continue to open as he leaned against the inner wall, preparing to fight whatever demons would appear. Sword in one hand, bow in the other and staff glowing intensely, still secured against his back, Orion glanced over at where his beloved wife was crouched behind a mature oak tree, clutching her gun, as Tilly and Arthur floated above the grassland summoning the spirits of the monks.

"Where are the monks?" Tilly said. "They usually come out to play with us."

"They might be scared?" Arthur said. "Maybe they can sense badness coming? … I can."

"Shall we wait in the café? Will you feel safer there?"

"Yes," Arthur said. The ghosts peered at the abbey, now surrounded by a haze, and returned to their retreat.

Marshall waited in the dungeon for his chance to assist Orion. Memories of Claire's kidnapping messed with his head. He was ashamed of his part in her suffering and decided he needed to take a lead, prove he'd turned over a new leaf. Leaving the safety of the jail, he sneaked along the corridor and spotted Orion.

"Get back," Orion said.

Marshall shook his head. "I want to help ... I'll keep out of your way."

The rift in the floor was ten feet wide with glowing lava clearly visible, bubbling in the depths below.

"Is this where Claire was taken?" Orion asked, his face reddened by the heat. Marshall nodded. Orion stepped closer, his shoe tips hanging over the edge. Taking a deep breath to compose himself, he bent his knees and prepared to jump.

"No!" Marshall said. "What the hell are you doing? You'll die, there's nothing but fire and brimstone. Claire travelled through a portal to the Egyptian underworld, a circle of light created by Osiris."

"Like that?" Orion said, pointing to a vortex forming above the molten river.

Marshall rushed over. "Yes ... Yes, that's it."

The rotating light ascended, eventually clearing the gaping precipice.

"Follow me," Orion said, running into a darkened corridor. The vortex accelerated, emitting lightning bolts spearing the abbey's walls, forcing Orion and Marshall to shield their eyes.

"Are we safe here?" Marshall yelled, pressing himself into Orion.

"I don't know. Was it like this before?"

"No!"

Before Orion could continue, the light dimmed and silence descended like a shroud. Removing their hands from their eyes, Orion and Marshall noticed a red line in the cloud. It widened, dispersing more light until a miracle occurred.

"Olly!" he yelled as the young adventurer magically appeared from the portal.

Olly seemed dazed and had difficulty finding his bearings. "Orion! Is that you?"

Katie and Claire were next, thrown from the portal, rolling across the floor until coming to a halt by the wall.

"Claire," Marshall said . "Are you okay?"

"I think so?" she said, still disorientated.

Olly helped Katie stand and hugged her tight as she regained her senses. "We made it."

"Where is he? … Where's my son!?" Orion yelled.

Olly watched as a shadow emerged from the white mist. He turned Orion around as Leo was thrust into his father's arms.

"My son, you're safe. Are you okay? Are you hurt?"

"I'm good, really. My slayer powers are back, thanks to Stumpy," Leo said.

"Stumpy's alive?"

"Sadly not, but I'll tell you later." Leo held his dad, aware of the transformation in him. "You're different dad – what are you doing here?"

"Marshall will tell you. He planned your escape."

"Well done, Marshall," Claire said. "I *knew* you were as good as your word."

Katie walked up to him. "Thanks, Marshall and I'm sorry for hitting you before." Marshall held out his hand which Katie ignored, instead giving him a hug.

"Yeah, well done," Olly said. "It's great to see you too Orion, but we've got to get away from here. We're not going to be alone for long."

They climbed out through the abbey windows onto the grass when Marshall realised something. "Wait. Where's Horace? He hasn't returned with you."

The seekers stopped, staring at each other.

"Well?" Marshall said.

"He didn't make it," Katie said.

"He made sure we did, though," Olly said.

"I hardly knew him … but he stood up for me and believed me … not many people have done that." Marshall reached into his pocket for a tissue but felt something else. "Here, this is for you Olly. Horace gave it to me to look after before you entered the portal. Your and Leo's names are on it. You keep it now."

Olly stared at the envelope until they were distracted by a screeching.

"What's that?" Orion said, glancing back at the abbey.

"Shirdal," Leo said. "One of Set's followers."

"It's also your dad," Olly told Marshall.

"My dad … how?"

"Your dad entered the portal so that Osiris could resurrect him, but the god refused. Instead, Victor discovered his evil brother Set, who reincarnated him as Shirdal, the griffin. The god's followers will come through this portal to retrieve Set's staff. It's the final piece, it ensures his domination of the Egyptian underworld."

"Set might need this as well," Leo said holding aloft Set's ankh.

"Good one son."

The news was hard for Marshall to take in. His dad was still keen on vengeance and had been reincarnated as a griffin. Marshall stared at his fellow adventurers knowing he was now on the right side, the good side. He'd forget his past. A red mist seeped through the abbey ruins, coinciding with high pitched screeching, forcing Olly and his friends to sprint across the expanse of grass.

"Look!" Katie said.

The group watched the mist being blown across the valley slopes as a shadowy figure emerged, flapping its giant wings.

"Quick," Olly said. "Inside the café, it won't spot us there."

With hearts pounding they ran to the courtyard and through the side door, rushing to one of the large bay windows that gave them a vantage point to view the abbey.

"Mum's not going to believe this," Leo said, keeping close to his dad. "Wait till we tell her this story."

"You won't have to," Orion said. He put a hand on his son's shoulder. "She's in those woods." The elder slayer pointed to the oak and pine trees dominating the right-hand side of the valley.

"What? Are you joking?"

"I told her to leave, but she wasn't having any of it ... you know what's she like."

"We need to get to her. If something spots her, she'll have no chance."

"Not sure we can mate ... look," Olly said.

Shirdal had moved onto the grassland, its golden plumage flickering as it surveyed the area for targets. Behind the beast, a myriad of creatures emerged from the nooks and crannies of the ruin.

"They were all in Set's temple," Katie said. "You were right, Olly. They're all searching for the staff and ankh."

A China cup vibrated on one of the tables in the café, behind them. It slid across the tablecloth before smashing to the floor, breaking the silence.

"Who did that?" Claire said.

"It's okay, calm down," Marshall said.

Katie scanned around. "Was that you Tilly! Arthur!?"

"It wasn't us, we promise," Tilly said, appearing through a wall.

"Aargh!" Claire said. "Who's that?"

"You're fine, it's Tilly," Katie said. "She died here a long time ago and is helping us. Where's Arthur by the way?"

Tilly floated over, dressed in her maid's outfit. "He's scared, so he's hiding down in the cellar."

"Something is vibrating the building," Orion said, as plates smashed in the kitchen. "What's out there?"

Olly blinked, trying to clear his vision. "Something is moving around the edge of the abbey ... something huge."

Katie joined him at the window, "Oh please no, don't let it be one of them."

"What is it?" Claire asked.

"A snake ... an absolutely ginormous snake, climbing up the side of the abbey tower."

"I've seen that before," Olly said. He pulled a book from his backpack and flicked through it. "There, I knew it ... its name is Apep, feared throughout Egypt."

"It would be," Leo said.

The dark green snake used its fifty-foot-long body to wrap itself around the ruin. Its body circumference was wider than a dustbin lid and it used its constriction skills to cause the tower to crumble. At the top of the tower, its tongue twitched and turned scenting its prey.

"We're all going to die! You should've just left me," Claire said, unable to control her fear. "Some of us don't even have weapons."

"Me and my old man will sort it," Leo said, trying to comfort her. It seemed an age since he'd first met Claire at the book signing, and nothing had changed in his feelings.

"Less of the old," Orion said. "And I'm *not* sure we can sort it. Even our slayer powers are no match for what's coming through there."

While Orion and Leo discussed a plan, Tilly waved to Olly – indicating for him to follow her. She drifted into the hall, disappearing through a doorway beneath the staircase. Olly opened the door, flicked on a light to reveal a flight of stairs descending to a basement. Walking carefully down the creaking steps, he spotted Tilly and Arthur on the floor apparently playing marbles.

"What have you brought me down here for?"

Around the room were artefacts from the café's past including Georgian furniture, oil paintings, marble statues, even army uniforms and helmets used during World War One training camps. On the wall something caught Olly's eye. "She looks familiar?" he said looking at a family portrait.

Tilly floated over. "Yes, that's me next to the Richmond family. Lord Richmond didn't want any

291

staff in the portrait, but Lady Richmond insisted. She sat me on a chair next to her. I was her favourite."

"Until you fell," Arthur said.

"No need for that," Olly said. "Hey! They're not marbles, that's ammo you're playing with!"

Tilly intervened, "Arthur likes playing down here; he loves the army stuff."

"I can show you more if you want?" Arthur said.

Olly was intrigued. "There's more?"

Arthur pointed to an oak dresser against the far wall. "Behind there. It was blocked years ago, everyone's forgotten about it."

Olly rushed over, sliding the piece of furniture across the dusty floor to reveal an alcove. He squeezed through but could see nothing in the darkness. "Arthur! Come over here."

The apparition drifted into the secret room, illuminating it with his glow.

"Wow!" Olly said. "Look at this."

Inside, cobweb ridden workbenches were strewn with rifles surrounded by ammo shells. As Arthur moved, his glow revealed boxes stacked to the ceiling, each stamped with the British army's emblem.

"These guns are amazing," Olly said, grabbing one along with a handful of shells. "Will you show me how to use one, Arthur?"

"I'm not sure," Arthur said. "I prefer pretending than real life."

"Oh, I'm so sorry, this is how you died, wasn't it?"

Arthur nodded. "I still want to help you and your friends … so I will."

CHAPTER 38

With everyone staring across the misty grassland at Shirdal and Apep, the portal continued to release the creatures from Duat.

Thousands of scarab beetles poured from the opening, scurrying over the floor like a moving carpet, seeping out through the windows. Seven-foot-tall mummies emerged next, covered in bandages. They stomped around the building, groaning with pain, crushing beetles underfoot. The sound of hideous laughter filled the abbey as hell goblins jumped from the portal. The two-foot creatures had a weathered crimson complexion, long noses, three talon fingers on each hand and sets of teeth akin to piranhas. They hunted in packs, ripping their prey to shreds, but also killed alone with the help of the creatures that followed them – Serpopards. The leopard-like animals sauntered from the portal, their reptilian necks stretching upwards, lizard heads sniffing the air in search of their prey.

Exiting the abbey, the serpopards walked onto the grass, their padded paws sinking into the soft ground. Hell goblins, eager to join in, jumped on the beasts' backs. They dug their talons in to the nape of the serpopards' necks, causing the beasts to release a burst of fire from their fanged jaws, setting alight some unfortunate mummies. From up above, Apep the snake spotted the movement from the creatures below. It was ambivalent about which side it supported. It noticed a hell goblin running in circles on the field and without hesitation, its fangs sank into its hapless prey. After the atrocity, Shirdal, killed in another life by the goblins, flapped its wings and rose into the night sky, seeking safety.

Over twenty serpopards were lined up across the field, guided by hell goblins gripping their backs. They marched forward blowing out fire balls in the café's direction with other creatures following suit.

"Olly!" Leo shouted. "Get up here."

Olly's pounding footsteps could be heard from below. He ran up the stairs into the main room. "What's happened?" he said, grasping a rifle. The two ghosts floated up through the floor to join him.

"Those things that attacked Stumpy, they're getting nearer," Katie said. "What shall we do?"

Olly saw the tip of Stumpy's walking stick poking out of Katie's jeans. "You're going to see if your wand works again. Are you ready?"

Katie nodded. "I'll try, but they're quite far away."

Stepping through the door onto the grass, she uttered the magic word, "Hesaraca!"

The wand spluttered, like a car starting on a cold winter's morning before kicking into life. "Hesaraca!" she repeated with added emphasis. A mist shot over the field towards its targets with Katie falling backwards. The spell lost both momentum and height, transforming the grass into an ice rink. Katie lifted herself to her feet and again repeated her spell. This time the ice spread further, reaching the serpopards, cementing them to the frozen surface.

A cheer erupted from inside the building but the euphoria was short lived. The serpopards used their fire to free the angry beasts.

"Get back in!" Claire shouted.

Katie was making her way to the comfort of her friends when a new noise distracted them.

"It's like someone popping bubble wrap," Leo said.

"Our friends, they've woken up," Tilly said with delight.

"Your friends?" Olly enquired.

"The monks of St. Prion Abbey," Arthur said. "They don't like the underworld. The creatures destroyed their abbey."

Cracks appeared on the icy surface of the frozen field as skeletons ascended.

"There are hundreds of them," Orion said.

"A thousand to be precise," Marshall said.

The dead monks climbed out of their resting place, holding their iron maces and swords aloft. A Gregorian chant filled the abbey's valley as they trooped forward.

"What are they singing?" Katie said. "It's beautiful."

"Not sure," Olly said. "But it appears the creatures don't know what to do."

The goblins pulled back on the serpopards, seeking guidance from above. "Attack them!" Shirdal shouted. "Attack them!"

The hell goblins kicked the serpopards and pressed their talons deeper into their necks, instructing them to move forward. The serpopards released a tirade of fire, melting the surrounding ice and turning the frontline of the monk army into ash. The skeletal monks wouldn't allow themselves to be beaten by fire again and sprinted onwards, thrusting their swords and spinning their maces at the flame-breathing beasts, removing their scaly heads. The goblins panicked, leaping off their steeds in retreat. Up above, Shirdal realised he had to intervene. The golden griffin swooped down and stretched out its immense wings. Shirdal sliced through the necks of the monks, leaving hundreds of skulls lying on the grass to be rolled away by the scarab beetles. Another foray of monks stepped forward, this time to be attacked by the mummies. The monks tried to stab and slice the bandaged zombies, but their weapons were no match for the walking dead. The mummies ripped the monk's limbs apart with ease before passing them on to Shirdal, who gripped his talons into the monks' ribcages. The griffin flew high above the abbey hall before dropping the skeletons, smashing them into pieces as they hit the stone building.

Orion and the seekers watched as line after line of monks were defeated by the underworld.

"What are they?" Claire said as a huge creature ripped apart the remaining monks.

"No idea," Marshall said, placing an arm over her shoulder. "Crocodiles with a hippo's body – odd."

"Crocohips." Arthur said, his childish mind trying to relieve the tension.

"Doesn't matter what they are, I won't let them get you," Leo said, seeing Marshall's closeness to Claire. "I reckon we go and kill these creatures once and for all."

"Steady son," Orion said. "Let's not rush. There are things out there we haven't dealt with before. We need to be careful."

The crocohips stampeded through the remaining monks, their bulbous bodies, pummelling the skeletons into the ground. With an ear-shattering shriek, Shirdal pointed his wings, prompting the monsters under his sway to move forward.

"Our friends," Tilly said. "They've broken them."

The remains of the valiant monks sank under the grassland, disappearing back to their muddy grave.

"This might help," Olly said holding up the rifle. "It's loaded."

"Thanks, but I think we'll need more firepower than that," Orion said.

"I'll use it," Marshall said.

"No you won't," Leo said.

"It's okay, I'll use it," Olly said. "Arthur told me what to do."

Arthur floated in front of Olly. "What about the boxes?"

Olly remembered seeing them downstairs. "The boxes Arthur … why? What's in them?"

"Bombs … that you throw."

Olly glanced at the floating apparition. "You mean we have hand grenades?"

"Yes, yes, that's what they're called."

"Oh my god! Guys, let's get them?"

"How many?" Leo said.

"As many as you can before those creatures reach us," Olly said.

Orion and Leo glanced at each other and jumped to their feet, following Tilly – deftly leading the way downstairs.

"This will make a difference, son. They won't know what's hit them."

After countless journeys, Leo placed the last of the boxes down in the café. Plates and cups and saucers were falling to the ground, smashing on the tiled floor around them.

"What's happening?" Leo said, puffing out his cheeks.

"It's the creatures," Claire said. "They're closer."

"Katie!" Olly yelled. "We need to slow the creatures down. Can you help?"

"No problem … leave it to me," she said, brandishing her wand.

CHAPTER 39

Katie waved her wand, launching fire bolts towards the crocohips. A gust of wind blew them off course and they hit the icy ground instead. Not to be deterred, Katie tried again, despite being blinded by the steaming haze rising from the grassland.

Inside the café, Olly and the slayers were opening boxes bought up from the basement.

"Unbelievable," Orion said.

"Will they still work?" Claire said, holding a hand grenade aloft.

"Put it down!" Olly said. Claire swiftly obliged. "We don't know if they'll work. They might be duds or blow up in our faces for all we know."

Orion reached for his bow. "There's only one way to find out," he said testing the bows elasticity. It had been over a year since he'd last used this weapon. He'd used it to defeat Hornbeam the dragon.

"Dad ... Dad!" Leo said on seeing his father enter a trance.

"I'm sorry, I ... I've bad memories... "

"I understand."

Olly peered through the window at Katie. "Quick, I don't think she can hold the creatures much longer."

Marshall grabbed a chair and launched it at the bay window.

"What the hell!" Olly said as shards of glass fell to the ground.

"No time to waste."

Tilly was unimpressed at the vandalism of her former workplace. "You're breaking our home, stop it. I can't watch." She waved Arthur over before they disappeared through the floorboards.

Orion selected a hand grenade and placed it on the taut bow. He moved to the shattered window and, unsure where the monsters were, fired the hand grenade blindly into the mist. Seconds of silence passed before, heavy with anticipation, a massive explosion eased their fears.

"It worked," Katie said from outside, before leaping back as a decapitated crocodile's head landed where she'd stood.

Marshall opened more boxes as Orion continued his archery. "Look in this one."

Olly reached in and grabbed a metal disc. "Mines! Leo, do you wanna practice discus throwing?"

"Do I ever," the slayer said. Leo snatched the mine from Olly and spun several times on the spot before launching the deadly mine into the mist. Moments that felt like hours passed until the noise of animal squeals filled the valley.

Katie ran back to her friends. "Keep going guys, it's working."

Orion and Leo launched further rounds at the creatures. Box after box were emptied, resulting in countless explosions. Monster's heads, arms, feet and tails flew out of the mist, often hitting the café's exterior.

"This is gross," Claire said, watching blood drip down the remaining windowpanes.

Marshall held her tightly and whispered, "It's okay, you'll be safe with me."

"Hey, can you hear that?" Olly said.

"I don't hear anything," Leo said.

"Exactly," Olly remarked. "No more squeals or shrieks."

They hesitantly moved closer to the damaged window. In front, the mist was drifting away in the breeze. With their eyes focusing, they could see the extent of their onslaught; once luscious green grass was now red, the resting place for creatures of the underworld. The few in-tact crocohips let out final breaths in defeat. Mummies were now piles of sodden red cloth scattered on the ground and the retreating hell goblins had been blown to smithereens, some catapulted to the tops of distant oaks.

"Wow," Marshall said. "You've nearly killed them all."

Orion fired an arrow at one last hell goblin. "We're not out of the woods yet," he said watching Apep slither down the tower. Shirdal the griffin was also stalking them from high up in the moon-lit sky. "Our biggest challenges are still to come."

"We've a couple of mines left, Dad … one for the griffin and one for the snake." Leo said.

"Okay, go for the griffin. You can throw them further than me."

"Hang on a minute," Olly said, seeing Marshall's eyes tear up. "Shirdal maybe our enemy but it's Marshall's father."

Marshall took a deep breath. "I'm not upset because the griffin is my father. I'm upset because I've never seen my father, except in this reincarnation. I've never played with him, kicked a football with him … even hugged him."

Claire was the first to speak. "Every child needs a father or a father figure."

"I did … Lance. Look how that turned out."

"I'm not sure what else to say, but I know you've got us."

Marshall smiled, moved forward and hugged her. "Thanks, it means a lot. Give that big, flying chicken hell, Leo."

The Seekers of Duat

Leo picked up the mine, spun around on the spot before launching it like a frisbee towards the target. Shirdal spotted the disc spiralling towards him. With a swish of one wing he swatted the mine across the sky before it exploded like a firework.

"Sorry everyone," Leo said.

"It's okay mate," Olly said. "We'll have to try something else."

Orion's turn came next. Apep the snake had slithered clear of the abbey and was gliding over the wet grass towards the café. Orion copied Leo's technique and launched the mine at the giant snake. The spinning disc hurtled through the air, straight into its fanged mouth causing Apep to rear-up, screeching.

"What a shot!" Leo shouted to cheers from everyone else.

"Wait, it's not exploded," Orion said.

"Oh my god, someone do something quick! It's coming straight for us," Katie yelled.

"I know what to do," Olly said brandishing his rifle. "Hasn't anyone seen the end of Jaws?"

Steadying himself, like Arthur had shown him, he stared down the sight and pulled the trigger. A deafening noise ripped from the gun, propelling the bullet towards Apep. The noise startled the snake who flipped its head releasing the mine from its teeth. As if in slow motion, they watched the mine leave the snake and spin wildly through the air, as the lone bullet pierced the snake's body barely making it flinch.

"The mine!" Orion shouted. "It's heading for the hillside."

A large explosion boomed through the valley, knocking the giant snake to the ground.

"Mum!" Leo screamed.

The tree-covered hillside lit up as the explosion ignited the undergrowth. Leo started to sprint but was held back by his father. "It's too dangerous son. She'll be safe. Your mum's braver than both of us put together."

"I hope you're right, dad."

"Me too, son," Orion said.

"Can you find a spell for water?" Claire said to Katie.

"I've got the ice one, but we're too far away."

Olly glanced over his shoulder at the two ghosts who had appeared from the basement. "What are you two whispering about?"

Before the ghosts could answer the ground rumbled again. Apep had awoke and was slithering over to the blazing woodland, ripping a burning oak from the ground using its powerful mandibles.

"What's it doing?" Katie said.

Apep span around and launched the flaming projectile directly towards the café.

"Move!" Orion shouted, as the tree speared through the air. They dashed for their lives as the projectile pierced the café's roof, setting it alight.

"I can't take much more of this?" Claire said.

"We must stay strong," Orion said. "We owe it to Stumpy."

"And Horace," Olly said.

Standing against the iron gates, they caught their breath, except the two ghosts of course, who floated over a wall to the lake where they stopped at one of the carved statues standing majestically in the water.

"What are they doing?" Marshall said.

"Not sure," Olly said trying to listen in on their conversation.

"When we met them in the café, Tilly pointed to the lake when she mentioned playing with their friends," said Katie.

"You're right, look."

Ripples of water gushed from the base of the stone statues. Dashing back, Tilly and Arthur flew to the gate to better see unfolding events.

"Is this what you were whispering about earlier?" Olly said.

Arthur nodded. "We thought our friends could help save Leo's mummy."

Large cracks and turbulent ripples of water sounded as the statues broke free from their plinths and three figures stretched out their limbs, stepping onto the lake.

"They're not sinking ... they're walking on water," Claire said.

"That's nothing, these are my magical friends," Tilly said.

The statues leant down into the lake, sucking in copious amounts of water. Satiated, they rose and flew over the café's inferno. The three figures, blurring as they arched over the building, released a fountain of water onto the burning café.

"The fire's going out," Katie said. "They've done it!"

"They're not finished yet," Tilly said.

The flying sculptures continued over to the ignited woodland where Apep awaited. Shirdal, reluctant to confront these strange beings, retreated to the abbey, watching from afar as the statues unleashed another barrage of water, extinguishing the flames. Gushing steam temporarily blinded the statues. This moment was all that Apep needed. It uncoiled higher than the tallest tree in the estate and plucked a statue from the sky.

Tilly and Arthur stared helplessly through the iron gates at their friend's despair, horrified as the snake crashed the sculpture back down to earth, smashing it into smithereens. "No!" Arthur shrieked.

The other two statues watched their friend's demise and headed back to the safety of the lake. They drifted down onto their plinths and again became solid stone where only their tears remained, trickling down their saddened chiselled faces before dripping into the lake below.

"I've had quite enough of that snake," Orion said, grabbing the gate. Pulling hard on the wrought iron bars he snapped the welded joints, passing one of the freed bars to Leo. "Let's do this, son."

Leo took the bar and nodded. Together the slayers launched the iron javelins at the mighty snake. Apep dodged the flying spears and made a beeline towards its adversaries.

"It's coming straight for us!" Claire shouted.

"Not for long," Katie said. The sorceress stepped forward and held out her wand. "Hesaraca!" A mist shot from the stick, engulfing the oncoming snake, freezing it to the ground.

"Now is your chance guys," Olly said. "Get it."

Orion and Leo snapped two further iron bars from the gate frame and launched them towards the stationary snake. Apep's slitted pupils transformed to dinner plates as the spears spiralled towards it – but it couldn't move, only its tail was free from its icy prison. The twisted iron bars penetrated Apep's thick scaly skin, impaling the beast to the ground.

"You did it," Marshall said.

Orion knew he had to finish off Set's disciple. "Look after this, we won't be long," he said, passing Olly the staff.

"His belly," Olly called after them.

"What about it?"

"One of the books … that's how to kill it."

The slayers sprinted over to the frozen reptile, their swords reflecting the moons glow. The snake wriggled, chunks of ice breaking from its torso as it strained to break free.

"Be careful, son."

Leo was still reeling from the thought of his mum being caught in the fire but nothing was going to stop him. Apep turned its head, spitting out its forked tongue directly at him. With a swift movement, Leo sliced off the appendage causing the snake to breach with a deafening roar, ripping apart its iron prison. With the serpent towering over Leo preparing to strike, Orion appeared, somersaulting through the air to land on Apep's neck. The snake tried to shake off the slayer but Orion held tight, sliding down towards its stomach. Thrusting his sword, he punctured the scaly green skin of the creature and slid the sword down further. A ten-foot wound glistened with oozing blood. Releasing its swan song of pain, Apep fell to the ground limply. Its wanton destruction was over.

CHAPTER 40

The death of Apep was cause for celebration. Olly and the gang ran from the gates cheering and thumping the air with delight, eager to greet the slayers.

"That was amazing," Claire said. "You're so brave."

"Thanks, it was nothing really," Leo said.

"It was a lot more than nothing. That snake was massive." Claire hugged Leo and gave him a kiss on his cheek, much to Marshall's annoyance.

"It does help when you're a dragon slayer," Marshall said. "If I had powers, I'm sure I'd have done the same."

"I'm sure everyone would Marshall," Orion said.

"Are you alright? You're not jealous are you?" said Olly.

"I'm fine … just think I've a connection with her." Marshall glanced over to Leo. "He seems to be getting in the way."

"Getting in the way! Leo and his dad have saved our lives. Of course she's ecstatic with him, and yes, maybe they like each other too, who knows? I'm pretty sure they're thinking of nothing else apart from sorting this mess out … like the rest of us. As for you and Claire? She's a nice girl, that's why she helped you. Don't think it's any more than that and anyway, we've got more things to concentrate on than your love life."

"Is that what you really think?" Marshall said.

"Well … yeah. Look, if Claire was to be interested in you, then sounding like a spoilt jealous teenager isn't the way to her heart."

"A spoilt jealous teenager! I know … sorry. Must be my family's genes popping their heads up. I need to learn how to be kinder and less selfish."

Olly put an arm around Marshall. "Well, that's a great start, admitting to your foibles. Come on, let's help the others."

Marshall nodded, following his friend back to the heroic slayers. The field was strewn with dead monsters, defeated in their quest to retrieve Set's staff and ankh. One creature eluded the slayers: Victor, reincarnated as Shirdal the griffin, was perched upon the abbey's roof, swaying in the wind, surveying everything before him. If Victor was to change back into human form again, he knew he had to capture Set's possessions.

Marshall gazed at the distant griffin until a hand on his shoulder interrupted his thoughts.

"This is it Marshall," Orion said. "There's only Victor left. Are you okay with this?"

Marshall turned around. "Yeah … I think so. In fact, I know so. I only ever think what he could have been – not what he was. He's evil, like Lance was."

Orion wrapped his arms around Marshall. "I'm proud of you. It would be so easy for you to follow their ways; it takes guts to be gentle and kind."

"Thanks, now finish that monster off for good."

Orion waved Leo over. "Let's do this, son."

"I'm ready," Leo said. "Do you want to go first? Can you hit him from here?"

"I'll have a go. This wind might be a problem – it's worse now than before."

Grabbing an arrow from his quiver, Orion drew back the bowstring, which tightened. A movement of his fingers released the projectile into the now overcast sky. Eager eyes followed the arrow's flight – and so did Shirdal. The griffin launched from its lookout as the arrow grazed its wing before continuing to arc towards the distant trees. Undeterred, Orion released multiple arrows towards the erratically swooping beast. Orion needed help, so Katie launched a torrent of fire from her wand and Olly joined in the attack, blasting the rifle. Not wanting to miss the action, Leo spotted swords and mace's abandoned by the fallen monks. He lobbed them at the golden feathered bird.

"He won't keep still and he's too fast!" Olly said, as the weapons missed their target.

Hit with a burst of inspiration, Leo ran to Katie and whispered in her ear. The sorceress's eyes lit up. "Jumudaca!" she shouted, pointing the wand at the circling beast. A ray of light gleamed from Stumpy's old walking stick, but the griffin continued to move. Refusing to be defeated she shouted twice as loud. "Jumudaca!" The wand's glow illuminated Shirdal's body releasing a negative bolt of energy back at Katie, knocking her to the floor. Remarkably, it paralysed Shirdal.

"What was that spell?" Olly said to Leo, helping a shaken Katie to her feet.

"Jumudaca." Leo said. "It's the spell the witch cast on me."

Shirdal was imprisoned in mid-air, unable to move, so Orion aimed his bow and released a single arrow. Finding its mark, it pierced the plumage of the griffin, boring into his heart causing the lion-like head to droop. Shirdal was dead and the creature, broken from his spell in death, plummeted like a rock, landing next to Apep.

Orion fell to his knees. Dropping his bow, he held his head in his hands and sobbed.

"You did it Dad," Leo said, leaping over to him. "Victor's dead, and Set hasn't his staff or ankh."

Orion turned and held his son tight. "We did it, Leo … you and me together."

The victory was muted, everyone drained by the adventure. Katie and Claire embraced each other in relief and above them, two friendly ghosts hugged as they spun in the air. Not everyone was happy though.

Olly walked over to a forlorn Marshall who was staring at the lifeless griffin.

"Not sure what to say, mate," Olly said.

"It's okay, I don't know how to feel. He died when I was a baby, so the only time I knew my dad was as a spirit. Not a nice one either."

"He was still your dad … I get it."

"Yes, he was." The words added little comfort so Olly embraced his friend. "Olly?"

"Yeah, what it is?"

"Look!" Next to Olly, lying on the ground, was the staff. "It's still glowing."

Olly stared in horror. Marshall was right, Set's staff was pulsating and hot.

Orion heard the conversation and rushed over. "Leo! Get over here." His son had begun to wander over to the blackened wooded hillside.

"I need to find mum."

"It's not safe, son. Something else could be out there."

Leo reluctantly headed over to his dad. "What is it? What do you want?"

"I need to see the ankh."

Pulling the ankh from his bag, Leo dropped it, grimacing. "It's hot!"

"There's a connection remaining," Olly said. "How? The creatures are all dead."

Attaching the staff and ankh onto his belt, Orion scanned around, "I'm not sure if they all are."

An eerie silence hung over the valley, interrupted by the first drops of rain and a murder of crows, startled from their vantage point on the abbey's tower.

"Something doesn't feel right," Orion said.

"I know what you mean," Claire said. "I've a chill down my spine."

"**YOU THOUGHT YOU HAD WON!**" boomed a deep voice resonating throughout the valley.

CHAPTER 41

"Who was that?" Claire said, clinging to Katie's arm.

"I don't know," Marshall said. "It didn't sound friendly."

Orion and Leo stood ahead of their friends, protecting them with outstretched arms while surveying the abbey.

"It sounded familiar," Leo said.

"I agree."

"Well?… are you going to share your thoughts?" Katie said.

"It's Set." Olly said.

"What! He's followed us through the portal?"

"Why not? The other creatures did. Plus, he's the one who needs the staff and ankh the most." Olly noticed Katie wasn't acting herself, "Have a sit down, I think you may have some concussion."

"I'll be fine!"

"Look!" Leo said and pointed. Eclipsing the portal, a shadowy figure appeared inside the abbey.

"I don't think I can handle any more of this?" Claire said.

Leo took Claire's hand. "You'll be safe, I promise."

"I want to go home." She pulled away from Leo. "This has been a nightmare for me. I wish I'd never come up here."

"We need to finish this off. Otherwise …"

"Otherwise, what!"

"Otherwise, it'll keep coming back."

"He's right," Olly said. "One way or another we're all involved in this and we all need to finish it."

The figure strode from the ruin, its bare feet sinking into the bloodied grass. An opening in the storm clouds allowed the moon glow to expose the image of Set.

"You were right," Orion said.

The seven-foot-tall Egyptian god Set was dressed in nothing but a pleated skirt. Once he collected his ankh and staff, his transformation from spiritual being to a resurrected god would be complete. His red hair draped over broad shoulders and muscular body resembled a Roman gladiator at the Colosseum. More noticeable was the shape of his head – like a dog's long snout.

The evil god swept his gaze over the battlefield and saw his henchmen and followers ripped apart, lifeless on the blood-stained grass. Raising his arms, he commanded, "My faithful, return to Duat and await your fate."

The gang stared at each other uncomfortably when Leo noticed something. "Did you see that?"

"What?" Claire said.

"That serpopard … it just moved."

"Really? It's headless. Are you sure?"

"Yes, look."

As sure as the moon glowed, the decapitated serpopard twitched. Its legs kicked out and sprang the body upright. With blood squirting from the open wound the creature headed towards its master.

"Look?" Katie shouted as more creatures resurrected. Battle-scarred hell goblins rose from the ground, joined by mummies – their bandages soaked in blood and mud.

"What shall we do?" Claire said.

Orion stepped forward and clutched his sword. "Stay back, all of you. Leo! We are needed again."

By now the field was alive with walking dead, each drifting towards Set. Orion and Leo needed to surprise the creatures before they were ordered to attack. The slayers ran forward, swords flailing in the air but they skidded to a slippery halt when the creatures exploded into a red mist.

"What's happening Dad?"

"I have no idea, but stay alert."

Set orchestrated the mist around the sky like a conductor as Olly, Marshall, Katie and Claire stared in amazement. Akin to a murmuration of starlings, the red mist flew from one side of the abbey to the other before Set used his powers to direct the mist into the abbey's hall, where the portal inhaled it.

The god spotted the staff and ankh tied to Orion's back. "I want what is mine!"

"Dad, we have to go!" Leo said, running past his father, back to his friends.

Orion refused and stood tall holding his sword. "You are not a match for a slayer. You may be a god in your world, but you are nothing here."

The god laughed deep and hollow before replying, "Foolish human!"

"Dad! Dad! Come back here."

Set raised his arms and levitated into the air. "You have taken what is mine!" The god brought his hands together, releasing a beam of energy towards Orion.

"Dad!" Leo screamed. The young slayer tried moving towards his father, but Olly and Marshall held him back.

The boys watched as a bright light shot across the sky, enveloping Orion and paralysing the slayer. Unable to move in his illuminated cocoon, the tractor beam dragged the slayer towards the god – dislodging hornbeams claw from his pocket. It fell into the mud below as Orion's feet forged a trough through the muddy field.

"Dad!"

Olly re-loaded the rifle and fired.

"You're not hurting him," Katie said, as the bullets bounced from Set's chest.

"That's it! I've had enough!" Leo said, shrugging off Marshall. "My dad needs me."

"Be careful," Claire said.

Olly and Katie tried to distract the god with further gun fire and magic while Leo ran towards Orion. He plunged his sword in the tractor beam, aiming to stop his dad's capture.

"Your slayer powers are no match for a gods," Set said.

With Set's increased power, Leo struggled to hold onto his sword, the heat becoming unbearable. Eventually, releasing his hands from its grip, the white-hot sword hovered before melting into a puddle. Leo sat on the muddy grass with his head hung. The sword that Stumpy had passed to him was nothing more than molten metal. With his dad being pulled towards the abbey, Leo glanced back at his fellow adventurers. He had to try something! Jumping to his feet, he sprinted towards Set. Leo knew that he possessed speed, agility and strength – he had to be a worthy adversary for this god. He leapt through the air, swinging a pumped arm towards the god. Set maintained control of the tractor beam with one arm while using his other to counter Leo's fist. Leo screamed.

"I told you once, your powers are weak … now die!"

Spinning Leo around like a rag doll, the god threw him towards the underworld aperture inside the abbey.

"**NO!**" screamed Claire as Leo disappeared towards the deep fiery chasm.

"Leo!" Orion screamed from inside his prison. Using all of his strength, he tried to escape but it was in vain, his powers were diminishing as the distance from the lost claw increased. "Let me see my son?"

Olly couldn't take any more so loaded his rifle before saying to Katie, "Closer, use your magic … Katie!"

Katie, recovering from her fall, stared at Olly in a haze. "It's not nice, not seeing your son."

"It's not," Olly said, puzzled.

"Well, if you're going, I am too," Marshall said, pulling a monk's sword from the ground.

"And me," Claire said, brandishing a mace.

"We've seen too many bad things," Tilly said. "It's time for us to keep safe."

"I understand," Olly said. "You've helped us more than enough. Thank you."

The ghosts disappeared into the remains of the café while the warriors marched onward, united in purpose. Stood in front of the abbey, Set pulled the weakened Orion nearer, his paralysed body leaving a furrow in its wake.

"Quick, let's attack before Set retrieves his items," Olly said, taking aim.

"Mwahahaha, you humans are naive. Look at you with your pathetic weapons!"

Olly stopped in his tracks and held the god's stare. "We may not be the strongest or have your firepower. We may not have hundreds of creatures doing our dirty work for us but we have something that you will never have … the heart to fight for someone from respect and love. Your followers worship you in fear … fear of dying if they do wrong. They have no respect for you. They wouldn't save you if you needed help but would leave you to rot in hell and then celebrate their freedom."

The god shrugged and turned his attention to Orion – angering Olly more. He lifted the rifle and released a shot aimed at the god's face, followed by Katie – feeling better – who shouted out numerous spells. Claire and Marshall joined in the throng, peppering the god with anything they could lay their hands on.

With each bombardment the god became angrier while swatting away the missiles. "I have warned you children of Earth!"

Like a magnet attracting iron, Katie's wand was ripped from her grasp to fly into Set's outstretched hand. Katie watched in despair as Set clenched his fist, crushing Stumpy's stick into tiny splinters. "There is no human who can hurt me," Set said, muscles bulging. "I reclaim my ankh and staff; the underworld will be mine."

"No human can hurt you … but a god can!" came a voice from behind Set.

CHAPTER 42

"It can't be?" Olly said.

Katie was confused. "Who? Who is it?"

Behind Set, exiting the abbey's ruins, came a familiar sight.

"Osiris!" Olly said. "It is you."

The green deity had travelled through the portal to offer his help. Set turned in shock as his old adversary appeared before him. "Brother, will you never learn. Will you never stop stepping in my way. I killed you once and I will kill you again."

Osiris, dressed in white robes, head dress and holding his crook, strolled forward. "Your words are not those of any brother of mine. They are the words of a maniac … you must be stopped."

"Your powers have weakened while mine have strengthened."

"The good in people will always prevail." Osiris held aloft his crook and pointed it toward his evil brother, releasing a bolt of charge. Set was too quick and moved to one side, reaching down to snatch his ankh and staff from the helpless Orion, paralysed in the tractor beam. The evil god released an almighty roar, causing parts of the already unstable abbey to collapse. Watching from afar, Olly and his friends watched as Set grew.

"This is not looking good!" Claire said, holding Marshall's arm. "He's nearly as tall as the abbey's tower."

"His height is the least of our problems," Marshall said, watching Set emit a red pulse of light.

The evil god moved in front of the oncoming energy beam, using it to increase his strength. Osiris' confidence in his own powers waned.

"Osiris is being beaten," Marshall said. "We have to help him and quick … look!"

Set lifted his staff into the air and called out a spell unknown to the seekers. Like a strobe light in a night club, a pulsing red beam appeared and propelled a force towards Osiris so powerful that it knocked the god to the ground.

"No!" Claire shouted.

"Oh my god!" Olly shouted, "I've just remembered something."

Before anyone could question him, Olly sprinted towards the abbey – feet sploshing through the blood and mud.

"What's he doing?" Katie said.

"It's hard to see," Claire said. "He seems to be heading for Osiris."

"He'll be killed," Marshall said. "We need to distract Set."

"**HEY YOU!**" Claire shouted causing Set to turn.

"Not exactly what I'd intended," Marshall said.

Set glared at the seekers. "Now Osiris is no more, **YOU** will be no more!"

With Set distracted, Olly rushed to Osiris' side. The god was wounded but alive. "Here," Olly said. "I've this. Will it help?" From his rucksack he produced the flail he'd grabbed from Set's altar. Osiris opened his eyes – his dying pupils brightened. He reached out a flaky green arm and took the flail. He inhaled a deep breath and sprang upright, knocking Olly over. Osiris was transformed – his limp body bulked with muscle and covered in green taut skin.

"My child, thank you."

"Please … help them."

As Set was about to unleash his power, Osiris stood and crossed the crook and flail against each other. Olly watched in awe as a white glow surrounded the deity.

"Can you see that?" Claire said. "That illumination in the distance."

"It's Osiris," Marshall said. "He's still alive."

Set, about to vent his fury, heard Marshall and turned to see his brother, Osiris, glowing like the full moon. Without hesitation, Set, funnelled his energy of hate through his giant torso, causing a red beam of light to exit his hands, heading straight towards his brother.

This time Osiris was ready.

From his crook and flail, Osiris channelled a tirade of lightning towards his evil brother. The streams of energy collided, causing the abbey and its surroundings to glow in an explosion of energy. As the abbey's tower lost more of its ancient stonework, Olly ran back to his friends.

"Are you all okay?" Olly said.

"We are," Marshall said, holding Claire close. "Not sure about Katie."

"Katie!" Olly knelt down beside his girlfriend. She looked at him but her eyes were empty and skin pale. "What's wrong with her?"

"I don't know," Claire said.

A wooden beam crashed from the abbey's rafters to the stone floor, distracting the seekers.

"Is Osiris winning?" Marshall said, temporarily blinded by the light.

"I think so … Set is weakening."

The god of war and chaos *was* tiring, red beam diminishing as Osiris' power grew, pushing his brother back.

"Look!" Claire shouted. "Set's body is fading."

"He's losing his powers," Olly said. "Only his spirit will be left soon."

Osiris continued to punish his brother with more bombardments until the dog-faced Set dropped to his knees. With one last thrust, Osiris straightened his arms and released a barrage of charge into his brother's body. It was so powerful that his crook and flail exploded into a thousand pieces.

"Aargh!" Set fell forward, body tissue vanishing, leaving a defeated, ghostly outline. The evil god had also relinquished its hold on Orion and released him from the tractor beam.

A weakened Orion rolled away from the conquered god. "Marshall! Now! Now! The time is now!"

Olly and Claire were bewildered at Orion's request, but Marshall knew what he had to do and delved into his bag.

"Oh my god!" Olly said. "The cube … quick, open it."

Marshall opened the lid and pointed it at Set's spirit before shouting the magical phrase, "**THIS WILL HOLD THE SPIRIT SAFE, AWAY FROM THE ENTIRE HUMAN RACE!**" A beam sprang from the box, travelling horizontally across the grass toward the evil spirit. With Set's spirit helpless, the glow encapsulated the god and absorbed his body. Marshall slammed the cube lid shut, imprisoning the evil god.

"You've done it!" Claire shouted.

Marshall, his slicked-back hair blowing in the wind, appeared dazed. He realised he had finally achieved something good in his life. "I have … haven't I."

"You have, my friend," Olly said. Marshall reached out to shake his hand but Olly hugged him tight instead.

CHAPTER 43

Calmness descended on the St. Prion estate. With Set captured the underworld was no more – except for Osiris who was pale and weak without his crook and flail. The god floated over to the seekers. "How can I ever thank you? You have not only saved your world, but mine too."

"But we couldn't save Horace and Leo," Olly said.

"And Melanie," Orion said. "She's vanished too!"

Osiris bowed his head. "I am sorry for your loss. I will make sure my evil brother is imprisoned forever." The god reached out towards Marshall, the early morning light reflecting off his wrinkly green arms.

"You want this?" Marshall said, grasping the cube.

"Yes, my child. It will be safe with me. It's where it belongs."

From the distant abbey, Claire noticed something. "Look … the light … it's fading."

"You're right," Orion said.

"The portal is closing. With Set captured, his powers are no more. I have to go or I will be trapped here forever."

Marshall passed him the cube before the god rushed back to the portal, his white robes flapping like the wings of a swan. Orion and the seekers looked on, watching the god wave a last time as the vortex encased him.

"**CHILDREN!**" Osiris shouted before disappearing.

"What did he want?" Olly said.

"He's seen something in the crevasse … I hope it's Leo!" said Claire, staying with the ailing Katie as the remaining seekers ran to the abbey.

"I can hardly breathe," Olly said. The heat from the boiling magma stopped them in their tracks.

"We must get nearer," Orion said, sweat dripping from him.

"Dad!"

"Son! … I can hear you."

Gazing through the steam, Orion ignored the intense heat. "**LEO! LEO!**"

"**DAD!**"

Orion fell to the floor and crawled to the edge of the fissure. Looking down, he saw movement, an arm waving. "Leo! I can see you."

"Dad. Can you jump down?" Leo shouted through the bubbling magma spitting up from below.

Wiping his brow, Orion gasped for air. "I can't, son. I've lost my powers. Can you jump up?"

"I can't … I dropped the piece of Stumpy's leg in the magma. I've lost my powers and it's so hot. I think I'm going to pass out."

"No, stay with me, Leo."

Olly and Marshall made their way alongside Orion, overlooking the gaping cauldron of fire. Leo was perched on the end of a long boulder above the fiery hell, his movement causing the rock to swing like a see-saw. Worst of all, the fissure was closing. "My son, we need to get him out."

"What can we do?" Marshall said. "One slip and he'll be cooked alive."

"Not the best thing to say," Olly said.

Feeling helpless without his powers, Orion sobbed; tears evaporating from his cheeks before they had chance to fall. A beam crashed down from above, splashing into the magma.

"Orion," Olly said. "We need a counterbalance."

"For what?"

"To fall on the other end of that boulder. It'll catapult Leo out."

He shouted to his son, "Leo, we'll be back soon, we have an idea."

"Hurry up Dad. I love you."

"I love you too."

Orion, Marshall and Leo headed back out of the abbey to breathe again. They bumped into Claire, walking arm in arm with Katie.

"Katie's really not well," Claire said. "I think we'll have to go."

"We're not going anywhere," Orion said. "Leo's dying in there and needs rescuing."

Olly tried his best to calm the situation and explained Leo's perilous situation to Claire and the semi-conscience Katie. Frantically they searched for rocks. Small ones were too light to be an effective counterbalance and the large ones were too heavy to move.

"Couldn't we use that?" Claire said, pointing to the stone table inside the abbey.

It was the perfect solution.

"Great idea," Marshall said.

The round table in the centre of the abbey had been damaged by an oak beam falling from the rafters, causing the top to dislodge from its base.

"We can roll it over to the crevasse," Orion said. "Come on."

Leaving Claire outside to care for Katie, Orion led the boys into the abbey's furnace once more, where Leo's calls were fading.

"We're back, mate!" Olly shouted . "We'll soon have you out."

"Hurry … please."

Keeping close together, they shuffled through the dense mist until they reached the table. "Listen carefully," Orion said. "We'll have one chance. Marshall, you stand at the front and guide it towards the crevasse while me and Olly push it … okay?"

"Got it," Marshall said.

With all their strength, Olly and Orion pulled the slab of stone up from its resting place and began to roll it across the floor. The heat caused the table to heat up.

"This is unbearable," Olly said.

"We're nearly there," Marshall said. "Just another five feet."

As the stone turned its last circumference, Leo gave out another cry. "Help … help!"

Orion knew there was no time to hesitate and glanced over the edge to check the positioning. "Let's do this."

Fighting through the pain barrier, Orion, Olly and Marshall rolled the stone one last turn until gravity took over. They watched the stone fall, pushing steam outwards as it plunged towards the boulder. With a crash it landed perfectly on the opposite side to Leo and, like a see-saw, the boulder moved, launching Leo upwards away from the magma.

Orion was first to react. He grabbed Leo's hands through the steam. "Got you!"

"Dad … my grip."

Their hands, both covered in sweat slid past each other. Orion tightened his grip but without his slayer powers, it was useless. "I need help! Marshall, reach down."

Marshall glanced out of the abbey window where Claire was watching the unfolding events. *This will make her like me more*, he thought. He slid himself over the edge as Olly held onto his legs. He reached down and gripped Leo's arm.

"Pull!" Orion shouted.

With Marshall's help, Orion recovered his grip on Leo's arm – who was now close to passing out.

"I'm not going to lose you again," Orion said, reaching for Leo's belt. With a final tug, Orion raised his lethargic son from the fire below back to safety.

"Watch out!" Claire yelled from outside.

Orion glanced up to watch a shadow falling towards them. He gripped Leo's waist and rolled him out of the way before an oak beam crashed to the floor.

"Move Olly!" Orion shouted. With a split second to think, Olly dived for cover – unintentionally releasing Marshall's legs.

"No!" Claire screamed.

"Aargh!" came the agonising scream of Marshall disappearing into the fissure.

On hitting the stone floor, the oak beam smashed and splintered into a hundred pieces, but Olly didn't flinch – his shocked state interrupted by Leo shaking his shoulders.

"I've killed him," Olly said. "I let him fall."

"No, you didn't," Leo rallied. "You had to move."

With the gap closing, Orion gazed down. "I can see him, he landed on a rock."

Olly and Leo joined Orion. "Is he moving?"

"His leg twitched," Olly said.

CHAPTER 44

Outside, Claire was having her own drama. She had told the drowsy Katie they had rescued Leo and that Marshall had fallen into the steaming opening. With this news, Katie fell backwards onto the grass, muscles starting to spasm.

"Err guys!" Claire shouted. "You need to see this."

Olly left Leo and Orion and ran to Claire. "Oh my god?" Olly said, sliding to a halt on the wet grass. "What's she doing?" Katie's eyes were as black as coals. Her skin was pale, veins pulsating in her neck while her head twisted violently from side to side.

"I don't know," Claire said. "One second I was telling her about Marshall … then this,"

"**MARSHALL!**" a loud croaky voice erupted from Katie's lips.

"What was that?" Claire said but there was no reply. "Olly?"

Olly stared in horror.

"Olly, what is it?"

"That v… v…voice," he said.

Katie's movements were becoming erratic. "Help me!" she said in her own voice, quickly followed by the deeper tone. "**MARSHALL, MY SON!**"

Claire looked at Olly. "That is Victor's voice isn't it … but how?"

"He must've possessed her body when she cast the spell on Shirdal, that's why she's ill. I don't know what to do."

Katie continued to flail her arms about, screaming obscenities like a character from The Exorcist.

"Hold her," Claire said.

Olly held her arms tight as Claire clamped her legs by sitting on them. Katie's screams became louder.

"Katie! Katie!" Olly shouted. "You've got to be strong. Get that demon out of you!"

"Olly!" Katie said.

"Yes, it's me, I'm right here. You must fight."

High pitch screeching followed with more muscle spasms.

"Look," Claire said.

From Katie's demonic torture, Victor's spectre rose from her body. "Aargh!" Katie screamed before fainting as her nemesis appeared above her.

Olly expected Victor to attack them, so signalled for Claire to move. To their surprise, the spirit dashed between them, heading into the abbey's hall.

"**MY SON!**" Victor roared, the echo vibrating the hall sending more stonework crumbling to the floor.

"It's Victor!" Leo said.

"We've got to get out of here," Orion said. "The whole place is going to collapse."

"What about Marshall? The floor is closing on him."

"We have to leave." Orion took his son's arm, dodging the debris while trying to find an exit through the steam.

"**DAD!**" came another haunting scream from the trapped Marshall. Victor's ghost flew down through the crack as the abbey floor locked together.

CHAPTER 45

"It's shut ... the floor's closed," Leo said.

Orion held his son tightly as masonry dropped around them. "We couldn't do anything."

Disorientated, Leo spotted a corridor. "This way, Dad." They ran hand in hand until they reached a door blocked by a boulder. "I remember this door. It's the dungeon. We came here on our school trip."

"Leo?" a faint voice called out from behind the oak door.

Leo recognised the voice. "Mum! Is that you?"

"Melanie!" Orion yelled.

"Orion, Leo! Yes, it's me. Help me get out."

Orion leveraged his body between the door and boulder while Leo pushed from the side. Inch by inch the giant stone scraped along the floor. Without their slayer powers they struggled – their oxygen deprived lungs struggling in the heat.

"One last push," Orion said.

"We've done it." Leo said as he opened the door. "Mum!"

Melanie ran out from her prison, embracing her son and husband. "My family! I thought I'd lost you both. I heard explosions. Are you both alright?" she said looking them up and down.

"We are … and you? What are you doing in here?" Orion said, unable to let go of his wife's hands.

"I ran from the burning hillside into the abbey. I remembered where the dungeon was … it was the only safe place I could think of. I closed the door and prayed as more explosions erupted. Then a giant rock blocked my way out."

"It's okay, you're safe now," Orion said hugging his wife once again – only to be distracted by Leo moving towards the door. "Everything alright?"

"I heard something." With the coast clear, Leo stepped back into the dungeon.

"What was that?" Melanie said, also hearing a noise.

Orion, Leo and Melanie peered from the dungeon's doorway. Leo knew what the hideous noise was. "It's a hell goblin … one survived."

The red creature scurried down the cobbled corridor, ushering them to the back of the dungeon wall. Orion stepped forward to protect his family as the goblin moved around the room.

"What shall we do?" Leo said.

"I'm not sure," Orion said. "Just don't do anything stup …"

Before Orion could finish his sentence, Melanie pushed between her loved ones.

"Mum!" Leo said, grabbing her in an attempt to hold her back.

Melanie shrugged off her son and brandished the gun given to her by Tilly and Arthur.

"Melanie!" Orion shouted.

Melanie wasn't going to stop. Pointing the gun at the hell goblin she yelled, "You might not be able to understand this, but nobody … or thing, is going to hurt my family any more." She cocked the hammer of the gun with the creature looking open-eyed back at her.

"I think we need to get out of here," Leo said as the goblin held its breath.

"Why?" Melanie said. "What's it doing?"

"It's going to explode!"

They rushed past the inflating goblin and slammed the cell door. They sprinted up the stone corridor towards the main hall when, "**BANG!**" An explosion ripped through the dungeon, knocking Leo, Orion and Melanie off balance into the hall.

"This way!" Olly shouted, waving them towards the window. They gained their footing and jumped to safety, as a giant dust cloud enveloped the hall. The blast had not only blown up the hell goblin and the dungeon, but it also damaged the foundations of the abbey. Cracks appeared at its base, zigzagging up the tower.

"We need to get out of here," Orion said. "The place is going to collapse."

"What's happening?" Katie said, opening her dazed eyes as rain drops splashed off her face.

"No time to explain," Olly said. With Claire's assistance, they pulled Katie up and dragged her across the field.

The forecasted storm was moving in as dawn broke. Dark clouds moved across the sky, bringing heavy rain, washing away the bloody residue. Thunder and lightning forced the seekers to speed up until one clap of thunder sounded different.

"Hey look!" Leo said as everyone skidded to a muddy stop. They glanced back at St. Prion's Abbey in time to see the tower come crashing down along with the main hall. The noise was deafening with vibrations felt afar, causing herds of deer to run for safety and birds to flee from the nearby trees.

"I can't believe Marshall was still under there," Claire said.

Melanie looked at her, "What?"

"She's right," Orion said. "He fell into the crevice. It closed before we could rescue him."

"It was my fault," Olly said. "I should've held him."

"Don't be daft, mate," Leo said. "I told you – you didn't have a choice."

Melanie sank to her knees and sobbed. "The poor boy."

"We'll never forget him," Claire said. "Without him we wouldn't have succeeded."

As the last wall of the abbey became a mound of rubble, Orion placed his hands on Melanie's shoulders. "Come on love, we need to get away from here before anyone shows up."

"Ouch!" Melanie said. "That hurt."

"But I haven't done anything."

Orion lifted his hands, realising they were bigger. "Dad!" Leo said flexing his biceps. "We're becoming slayers again."

"But how?" Melanie asked.

Olly noticed the rain uncovering something in the mud. "I think you'll find this is the reason," he said plucking the dragon's claw from the ground.

"Well spotted Olly," Orion said scooping Melanie up from ground with ease.

"Hey, I want it! I need the powers as well," Leo said.

Melanie took the claw from Olly and moved it around her fingers, pondered for a moment. "I know what I'm going to do."

The slayers looked at her like two Labradors waiting for a bone.

"*I'm* going to keep it," she said.

"What?" Leo said.

"I've made up my mind. I prefer you both without this power. When we arrive home, I'm going to keep it safe in a lead box so it can't connect with you both."

"But Mel," Orion said.

"But nothing, you'll still be strong enough," she said holding his hand.

"You pulled Leo out of the crevice without your powers," Olly said.

"Well, there you go," Melanie said. "That takes inner strength … I'd be more concerned if you lose that. You were strong enough when you needed to be and that's what life's all about. In the time of adversity, you had the mental and physical strength to fight … and I love you for that. You've proved what a great father you are. And anyway, we'll still have it … just in case."

"She's right," Claire said interlocking arms with Leo. "You're the bravest lad I know. You don't need it either."

CHAPTER 46

Orion and Melanie led the way in the pouring rain, across the grassland towards the iron gates where the car and the two remaining bikes were left.

"How are you feeling?" Olly asked Katie.

"A bit better. Can't believe I was possessed."

"I know, that was scary. I thought you were a gonner." His eyes welled up.

"Aww you big softy." Katie turned and kissed him. "It'll take more than that to get rid of me."

"Come on you two!" Leo said. "Let's get out of here."

They climbed through the damaged gates as Olly spotted a piece of paper fall from his pocket. He went to pick it up, but the lively winds had other ideas. The paper disappeared in a mini cyclone, spinning around with speed. Katie and Claire tried to grasp it, but couldn't and even Leo with his returning powers couldn't grab it as it rose higher.

"Out of the way," Olly said, holding a piece of the iron gate. He thrust the spike into the air and pierced the paper. "That's how you do it."

"Well, that was pure luck," Leo said.

Olly took the paper. "I'd forgotten about this. Marshall gave it to me earlier. It's from Horace, apparently."

"Well? What are you waiting for?" Orion said. "Read it."

Opening the message, Olly's eyes flicked through the contents.

"Olly … Olly!" Leo said, eager to know what it said. "Come on, Marshall said it was for me as well."

"Sorry," Olly said. "It's Horace … he's left us something."

"Really? I hope it's not one of those masks or skeletons; we've seen enough creepy stuff lately."

"I'll read it out to you."

Dear Olly and Leo,

If you are reading this, then my worst fears have been realised. I'm sure my death wasn't in vain and that you succeeded in your quest.

When I first heard your story, it brought so many memories back to me. I was delighted to know there were two boys in my home town of Brunswick linked to my father's club. And when I met you, your enthusiasm for my stories and my dad's history left me immensely proud.

Over the last few days, I've sorted out the paperwork with my solicitors, in case of this eventuality.

As I am an only child and don't have any close family, I have decided to leave you both my dad's club and snooker hall, including its contents – with your parents as custodians until your rightful age, of course.

I don't think I could leave it in any better hands than the both of yours. And who knows, another adventure might be waiting for you, hidden in a box on a dusty shelf.

With sincere gratitude
Horace Griffin.

Leo had a glazed look in his eyes. He wasn't really sure if he'd heard Olly's words correctly. "It's ours?"

"Sounds like it. He's left it all to us."

Orion took the letter. "It does have a counter signature from a solicitor. It must be legitimate."

"We're going to own the Art of Darkness," Olly said.

"Yeah, it'll be the best club in town!" Leo shouted.

"Just hold your horses for one second," Melanie said. "Me, your father, and Olly's parents will have to meet up with these solicitors first and get everything verified. Even then, you'll have to wait until you're eighteen before you legally own it."

"We can still tidy it up, can't we?" Olly said. "There's tonnes of stuff to sort out."

"We'll see," Orion said. "First of all, we need to get everyone home. Katie and Claire, you come with us. Leo and Olly, you cycle back."

"Are you joking, Dad?" Leo said. "I'm knackered."

"Do as your dad says. We can't fit everyone in the Beetle, and we can't leave the bikes. You have no other choice."

"Your mum's right," Olly said, mounting one of the bikes. "We can't leave any evidence we were here. Look at the state of this place; café's roof is burnt to a crisp and the abbey's turned into a pile of rubble. There will be questions asked about this."

A distant rumble of thunder followed by a flash of lightning hastened their exit. The boys sped off down the lane while Melanie started the Beetle.

"I hope they'll be able to save the café," Claire said, seeing a piece of charcoaled wood fall from the smouldering roof.

"I'm sure they will," Katie said. "Hey, look."

A pair of familiar faces waved back through a bay window. Tilly and Arthur smiled at seeing their friends, especially pleased that Melanie had survived.

"We owe a lot to the ghosts," Orion said.

"We sure do," Melanie said. The green Beetle chugged its way from the gates along the lake side, then up between the avenue of oak trees before leaving the St. Prion estate for the last time.

EPILOGUE

A month had passed for the seekers. Claire left to go home after an emotional farewell with her cousin Katie and her new friends, Olly and Leo. She promised that she would never speak about what had happened to her and her friends over the Easter holidays of 1991. After all, if she did tell her parents the truth, she would never be let out of her house, or see Katie and the boys again.

Katie struggled the most. She became withdrawn and quiet, apart from her nightmares. Screams were a nightly occurrence as she imagined Victor possessing her body and creatures attacking her. Her parents, who weren't told the truth, thought she was going through 'moody teenager years', leaving her to get on with it.

Melanie and Orion had found normality in their lives again. True to her word, Melanie locked the dragon's claw away in a lead air-tight box, keeping the key safe in her possession. Orion kept himself busy with frequent visits to the solicitors, trying to resolve the ownership of the Art of Darkness club and snooker hall – as Horace had mentioned in his letter, Olly and Leo's parents would be custodians until the boys reached eighteen.

The big question the authorities were all asking was: where was Horace? He'd disappeared off the face of the earth. Of course, the seekers knew what had happened, but would anyone believe them? Don't be silly!

The adventures in the Brunswick tunnel a year earlier helped Olly and Leo come to terms with what had happened but it was those they'd lost which affected them most. Marshall, once their nemesis, had turned his life around. Without him they would never have defeated Set and his followers. Horace, the mild-mannered, gangly gentleman who strode into their lives, who morphed into the colossal, flying Egyptian god Horus, and guided them to Osiris's temple and beyond. Then there was Stumpy, the cave troll, who was once the mighty dragon slayer Bellafino who connected with Leo, signalling the turmoil in Duat.

"We should go to this?" Leo said. "It'll take our minds off things."

"What's that?" Olly said.

Leo turned the NME paper around. "This Happy Monday's concert, they're playing an all-day gig next month."

"Err yeah, sounds good … Sorry mate, I'm still getting used to all this being ours. That and everything that's happened."

"It feels like a dream," Leo said, seated opposite Olly at the Victorian wind-out table in the Art of Darkness club.

"More like a nightmare," Olly said, glancing at a copy of the Brunswick Bugle. "Luckily for us we've kept our names out of the papers this time."

The demise of St. Prion abbey had made both the local and national news. The story had been on the front page of every newspaper and related how a localised storm had struck the estate, turning the abbey from a resplendent ruin and national treasure to a pile of rubble. The police were involved when a site worker, removing the debris, found the remains of a body.

An extract from The Brunswick Bugle read:

The deceased was named as Lance Golding, a fugitive who had escaped from prison a week earlier. His nephew James Marshall Golding, who escaped on the same day, has not been found and is still evading the police.

"Looks like we're in the clear," Leo said. "The police will think Lance was hiding when the abbey crashed down on him."

"Possibly," Olly said. "And Marshall? Do you think he's dead?"

Leo scrunched up his face. "You what? Course he is. You saw it with your own eyes. The floor closed up over him … with a river of molten lava for company! Believe me, he's dead."

"Suppose you're right. Just glad we got out alive."

Katie walked into the room, hearing part of the conversation. "I think it was Osiris somehow helping us?"

"True. There was definitely divine intervention from somewhere."

"Hey, you three!" Melanie shouted from the back door. "Someone's here to welcome you."

"Sidney!" Olly said, seeing the old man from the neighbouring sweet shop shuffle his feet up the hallway.

"Well, hello there," Sidney said holding a carrier bag. "I've brought you all some sweets as a welcoming gift."

"Aww, well isn't that lovely," Melanie said. "But it'll be a while till we're officially open in here. In fact, we're only here today to find some more paperwork. I'm sorry, where are our manners, Katie, grab a chair for Sidney."

Katie picked up an oak chair from the side of the room.

"Not that one!" Leo shouted.

"What? Why not?"

"Horace told me never to sit in that chair. He looked pretty serious about it as well."

Sidney coughed to interrupt. "He's correct, young lady. I've been next door a lot of years, too many years to remember, and a lot of strange people holding even stranger objects have past my shop to enter this club." An eerie silence filled the room not felt since Horace told his story. Sidney continued. "I was good friends with Archibald Griffin. We used to chat and tell each other stories, mainly to fill in the time. There were countless tales about his archaeological trips and me talking about my exploits in the Great War, but there was one story I'll always remember. That chair … Archie called it the executioner's chair. It has a long past. A long dark past."

"How can a chair have a dark past," Leo quipped.

Olly gave Leo a kick under the table. "Shh, he's going to tell us."

Sidney stared deeply into Leo's eyes. "Five hundred years ago, legend has it that a man, possessed by the devil himself, sat on this chair awaiting execution. The man cursed everything in the room, including the chair. Throughout the centuries whoever has sat on the chair has died an untimely and mysterious death."

"That's amazing," Leo said.

"It is," Melanie remarked. "I think we should store this away, just in case."

"Wow," Olly said. "That's unbelievable. This place is full of crazy stuff."

Katie went quiet and gulped.

"What's wrong? You look like you've seen a ghost."

"Last time I was here … I sat on that chair."

THE END

LAST WORD

If you enjoyed The Seekers of Duat, please consider leaving a review on Amazon and Goodreads as these can make a huge difference to an author and help other readers find and enjoy this book.

Keith Robinson writes as Keith Cador and was born in 1975 in the Spa town of Harrogate in North Yorkshire. He now lives in Ripon in the same county with his wife Melanie and son Ryan.

This is the second in the Art of Darkness Series and continues the exploits of Leo and Olly – of *The Search for Orion* fame – joined in this adventure by Katie and Claire, exploring a supernatural world while battling gods and a cast of fierce creatures.

Thank you *Father Time* for giving me the opportunity to complete the second novel in this series. My gratitude to Paul Smith of Wise Grey Owl who performed the final edit, formatting and helped me prepare it for publication.

Printed in Great Britain
by Amazon